D0012867

Books by Tom Robbins

ANOTHER ROADSIDE ATTRACTION
EVEN COWGIRLS GET THE BLUES
JITTERBUG PERFUME
STILL LIFE WITH WOODPECKER
SKINNY LEGS AND ALL

Available now in hardcover

HALF ASLEEP IN FROG PAJAMAS

STILL LIFE WITH WOODPECKER

TOM ROBBINS

BANTAM BOOKS

NEW YORK · TORONTO · LONDON · SYDNEY · AUCKLAND

NOTE

The original 12 Most Famous Redheads list appeared in *The People's Almanac® Presents the Book of Lists* by David Wallechinsky and Irving Wallace. I have tampered with it. T.R.

STILL LIFE WITH WOODPECKER

A Bantam Hardcover Book/August 1980
Bantam Trade edition/August 1980
Bantam rack-size edition/November 1981

ISBN 0-553-27093-1

Published simultaneously in the United States and Canada

Bantam Books are published by Bantam Books, a division of Bantam Doubleday Dell Publishing Group, Inc. Its trademark, consisting of the words "Bantam Books" and the portrayal of a rooster, is Registered in U.S. Patent and Trademark Office and in other countries. Marca Registrada. Bantam Books, 1540 Broadway, New York, New York 10036.

PRINTED IN THE UNITED STATES OF AMERICA

OPM   22   21   20

To the memory of
Keith Wyman and Betty Bowen:
if there is a place where people
go after death, its proprietors have
got their hands full with those two.

To everybody whose letters
I haven't answered.

And to G.R., special delivery.

You don't need to leave your room.
Remain sitting at your table and listen.
Don't even listen, simply wait.
Don't even wait.
Be quite still and solitary.
The world will freely offer itself to you.
To be unmasked, it has no choice.
It will roll in ecstasy at your feet.

—Franz Kafka

Here should be a picture of my favorite apple.
It is also a nude & bottle.
It is also a landscape.
There are no such things as still lifes.

—Erica Jong

PROLOGUE

If this typewriter can't do it, then fuck it, it can't be done.

This is the all-new Remington SL3, the machine that answers the question, "Which is harder, trying to read *The Brothers Karamazov* while listening to Stevie Wonder records or hunting for Easter eggs on a typewriter keyboard?" This is the cherry on top of the cowgirl. The burger served by the genius waitress. The Empress card.

I sense that the novel of my dreams is in the Remington SL3—although it writes much faster than I can spell. And no matter that my typing finger was pinched last week by a giant land crab. This baby speaks electric Shakespeare at the slightest provocation and will rap out a page and a half if you just look at it hard.

"What are you looking for in a typewriter?" the salesman asked.

"Something more than words," I replied. "Crystals. I want to send my readers armloads of crystals, some of which are the colors of orchids and peonies, some of which pick up radio signals from a secret city that is half Paris and half Coney Island."

He recommended the Remington SL3.

My old typewriter was named Olivetti. I know an extraordinary juggler named Olivetti. No relation. There is, however, a similarity between juggling and composing on the typewriter. The trick is, when you spill something, make it look like part of the act.

I have in my cupboard, under lock and key, the last bottle of Anaïs Nin (green label) to be smuggled out of

Punta del Visionario before the revolution. Tonight, I'll pull the cork. I'll inject ten cc. into a ripe lime the way the natives do. I'll suck. And begin . . .

If this typewriter can't do it, I'll swear it can't be done

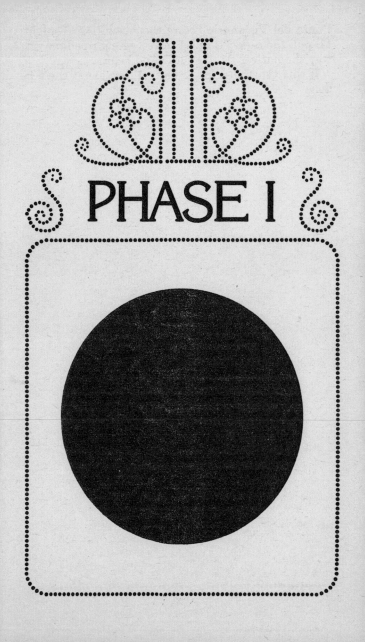

PHASE I

1

In the last quarter of the twentieth century, at a time when Western civilization was declining too rapidly for comfort and yet too slowly to be very exciting, much of the world sat on the edge of an increasingly expensive theater seat, waiting—with various combinations of dread, hope, and ennui—for something momentous to occur.

Something momentous was bound to happen soon. The entire collective unconscious could not be wrong about that. But what would it be? And would it be apocalyptic or rejuvenating? A cure for cancer or a nuclear bang? A change in the weather or a change in the sea? Earthquakes in California, killer bees in London, Arabs in the stock exchange, life in the laboratory, or a UFO on the White House lawn? Would Mona Lisa sprout a mustache? Would the dollar fail?

Christian aficionados of the Second Coming scenario were convinced that after a suspenseful interval of two thousand years, the other shoe was about to drop.

And five of the era's best-known psychics, meeting at the Chelsea Hotel, predicted that Atlantis would soon reemerge from the depths.

To this last, Princess Leigh-Cheri responded, "There are two lost continents. . . . Hawaii was one, called Mu, the mother, its tips still projecting in our senses— the land of slap dance, fishing music, flowers and happiness. There are three lost continents. . . . We are one: the lovers."

In whatever esteem one might hold Princess Leigh-Cheri's thoughts concerning matters geographic, one must agree that the last quarter of the twentieth century was a severe period for lovers. It was a time when women openly resented men, a time when men felt betrayed by women, a time when romantic relationships took on the character of ice in spring, stranding many little children on jagged and inhospitable floes.

Nobody quite knew what to make of the moon any more.

2

Consider a certain night in August. Princess Leigh-Cheri was gazing out of her attic window. The moon was full. The moon was so bloated it was about to tip over. Imagine awakening to find the moon flat on its face on the bathroom floor, like the late Elvis Presley, poisoned by banana splits. It was a moon that could stir wild passions in a moo cow. A moon that could bring out the devil in a bunny rabbit. A moon that could turn lug nuts into moonstones, turn Little Red Riding Hood into the big bad wolf. For more than an hour, Leigh-Cheri stared into the mandala of the sky. "Does the moon have a purpose?" she inquired of Prince Charming.

Prince Charming pretended that she had asked a silly question. Perhaps she had. The same query put to the Remington SL3 elicited this response:

Albert Camus wrote that the only serious question is whether to kill yourself or not.

Tom Robbins wrote that the only serious question is whether time has a beginning and an end.

Camus clearly got up on the wrong side of bed, and Robbins must have forgotten to set the alarm.

There *is* only one serious question. And that is:

Who knows how to make love stay?

Answer me that and I will tell you whether or not to kill yourself.

Answer me that and I will ease your mind about the beginning and the end of time.

Answer me that and I will reveal to you the purpose of the moon.

3

Historically, members of Leigh-Cheri's class have not much fallen in love. They mated for power and wealth, for tradition and heirs, and left "true love" to the masses. The masses had nothing to lose. But this was the last quarter of the twentieth century, and with the exception of a few savage buffoons in Africa, the royalty of the world had long since resigned itself to the fact of its mortal, if not quite democratic, dimensions. Leigh-Cheri's family was a case in point.

Since his exile, more than thirty years before, the King had made gambling a career. Poker was his work. Recently, however, he had had a taste of open-heart surgery. A major valve had been removed and replaced with a Teflon substitute. The artificial valve functioned efficiently, but it made a metallic noise as it opened and shut. When he was excited, everyone in the room knew it. Due to the audible sound of his heart, he was no longer able to practice poker, a game with necessary concealments and bluffs. "Jesus," he said. "When I draw a good hand, I sound like a Tupperware party." He spent his hours watching sports on television, pining for the good old days when he could have ordered Howard Cosell to the garrote.

His wife, the Queen, once the beauty of seven capitals, was understimulated and overweight. She had attended, in America, so many second-rate society teas, charity fashion shows, and gala this and gala thats, that she'd begun to exude a kind of pâté de fois gras gas, and the expulsion of this effluvium propelled her from party to ball as if she were a sausage skin inflated by Wagner. With no lady to attend her, she required two hours to dress, and since she changed clothes thrice daily, the draping, bejeweling, and painting of her bulk amounted to a full-time job. The Queen had long ago abandoned her husband to the tube and her daughter to the attic. Her sons (she could scarcely recall their number) were scattered about Europe, entangled in endless financial adventures of a primarily shady nature, and were lost to her. She had one intimate: a Chihuahua that she clutched to her bosom.

If asked what he expected from the last quarter of the twentieth century, the King would have replied, "Now that it is no longer reasonable to hope for the restoration of the monarchy, my fondest wishes are that the Seattle Mariners win the pennant, the Seattle Sonics make the NBA playoffs, the Seattle Seahawks go to the Super Bowl, and that the play-by-play announcers be replaced by Sir Kenneth Clark."

The same question directed to the Queen would have educed this reaction: "Oh-Oh, spaghetti-o." (Her favorite Americanism.) "Vat can you expect of crazy peoples? I'm happy only zat mein vadder and mama mia are in zee Heaven and not hafing to suffer from no stinking modern times. *Sacre bleu!* I do my duty to zee crown and das ees zat." The Queen had learned English in seven capitals.

Each night on a worn but opulent Kashan rug, beside a canopied barge of a bed, Queen Tilli lowered herself onto knees that resembled great wads of bubble gum, and prayed for the deliverance of the crown, the health of her Chihuahua, the state of grand opera, and not much else. Each night, King Max would steal into the kitchen to eat by the spoonful the salt and sugar that the doctors had eliminated from his meals.

6

"It's something other than five centuries of inbreeding that's queering this royal family," thought Princess Leigh-Cheri, whom gossip columnists recently had characterized as "a retired cheerleader, a moonstruck social activist, a tragic beauty who has sequestered herself in an attic."

"This family has got the Last-Quarter-of-the-Twentieth-Century Blues."

4

Palace-in-exile for the Furstenberg-Barcalonas, which was quite their name, was a voluminous three-story yellow frame house on the shore of Puget Sound. The house was built in 1911 for a Seattle lumber baron, who, in reaction against the turrets, cupolas, and dormers that embellished the Frontier Gothic mansions of his peers, ordered "an American house, a house without frills," and got just that. It was a barn, a box with a peaked roof. It sat among ten acres of blackberry brambles, like an abandoned radio, broadcasting creaks and whispers to the rain. The house was given to Max and Tilli by the CIA.

The Furstenberg-Barcalona homeland was now ruled by a right-wing military junta, supported by the United States government and, of course, the Roman Catholic Church. While the U.S. publicly regretted that the junta permitted so few civil liberties, it was loath to interefere in the internal affairs of a sovereign nation, particularly a nation that could be relied upon as an ally against those left-leaning nations in whose internal affairs the U.S. did regularly interfere. It irritated the U.S. that royalists still loyal to Max and Tilli might disturb political stability in that part of the world. The U.S. paid King Max a modest stipend to keep a low profile and not fan any flames. Each year at Christmas, the Pope sent Queen Tilli a crucifix, candlestick, or some other knickknack that he had personally blessed.

Once, Princess Leigh-Cheri used a papal candlestick for the purpose of self-gratification. She had hoped that at the appropriate moment she might be visited by either the Lamb or the Beast, but, as usual, only Ralph Nader attended her.

5

If the CIA imagined that its hospitality would charm the monogrammed socks off of Max and Tilli Furstenberg-Barcalona, it was once again wrong. During the first decade of their residency, the royal couple never complained about the drafty old mansion, for fear the place was bugged. In later years, however, made brazen by advanced age (the bravery of childhood returning, like salmon, to the source), they griped as much as they pleased.

The King would stand at a window (during halftime or the seventh-inning stretch) and stare apprehensively at the creeping tide of brambles. "I may be the first monarch in history to be assassinated by blackberries," he would grumble. His Teflon valve grumbled with him.

The Queen caressed her Chihuahua. "You know who lifed here bevore ve did? Smokey zee Bear."

Encouraging her parents to move was futile, Leigh-Cheri learned.

Max, a tall, horse-faced man with a Hitlerian mustache, shook his head so hard and long that were he wearing his crown it would have toppled off and tumbled into the berry vines. "Changing places at the table doesn't fool the cards," Max said.

"Moof? I got three teas this veek," said Queen Tilli. "No! I forget. I got *four* teas. Oh-Oh, spaghetti-o."

Like a pair of *r*'s trapped in a Spanish songbook, Tilli and Max lurked in their shoebox castle, waiting to be rolled.

6

The Princess lived in the attic.

As a child, it had been her favorite playroom. It was private and cozy up there. She had liked the low, slanted ceiling and the complete absence of coat-of-arms wallpaper. As a child, she had appreciated the view of Puget Sound from the attic's west window and the view of the Cascade Mountains from the window facing east. There was one mountain in particular, a white beak, broad and cloud-snagging, that would nearly fill the east window on those days when vision was not obscured by mist or rain. The mountain had a name, but Leigh-Cheri could never remember it. "It's an Indian name, I think."

"Tonto?" asked the Queen.

Now the windows were painted black—except for a single small pane through which the Princess could entertain an occasional corner of the moon.

The Princess lived in the attic and did not come out. She could have come out, but she chose not to. She could have raised the windows or scraped off the paint, but she chose not to do that, either. Having the windows nailed shut and painted black was her idea. The attic was illuminated by one forty-watt bulb. That was also her idea. The Princess had furnished the attic, as well.

The attic was furnished with a cot, a chamber pot, and a package of Camel cigarettes.

7

Once, Leigh-Cheri had lived much as any other young woman within her parents' domicile. She had a room in the north end of the second floor, a room with a full-sized bed and a comfortable chair, a desk at which to do her schoolwork, and a dresser filled with cosmetics and underwear. There was a phonograph dedicated to the faithful reproduction of rock 'n' roll and a mirror dedicated to the flattering reproduction of her own image. There were curtains at the windows and heirloom carpets on the floor, while upon the walls posters of the Hawaiian Islands rubbed edges with photographs of Ralph Nader.

The room sometimes seemed pinched and stifling to her, compared to that "big wide world out there" for which she yearned, yet she was fond enough of her quarters and returned to them agreeably each evening when classes were over and this or that committee for this or that ecological cause was adjourned.

Even after she was forced off the cheerleading squad at the University of Washington, a humiliating experience that provoked her to withdraw from college, she occupied her room as correctly as a cephalopod its shell. Those days, she shared the room with Prince Charming.

Prince Charming was a toad. He lived in a terrarium at the foot of Leigh-Cheri's bed. And yes—you nosy ones—she *had* kissed the toad. Once. Lightly. And yes, she'd felt silly as shit. When one is a princess, however, one is tempted by things that we common people barely comprehend. Besides, the circumstances under which she had acquired the toad encouraged superstitious behavior, and, moreover, was a little teenie quick peck on the top of a frog's head so much sillier than kissing the picture of a desired one—and who hasn't kissed a photograph at one time or another? Leigh-Cheri kissed Ralph Nader's photo fairly frequently.

It might be noted here that Freudian analysts of fairy tales have suggested that kissing toads and frogs is symbolized fellatio. In that regard, Princess Leigh-Cheri was, on a conscious level, innocent, although not so naive as Queen Tilli, who thought fellatio was an obscure Italian opera and was annoyed that she couldn't find the score.

8

Prince Charming was given to Leigh-Cheri by old Gulietta, the last living of the servants who had accompanied Max and Tilli into exile. At Leigh-Cheri's birth, in Paris, four of those loyalists were still in service, but all but Gulietta died soon after the royal family took up residence in the Puget Sound palace. Perhaps it was the dampness.

The U.S. government provided a servant, also, a man named Chuck who was to function as gardener, chauffeur, and general handyman. He was, of course, a CIA informer. As age added infirmity to his native indolence, Chuck was no match for the Great Northwest blackberries, and they edged ever closer to the walls of the house. At the wheel, he was terrifying. King Max and the Princess had for some years refused to ride with him. Chuck still drove the Queen to her galas and teas, however, seemingly oblivious to the Hail Marys and Oh-oh, Spaghetti-O's bubbling in rank fear from the back seat.

Regularly, each fortnight, Chuck sat down to poker with the King. Even with a telltale ticker, the King regularly, each fortnight, took Chuck to the cleaners. Thus, Max added Chuck's salary to his own. "It's all he's good for," said Max, whose great mule face would smile faintly at what he must have considered a little joke on the CIA.

Gulietta, on the other hand, was in her eighties, both efficient and energetic. Miraculously, she had kept the huge house free of cobwebs and mold while doing the royal wash and preparing six meals a day: since Max and Tilli were carnivores and Leigh-Cheri vegetarian, each meal had been, in fact, two.

Old Gulietta spoke no English, and Leigh-Cheri, who was brought to America when she was not much taller than a jug of wine, spoke nothing else. Yet, it was Gulietta who told Leigh-Cheri her bedtime story each night until she was fifteen, always the same story, a story so frequently repeated that the girl came not only to comprehend its general meaning but to actually understand every word, though pronounced in a foreign tongue. And it was Gulietta who sensed the true dimensions of Leigh-Cheri's depression after the Princess suffered a miscarriage during the UW homecoming game. (She was in midair—all a-leap— when the blood broke loose, rivulets racing as if to hemophilic touchdowns from beneath her diminutive cheerleading skirt.) It was Gulietta who sensed that her young mistress had lost more than a baby that autumn afternoon, had lost more, indeed, than the baby's father (the second-string quarterback, a pre-law student who headed the campus chapter of the Sierra Club and intended to work for Nader someday), although the memory of him sitting on the bench pretending not to notice as she was whisked from Husky Stadium in embarrassment and fear haunted her mind and her heart like an ugly specter in muddy shoes.

It was Gulietta who, during that unhappy aftermath, came to her with hag hands cupped around a toad. The Princess was not immediately overjoyed. But she had heard tales of Old World totems, and if toad magic could help, she'd give it a try—and let the warts fall where they may.

Alas, Gulietta, this was an American frog of the last quarter of the twentieth century, a time when wishing apparently no longer led to anything, and Leigh-Cheri eventually named it Prince Charming after "that son-of-a-bitch who never comes through."

9

Sandwiches were invented by the Earl of Sandwich, popcorn was invented by the Earl of Popcorn, and salad dressing by the Oil of Vinegar. The moon invented natural rhythm. Civilization uninvented it. Princess Leigh-Cheri would have liked to reinvent it, but at that point she hadn't a clue.

She had ovened that rubber cookie called the diaphragm and gotten pregnant anyway. Many women do. She had played hostess to that squiggly metallic houseguest who goes by his initials, IUD, and suffered cramps and infections. Many women do. She had, in desperation and against her fundamental instincts, popped the pill. She became ill, physically and emotionally. Many women do. She had experimented with the jellies and jams, creams and goops, sprays and suppositories, powders and foams, gels and gunks only to discover her romantic personality—she had grown up with European folk tales (*one* tale, at any rate)—repulsed by the technological textures, industrial odors, and napalm flavors. Many romantic personalities are.

This constant battle with the reproductive process, a war in which her only allies were pharmaceutical robots, alien agents whose artificial assistance seemed more treacherous than trustworthy, was gnawing with plastic teeth at her very concepts of love. Was it entirely paranoid to suspect that all those stoppers, thingamajigs, and substances devised to prevent conception were intended not to liberate womankind from the biological and social penalties imposed on her natural passions but, rather, at the insidious design of capitalistic puritans, were supposed to technologize sex, to dilute its dark juices, to contain its wilder fires, to censor its sweet nastiness, to scrub it clean (clean as a laboratory autoclave, clean as a hospital bed), to order it uniform, to render it safe; to eliminate the risk of uncontrollable feelings, illogical commitments, and deep involvements (substituting for those risks the less mysterious, tamer risks of infection, hemorrhage, cancer, and hormone imbalance); yes, to make sexual love so secure and same and sanitary, so slick and frolicsome, so *casual* that it is not a manifestation of love at all, but a near anonymous, near autonomous, hedonistic scratching of a bunny itch, an itch far removed from any direct relation to the feverish enigmas of Life and Death, and a scratching programmed so that it would in no way interfere with the real purpose of human beings in a capitalistic, puritanical society, which is to produce goods and consume them?

Since she could not possibly answer that question—she couldn't even ask it without getting winded—and since the lunch-hour, parking-lot rendezvous in the back of her boyfriend's van were frankly deficient in certain romantic details that she'd always associated with sex, the Princess decided that she would enter a second exile: celibacy. Before she could steal safely across the border, however, the biological IRS caught up with her and exacted its stubborn price.

10

When her lover, the quarterback, implored her to have her pregnancy "taken care of," Princess Leigh-Cheri rested her forehead against the plate glass of the vegetarian restaurant in which they were dining and wept. "No," she said. "No, no no."

At nineteen, she had already undergone one abortion. She would not tolerate a second. "No," she said. A teardrop hung out of each blue eye, like a fat woman leaning out of a tenement window. They bobbed, balanced, and bobbed again, as if dreading the uncertain journey down her cheeks. Wavering there, her teardrops reflected for a moment the sheen of the soybean curd upon her plate. "No more vacuum cleaners, no more steel. They can scrape my heart, they can scrape my brain before they'll scrape my uterus again. It's been over a year since my last D and C, and I still feel raw in there. It feels bitter when it should feel sweet, it feels ragged when it should feel smooth, it feels deep purple when it should feel pink. Death has thrown a stag party in the most sacred room in my body. From now on, that space belongs to life."

Any time that technology subverts a benevolent natural process, the sensitive smell sulfur. For Princess Leigh-Cheri, abortions had not only the reek of totalitarianism but the shriek of betrayed meat. If another D and C was an intolerable idea, however, the prospect of inopportune maternity was equally distressing—and not just for the usual reasons. Furstenberg-Barcalona was an ancient lineage in which strict codes had evolved. If a female member of the family wished to possess full privilege, if she would someday be queen, then she must neither marry nor mother before the age of twenty-one, nor could she before that age forsake her parents' domicile. And although she considered herself one of the people, Leigh-Cheri did very much indeed desire full royal privilege. Leigh-Cheri believed that she could use that privilege to help the world.

"Fairy tales and myths are dominated by accounts of rescued princesses," she reasoned. "Isn't it about time that a princess returned the favor?" Leigh-Cheri had a vision of the princess as hero.

As Queen Tilli put it when Max asked her what she thought their only daughter wanted out of life, "She vants to buy zee vorld a Coke."

"What?"

"She vants to buy zee vorld a Coke."

"Well," said Max, "she can't afford it. And the world would demand Diet Pepsi, anyhow. Why doesn't she buy *me* a martini, instead?"

11

It was autumn, the springtime of death. Rain spattered the rotting leaves, and a wild wind wailed. Death was singing in the shower. Death was happy to be alive. The fetus bailed out without a parachute. It landed in the sideline Astroturf, so upsetting the cheerleaders that for the remainder of the afternoon their rahs were little more than squeaks. The Huskies won anyway, knocking off favored UCLA, 28-21, and at nearby University Hospital, where Leigh-Cheri had to have a pint of common blood pumped into her royal conduits, the interns were in a festive mood.

Leigh-Cheri's dilemma was resolved, for the time being, but she felt like a black candle at a wake for a snake. When an intern whistled "Proud Mary," she had no inclination to sing along.

Her boyfriend telephoned about eight that evening. He was at his fraternity house. They were having a victory party. He said he'd drop by the hospital the next day, but he must have lost the address.

When her identity was learned, the Princess was moved to a private room. She was given the best sedative in the house. Château du Phenobarbital 1979. Asleep at last, she dreamed of the fetus. In her dream, the fetus went toddling off down some awkward dirt road like Charlie Chaplin at the end of a silent movie.

By Tuesday, she was physically recovered to the degree that she could return to campus, where she learned that her status as the only genuine princess west of New York was insufficient to deflect the moral indignation of the committee on cheerleaders. Asked to resign from the yell squad, she resigned from classes, as well. She also resigned from men, but rather late to appease the King and Queen.

Max's heart was rattling like a full set of dishes when he told Leigh-Cheri that she must shape up or ship out. "We've been liberal with you," said Max, "because, well, after all, this is America. . . ." Max neglected to point out that it was also the last quarter of the twentieth century, but that, no doubt, was self-evident.

"Adolf Hitler vas a wegetarian," Queen Tilli reminded Leigh-Cheri for the three-hundredth time. Tilli was attempting to discourage her daughter from joining a natural foods commune in Hawaii, an option that appeared to be open to her if she elected to relinquish royal privilege. In turn, Leigh-Cheri might have reminded the Queen that Hitler ate two pounds of chocolate a day, but she'd grown weary of that dietary debate. Besides, she'd decided to protect her claim on royal privilege, even though it meant subjecting herself to tighter social restrictions.

"You goan be a gut girl, then?"

"Yes, mother."

"If we deal you a new hand, will you play by the rules?"

"Yes, father."

They observed her as she turned to go upstairs. They observed her as if it were the first time they'd really looked at her in years. Despite her pale color and the unhappiness that clung to her the way a bad dream clings to a rumpled pillowcase, she was lovely. Her hair, as straight and red as ironed ketchup, rode gravity's one-way ticket all the way to her waist; her blue eyes were as soft and moist as *huevos rancheros,* and the long curl of their lashes caused fimbrillate shadows to fall on the swell of her cheeks. She was not tall, yet the legs that hung out of her skirt seemed a tall woman's legs, and beneath her No-Nukes-Is-Good-Nukes T-shirt, her astonishingly round breasts jiggled ever so slightly, like balls balanced on the noses of Valium-eating seals.

Tilli stroked her Chihuahua. Max's heart made a sound like the sleigh bells on Mrs. Santa Claus's dildo.

⚬⚬ 12 ⚬⚬

Neoteny. Neoteny. Neot— Oh how the Remington SL3 enjoys that word! Unrestrained, it would fill the page with neotenyneotenyneotenyneoteny. Of course, it bothers the Remington SL3 not a comma's worth that very few readers know what the word means. Given an opportunity to write it again, however, the machine would be inclined toward definition.

"Neoteny" is "remaining young," and it may be ironic that it is so little known, because human evolution has been dominated by it. Humans have evolved to their relatively high state by retaining the immature characteristics of their ancestors. Humans are the most advanced of mammals—although a case could be made for the dolphins—because they seldom grow up. Behavioral traits such as curiosity about the world, flexibility of response, and playfulness are common to practically all young mammals but are usually rapidly lost with the onset of maturity in all but humans. Humanity has advanced, when it has advanced, not because it has been sober, responsible, and cautious, but because it has been playful, rebellious, and immature.

One needn't feel excessively ignorant if one was unfamiliar with neoteny. There have been queens and kings and princesses who also were oblivious to it, in word and in action.

During the period following Leigh-Cheri's miscarriage, the supposed virtue of maturity was cardinal in the Puget Sound palace. Although understandably vague about what maturity might actually be, Leigh-Cheri strove, with her parents' encouragement, to acquire more of it. Nightly, until the age of fifteen, and on a few evenings thereafter, she had been told a bedtime story; until a few weeks prior, she had been flailing about paroxysmally amidst pompons, shouting incomprehensible incantations meant to further the fortunes of a band of innocent sprites worshiping a sacred fruit (upon the fortunes of that same football team habitually rode much of mature King Max's bank account, but that's another matter). It was about time she grew up. Princesses were not exactly a dime a dozen. And this princess, it had suddenly dawned upon Tilli and Max, was a sexpot.

She might be expected, upon attaining the age of twenty-one, to marry well, very well, indeed. In fact, there was probably no man, from Prince Andrew to the U.S. president's son, whom she might not fairly mate. Those prospects pleased the King and Queen. Heretofore, living under the stare of the CIA, having agreed to "retire" from the royalty circuit, the Furstenberg-Barcalonas sheltered no particular ambitions for their daughter and were content to have her indulge a normal American girlhood (although they were unconvinced that developments such as vegetarianism and ecology were normal). Now, it occurred to them that if this young woman were to attract the attention of the right man, one of the emerging Arab rulers, for example, even the CIA probably would be powerless to prevent a most propitious union.

It was the wrong time to speak of marriage to Leigh-Cheri. Leigh-Cheri had driven a wooden stake through the valentine. Yet, on the premise that it would aid preparation for her mission in life; on the premise that were she ever to resume her studies in environmental sciences she might not be so easily distracted by vibrations from the half-shellfish half-peach that occupied the warm, watery bowl of her lower regions, she made herself available to maturation, if maturation would have her.

Put away was her teddy bear. Put away were her Beach Boys records. Put away was her fantasy of a Hawaiian honeymoon with Ralph Nader, her daydream of Ralph and her driving off together into the Haleakala sunset with their seat belts fastened. Not that she'd changed her mind about how perfect she'd be for him—he worked too hard, smiled too little, and dined as one indifferent to both flavor and fate; he clearly was a hero in need of rescue by a princess—it was just that romantic fantasies were . . . *immature*.

Leigh-Cheri read books on solar radiation. She perused papers on overpopulation. To keep abreast of current events, she watched every news telecast that she could, fleeing the TV room immediately whenever a love story was dramatized. She gave her ears to Mozart and Vivaldi (Tchaikovsky was painful). She fed flies to Prince Charming. And she worked at keeping her person and her room exceedingly clean.

"Cleanliness is next to godliness" was one slogan of maturity to which Leigh-Cheri could faithfully subscribe—not stopping to consider that if by the last quarter of the twentieth century godliness wasn't next to something more interesting than cleanliness, it might be time to reevaluate our notions of godliness.

•☺ 13 ☺•

Gulietta didn't work on Sundays. It was only fair. Even Friday got Thursday off, thanks to Robinson Crusoe. On Sundays Queen Tilli would lumber into the kitchen, her Chihuahua affectionately clasped, and make brunch.

The odor of frying bacon, sausage links, and ham tiptoed on little pig feet all the way to the north end of the second floor. Inevitably, the odor would awaken Leigh-Cheri. Inevitably, the odor made her simultaneously ravenous and nauseated. She hated the sensation. It reminded her of pregnancy. Every Sunday morning, celibacy notwithstanding, Leigh-Cheri awoke to a pan of fried fear.

Even after the panic had subsided, she found little to admire about a Sunday. To her mind, Sunday was where God kept his woolly slippers. It was a day with a dull edge that no amount of recreation could hone. Some might find it relaxing, but the Princess guessed that a great many people shared her feeling that Sunday generated a supernatural depression.

Sunday, a wan, stiff shadow of robust Saturday. Sunday, the day divorced fathers with "visitation" rights take their children to the zoo. Sunday, forced leisure for folks who have no aptitude for leisure. Sunday, when the hangover knows no bounds. Sunday, the day the boyfriend didn't come to the hospital. Sunday, an overfed white cat mewing hymns and farting footballs.

The day of the full moon, when the moon is neither increasing nor decreasing, the Babylonians called *Sa-bat,* meaning "heart-rest." It was believed that on this day, the woman in the moon, Ishtar, as the moon goddess was known in Babylon, was menstruating, for in Babylon, as in virtually every ancient and primitive society, there had been since the earliest times a taboo against a woman working, preparing food, or traveling when she was passing her monthly blood. On Sa-bat, from which comes our Sabbath, men as well as women were commanded to rest, for when the moon menstruated, the taboo was on everyone. Originally (and naturally) observed once a month, the Sabbath was later to be incorporated by the Christians into their Creation myth and made conveniently weekly. So nowadays hard-minded men with hard muscles and hard hats are relieved from their jobs on Sundays because of an archetypal psychological response to menstruation.

How Leigh-Cheri might have chuckled had she known that. On a particular Sunday in early January, January being to the year rather what Sunday is to the week, she wasn't aware of it, however, and she awoke in mean spirits. She pulled a robe on over her flannel pajamas (she'd discovered that silk had a tendency to agitate the peachfish), brushed the knots out of her hair, knuckled the crunchy granola from the corners of her eyes, and descended, yawning and stretching, into the hot hog hell of brunch. (She knew without tasting that her soybean curd would have soaked up some of the essence of bacon.)

As it has for so many for so long, the Sunday paper helped her through the day. Regardless of what else the press might have contributed to our culture, regardless of whether it is our first defense against totalitarianism or a wimpy force that undermines authentic experiences by categorizing them according to faddish popular interest, the press has given us big fat Sunday papers to ease our weekly mental menstrual bloat. Princess Leigh-Cheri, wriggle into your cheerleader uniform one last time and show us the way to hooray: two, four, six, eight, who do we appreciate? The Sunday papers, the Sunday papers, yea!

It was in the Seattle paper, on that particular Sunday in early January, that Leigh-Cheri initially read of the Geo-Therapy Care Fest, the what-to-do-for-the-planet-until-the-twenty-first-century-arrives conference. It was an event that would have speeded up her pulse even had it not been scheduled to occur in Hawaii. As it was, she bounced in her mother's lap—hardly the ultimate mature act—for the first time in years and began her petition to attend, for under the Furstenberg-Barcalona code to which they now strictly adhered, the Queen would have to accompany her. Tilli on Maui? Oh-Oh, spaghetti-o.

This may be said for the last quarter of the twentieth century: the truism that if we want a better world we will have to be better people came to be acknowledged, if not thoroughly understood, by a significantly large minority. Despite the boredom and anxiety of the period, or because of it, despite the uneasy seas that separated the sexes, or because of them, thousands, tens of thousands seemed willing to lend their bodies, their money, and their skills to various planetary rescue missions.

Coordination of those far-flung projects was a primary aim of the Geo-Therapy Care Fest, slated for the last week in February at Lahaina, Maui, Hawaii. Leading experts in the fields of alternative energy sources, organic farming, wilderness preservation, alternative education, holistic medicine, nutrition, consumer protection, recycling, and space colonization were to lecture and lead panel discussions and workshops. Proponents of many diverse self-help systems and consciousness cures, ranging from ancient Oriental to contemporary Californian, would also be in attendance. Moreover, certain futurists, artists, visionary thinkers, shamans, and poetic seers had been invited to participate, although several of the poets and one of the novelists were suspected by the organizers to register on the lunatic scale.

Don't think the news of that conference didn't melt the ice off the dog dish at thirty paces. If her life span were a salad, Leigh-Cheri would have dived into the dressing to present that conference with a perfect crouton. Not the least of her excitement was the information that Ralph Nader would deliver a key speech there and that one whole evening would be devoted to the subject of alternative methods of birth control. Even in the Siberia of celibacy, Leigh-Cheri was concerned with contraception. The problems associated with it had been more frustrating to her than the aggressive, competitive, assertive, egocentric, and crude behavior of the men with whom those problems *should* have been shared, and although she was presently free of the problem, she was too intelligent to mistake flight for victory.

The King and Queen hadn't seen their daughter so animated in months. True, this animation was a relative thing: Leigh-Cheri moved about like a zombie, yet a few days earlier she had more closely resembled a corpse. That was progress. Now there were moments when, speculating about the Care Fest, she actually appeared on the verge of smiling. What would any compassionate parents do? Give in, of course. Allow her her conference.

As the date approached, Queen Tilli decided that Maui was simply too barbarous. It was bad enough being stuck on the outskirts of Seattle, it raining trout teeth night and day, blackberry vines trying to force their way into the privacy of her own chamber, without transporting her posh poundage to some jungle island inhabited by surfer boys and vacationing strumpets, to whose company on that particular week would be added a couple thousand coocoos intent on saving a world they didn't fit into anyway. The Seattle Opera Company was opening *Norma* with Ebe Stignani that same week, and although Stignani was well past her prime, she provided true legato, a rare commodity in those jagged times, and the Queen had been invited to be honorary hostess at a reception for the aging soprano. Since Max dare not travel because of his valve, it was agreed about the middle of February that Gulietta would chaperon the Princess in Hawaii.

Gulietta was antique and couldn't mouth ten words of English, but she was so generally competent and so fond of Leigh-Cheri that Max and Tilli were convinced that her chaperonage would be adequate. They looked at one another nervously, however, when the skinny old servant, upon learning of her assignment, went to J. C. Penny and bought herself a bikini.

15

The sky is more impersonal than the sea. Above the birdline, higher than the last referential cloud, at an altitude that oxygen will not voluntarily frequent, across a zone where light drives the speed limit and never stops for coffee, crossing that desert in which gravity is the only sheik, a vehicle, owned and operated by Northwest Orient Airlines, whistled through its nostrils as it bucked the current of the Pacific jet stream. Leigh-Cheri turned from the window through which she'd been gazing down upon cloud top and ocean top. Leigh-Cheri looked at the old woman asleep in the adjacent seat. Leigh-Cheri had to smile. Rippling the canned air of the first-class cabin with her gentle snores, Gulietta was so serene that it was difficult to imagine her causing all the trouble she'd caused back at Seattle-Tacoma International Airport a few hours before.

Leigh-Cheri had been as surprised as anyone by the frog. Although the frog was relatively large and uncommonly green (a distant cousin, at best, of Prince Charming), there had been no hint of its presence in Gulietta's little wicker case. No sign of frog at all until the sudden shriek of the uniformed woman at the security check station.

A bit of a row had resulted. PLEASE, NO JOKES

said the sign above the checkpoint, and this *must* be a joke. Mustn't it? The incident was complicated by the fact that Gulietta could offer no English explanation, that her surname resembled a line from an optometrist's examination chart.

Security guards conferred. Gulietta and the Princess were searched a second time. Their hand luggage was reexamined. The frog was X-rayed to ascertain that it wasn't some kind of weapon. Could they be positive it wouldn't explode? "It's her pet," said Leigh-Cheri, who, in fact, had such a dim idea what the frog was doing in the old woman's case that even the memory of a European folk tale couldn't illuminate it. "It's her little pet." Leigh-Cheri batted her lengthy lashes, breathed in such a way that her round breasts seemed to rotate twelve degrees on their axes, and smiled so broadly that certain tiny mouth muscles, long neglected, struggled painfully to break free. "It's her little widdle pet."

Having extracted a promise that Gulietta would keep the amphibian enclosed—it was nestled in damp towels inside her bag—the charmed guards decided to let the two women and their widdle pet proceed. Aboard the jetliner, however, moments before takeoff, a different set of guards, accompanied by an official of the airlines, abruptly appeared and demanded the frog. "You can't take a live frog into Hawaii!" one of them exclaimed. They were quite agitated.

At that point, Leigh-Cheri recalled her previous visit to the islands. She remembered how adamant they'd been about restricting travelers bringing in pets of any kind. She remembered that bringing in fresh fruit or flowers was prohibited. She saw in her mind's eye the Honolulu airport's exhibition of insects, a collection of mounted bugs and beetles that had been discovered aboard visiting aircraft. She remembered that at Paradise Park the performing parrots and cockatoos had all had their wings clipped so that they might never escape and breed in the wild. The ecology of the islands was so delicately balanced that the introduction of one new species of mammal, bird, or reptile might throw it into chaos; one nonindigenous plant disease or invading female insect might ruin a billion-dollar business, be it pineapple for eating or palm trees for viewing.

Leigh-Cheri motioned to Gulietta, who was lashing the guards furiously with the vilest invectives in her strange language. Leigh-Cheri motioned for Gulietta to give up the frog. The crone was unconvinced. She hesitated. The captain, copilot, and flight crew had joined the administrator and guards in the first-class cabin. Passengers in coach and economy were in the aisles, peering up front to learn what the commotion was about. One of the guards yanked the wicker case from Gulietta's gnarled hands. The lid flew open. The frog took a tremendous leap. It landed on the head of a stewardess, who sent shocked whispers the length and breadth of the plane by screaming, "Aiii! Get that fucking thing off of me!"

The frog took another leap and came down on an empty seat. Several men dove for it. They missed. Dives and misses continued for a while, until the frog was cornered in the cockpit, where a guard captured it, but not before he had slammed his elbow into a navigational instrument, causing a possible malfunction. The device had to be checked and rechecked. All in all, the flight was delayed one hour and forty-six minutes.

Gulietta hadn't flown before. She was confused by the objections to the contents of her luggage. She refused to eat the snack served by the still-flustered stewardess.

How could Leigh-Cheri make Gulietta understand the Great Hawaiian Mongoose Reaction?

Hawaii once had a rat problem. Then, somebody hit upon a brilliant solution. Import mongooses from India. Mongooses would kill the rats. It worked. Mongooses did kill the rats. Mongooses also killed chickens, young pigs, birds, cats, dogs, and small children. There have been reports of mongooses attacking motorbikes, power lawn mowers, golf carts, and James Michener. In Hawaii now, there are as many mongooses as there once were rats. Hawaii had traded its rat problem for a mongoose problem. Hawaii was determined nothing like that would ever happen again.

How could Leigh-Cheri draw for Gulietta the appropriate analogy between Hawaii's rodents and society at large? Society had a crime problem. It hired cops to attack crime. Now society has a cop problem.

The answer, of course, is that Leigh-Cheri could not draw that parallel at all. That parallel had never occurred to her. It had occurred to Bernard Mickey Wrangle, however.

Bernard Mickey Wrangle sat in the economy cabin of the Northwest Orient airliner and pondered the rat/mongoose-crime/cop analogy. Bernard Mickey Wrangle sat in the rear of the aircraft with seven sticks of dynamite strapped to his body.

Bernard Mickey Wrangle was clever. Most likely, he could have successfully boarded the flight to Hawaii with seven sticks of dynamite strapped to his body under any conditions. Certainly, though, the frog had helped pave his way.

(The frog, incidentally, was released at a pond near the Sea-Tac runways. For being close to a busy airport, it was a pleasant pond. It featured lily pads and cattails and fat mosquitoes for lunch. But let's face it, damn it all, it wasn't Waikiki.)

16

The jetliner, missing one small green traveler but carrying a bonus seven sticks of dynamite, continued its crossing of what every novice surfer knows to be the most inappropriately named body of water on earth. The jetliner whistled to conceal its fear of gravity. Leigh-Cheri read magazines to conceal her excitement.

Excitement widened in her eyes like periods at the end of billboard sentences. Commas of excitement wobbled in her tummy, and question marks squirmed in there as well. Every once in a while, she felt as if she were sitting on an exclamation point.

Such a wonderful idea was the Geo-Therapy Care Fest that it was surprising to her that it hadn't happened before. An assembly of the best thinkers, the most advanced technicians, the most concerned scientists, the most enlightened artists, pooling their knowledge and their dreams for the betterment of all. That was what the United Nations would be were the United Nations not in the hands of the dull and the corrupt. Were it not in the service of ego-politics.

At the Maui conference, Buckminster Fuller would deliver a paper on "Harvesting Pollution: Thar's Gold in Them Thar Spills." Gary Snyder would talk about "The Buddhist Approach to Fighting City Hall." The lecture by the environmentalist Dr. Barry Commoner (his name induced in the Princess a twinge of superiority followed by a deeper twinge of guilt) would be entitled, "There's No Such Thing As a Free Lunch." The Alternative Birth-Control Workshop would be led by Linda Coghill, the woman who singlehandedly slashed the illegitimacy and abortion rates in Portland,

Oregon. On the morning of February 26, Leigh-Cheri would have to choose between a demonstration of the photovoltaic cell (a breakthrough in reducing the expense of solar power) and a panel discussion led by Dr. Linus Pauling on Vitamin C as a prevention and a cure. Oh my, this *was* exciting. Was there any planetary problem of significance that the Care Fest overlooked? Leigh-Cheri couldn't think of one.

Maybe Leigh-Cheri would admit nothing significant in the fact that the articles in the magazines she was perusing were largely about romance: who was breaking up—or taking up—with whom, what to do when husbands lose interest, how to cope with loneliness and rejection, and so forth. The advertisements in the magazines were almost exclusively concerned with making oneself attractive to the opposite sex. Moreover, the movie that was screened aboard the plane was a love story. The movie had an unhappy ending and thus was considered "realistic." And when the Princess put on a headset to listen to the taped music that Northwest Orient provided its passengers, the songs she heard were about hearts breaking and hearts aching, or hearts quaking as they slid, spewing sparks, across the electrified threshold of new love.

Maybe Leigh-Cheri elected to disregard the evidence because it was just too personal. If beneath the great issues and all-encompassing questions (as underplayed as they were in the last quarter of the twentieth century) a more intimate struggle raged, a struggle whose real goal was romantic fulfillment, maybe it was courageous and honorable to attempt to transcend that struggle, to insist on something more than that.

Maybe.

In the rear of the aircraft, Bernard Mickey Wrangle reached inside his jacket . . . and pulled from his breast pocket . . . not a detonator . . . nor a fuse . . . not yet . . . but a package . . . of Hostess Twinkies.

Too bad the Queen insisted that you fly first-class, Leigh-Cheri. Too bad you're sitting next to your snoozing old chaperon instead of next to Bernard Mickey Wrangle. Since Hostess Twinkies always travel in pairs—because like the coyote, the killer whale, the gorilla, and the whooping crane, Hostess Twinkies mate for life—there would have been a Twinkie each for you to share.

17

The airliner circled Honolulu the way a typing finger circles a keyboard, awaiting the message from the control center that would instruct it when and where to land.

And they land . . .

. . . on A.

Runway A.

A for "attic."

A for "amore."

What we have here is an unexpected touchdown on the runway of the heart. This flight could only terminate in a room close to the moon.

The No Smoking sign was on. (In the attic, the Camel cigarettes were never to be lit.) The signal to Fasten Seat Belts was given. (In amore, belts fasten and unfasten at delicious intervals.) Gulietta clutched her wicker case, which now bore but the slightest spoor of frog. Leigh-Cheri clutched her thighs, as dry now as princess thighs ought to be. Bernard Mickey Wrangle, listed on the passenger manifest as T. Victrola Firecracker but once known to millions as the Woodpecker, clutched nothing, not even his black powder underwear. The Woodpecker knew better than to clutch and to hold. The Woodpecker simply grinned.

He grinned because he had reached Hawaii without detection. He grinned because Twinkie cream always made him grin. He grinned because it was the last quarter of the twentieth century, and something momentous was happening.

INTERLUDE

Maybe I'm mistaken about the Remington SL3. I'm no longer convinced that it will do. Oh, it's a superb tool—for the proper desk in the proper office. If there's a treatise you wish to compose, a letter to the editor, an invoice, a book review, why it will cross your *t*'s before you come to them, and I'm positive that there are secretaries who would prefer it to their mates. But for the novelist, any typewriter is a formidable thing; and the Remington SL3, with its interchangeable printing units, its electric margins, variable line spacer, paper-centering scale, personalized touch control, automatic paragraphing button, vertical and horizontal half-spacing, express backspacer, skip tabulation, improved umlaut maker, and misspell alarm, well, to face that degree of mechanical sophistication in the midnight of your sanctum is to know a brand of fear.

First of all, it hums, purrs like a seductive housecat, fairly trembles upon the table; it seems eager—too goddamned eager—to get to work. Hey! Relax, fella. I'm thinking. Don't push me.

Then there's its color: blue. Not matte black; mysterious, deep, absorbent, accepting, noncommittal, priestly black like typewriters of old, but a harsh, chill, modern blue that causes it to affect, even by candlelight, the suspecting, censorious glare of the customs inspector or efficiency engineer. It appears to be looking over my shoulder even as I am looking over its.

All right, those toadstool spores I inadvertently

snorted while cleaning out my refrigerator *may* be magnifying sensation, but this is not the first time that intimidation by typewriter has caused me to consider the pen. Pencils are out of the question, their marks are impermanent. Of course, fountain pens leak; ballpoints have no style, and, moreover, always run away from home. The peacock quill appeals to me, the woodpecker quill even more so, but the last are hard to come by and the first scratchy and slow.

Perhaps what a novelist needs is a different sort of writing implement. Say, a Remington built of balsa wood, its parts glued together like a boyhood model; delicate, graceful, submissive, as ready to soar as an ace.

Better, a carved typewriter, hewn from a single block of sacred cypress; decorated with mineral pigments, berry juice, and mud; its keys living mushrooms, its ribbon the long iridescent tongue of a lizard. An animal typewriter, silent until touched, then filling the page with growls and squeals and squawks, yowls and bleats and snorts, brayings and chatterings and dry rattlings from the underbrush; a typewriter that could type real kisses, ooze semen and sweat.

Or—a typewriter constructed of tiny seashells by a retired merchant sailor, built inside a bottle so that it can be worked only by the little finger of the left hand of a right-handed person. A left-handed typewriter for a left-handed task. (You're aware, I assume, of the scientific discovery that our universe lives side by side with a parallel universe. The two universes, identical in many respects, are opposite in electrical charge and magnetic property: the "anti-universe," so called, is in effect a mirror image, a reverse copy. Well, certain amino acids are left-handed, some are their reflection, right-handed. But the proteins in living organisms are always left-handed. The right-handed amino acids are impossible to digest and can be harmful to life. It's smart not to eat anything you find in a mirror. As for those novels that claim to "mirror" reality . . . may a word to the wise be sufficient.

(Toward the wind-down of the Second World War, an American flyer parachuted from his burning plane to land in an isolated village near Japan's Inland Sea. The villagers, devout Buddhists far removed from the hot arena of events and the Shinto/fascistic/industrial philosophies that had spawned the events, took in the broken pilot and nursed him. They kept him concealed and alive for several months, but eventually he died.

(Since Buddhists have reverence for all life, they also respect the proprieties of death. The villagers wished to award the dead foreigner his entitled burial, but the only funereal customs with which they were familiar were Buddhist, and those, of course, would have been inappropriate.

(Having packed the corpse in pond ice, they set out to make inquiries about Christian burial procedures, all very discreetly so as not to arouse the suspicion of the authorities. Their luck was small.

(At last, someone smuggled into the village a Japanese translation of an English language book that promised to provide the information they sought. The book was called *Finnegans Wake*.

(If you can picture those remote 1945 Japanese peasants earnestly trying to hold a drunken Irish wake, complicated by the experimental wordplay of James Joyce, you can picture the relationship between an author, his typewriter, and that reality to whose recreation he's obliged to apply the southpaw touch, even though he knows only too well the function Arabs and Hindus assign the left hand.)

I'm not so far gone that I expect technologists to be interested in designing machines for artists—why, if novelists got wooden typewriters, poets would demand that theirs be ice. What is more likely is that technology will bypass artists, that a day is coming when our novels will be written by computers, the same devices that will paint our murals and compose our tunes. If I'm chuckling, it's because I'm imagining a computer, programmed to produce logical variations on the eighteen possible literary plots, I'm imagining that computer trying to deal with what happened in Leigh-Cheri's attic. If I'm chuckling, it means that the Remington SL3 had better watch its P's p's and Q's q's.

PHASE II

18

It was mid-afternoon, a good five hours before moon-rise, when the flight touched down in Honolulu, but already the mai tais were swaying, the pineapples were jiggling, the mongooses were mating, and coco-nuts were rolling in ecstasy. The Hawaii sun, in con-trast to, say, the Nebraska sun, had obviously fallen under the influence of the moon and was given to deporting itself in a fairly feminine fashion. Not that the Hawaii sun wouldn't fry your hide off should you show it disrespect, but it had a romantic aura, a decidedly lunar attitude toward amore that the sun of Mexico would consider soft and weak. Despite the tangle of traffic, the din of condominium construction, the smoking sugar refineries, and the strange specta-cle of Japanese tourists roaming the hot beaches in business suits and street shoes, Hawaii was, indeed, a travelogue tableau; a living Pap smear for the paradise flu.

So goofy/erotic was the Hawaiian language that the street signs read like invitations to pagan whoopjam-boreehoos, and "nookie" was on the tip of every sober tongue. Hawaiian was a language that could name a fish "humuhumunukunukuapua'a" and a bird "o-o," and never mind that the bird was larger than the fish. Humuhumunukunukuapua'a (a typewriter that enjoys that word as much as the Remington SL3 couldn't be all bad) still played in Hawaiian waters, not fifty yards from the leather soles of Sony execu-tives, but the o-o, that gorgeous honeysucker, was long gone. Hawaiian royalty favored the tail feathers of the o-o for their ceremonial capes. Hawaii's rulers were mammoth, their capes were very long. It took a lot of tail feathers to make a king a cape. The o-o was plucked into extinction. O O spaghetti-o.

Although the ecological implications would have appalled her, Leigh-Cheri could fancy herself in o-o. If our pale Princess could have chosen a land to be queen of, Hawaii was it. The instant she stepped off the jetliner, her heart began to pump pure hibiscus juice. If her hands were tied behind her and the world had Hawaii in its wall safe, she would have figured a way to get it out. Hawaii made the mouth of her soul water.

Alas, Leigh-Cheri hadn't much opportunity for reverie. Because of frog problems, her plane had landed on Oahu merely minutes before her connecting flight on inter-island Aloha Airlines was scheduled to depart for Maui. She and Gulietta had to run, if you could call Gulietta's scurrying a run, from one end of Honolulu's airport to the other.

So intent was their dash that they failed to notice that Bernard Mickey Wrangle was loping along beside them.

⣿ 19 ⣿

The flight to Maui was as bumpy as a kite's. As the small plane was tossed about by drafts, several passengers acquired the hue of Hawaiian foliage. Leigh-Cheri, however, had been driven to the airport that morning by Chuck the chauffeur, and after such a ride, it would have taken more than a little turbulent air to unnerve her. Gulietta was simply too old to be unnerved by anything, although she was still pouting about the confiscation of her totem. As for Bernard M. Wrangle, who sat behind the Princess studying her red hair, his heart thumped peacefully against the explosives taped to his chest.

As the aircraft bobbed, so did Leigh-Cheri's mind, up and down, from one level to another, thinking one moment of the charms of Hawaii, to which she had a mild addiction; thinking the next of the Care Fest and the great good that might come from it; bouncing to thoughts of herself, who she was and who she might be.

"I'm a princess," she reminded herself, with a minimum of conviction, "a princess who grew up in a blackberry patch near Seattle, who's never so much as set a tennis shoe in the nation where her royal blood was formed, a princess who doesn't know diddly squat about princessing, a princess who's behaved like a twit and a twat; who's been, well, *disappointed* in men and romance, who's a bit confused, who's got a lot to learn, but a princess, after all; just as fucking much as Caroline or Anne, and although in the last quarter of the twentieth century the very idea of royalty may seem artificial, archaic, and somewhat decadent, I insist on my princess-hood because without it I'm just another physically attractive woman with that I-went-to-college-but-it-didn't-do-me-any-good look and nothing much to offer anyone. If I'm lost as a lover, I'm still right here as a human. I feel the pain of humanity inside me, in my tummy, about eight inches above the peachfish. Whether I'm unduly sensitive to this pain because I'm a princess—could the whole world be the pea under my mattress?—I don't know, but because I'm a princess, I might be able to do something to help lessen humanity's pain. And the Care Fest just may show me the way to do it. I wonder if Ralph is staying at our hotel? I hope I packed my No Nukes T-shirt. Don't Crosby, Stills, and Nash hang out in Lahaina? Can I drink more than one mai tai without taking on the aroma of an aroused butterfly?"

Her thoughts dipped and lifted in unstable air.

Before long, they had passed over Molokai and could see the reddish corona of Haleakala rising in the southeast like the stone in a Truman Capote mood ring. "Maui," whispered Leigh-Cheri to Gulietta. "Maui." Her own red top bounced as she sat up straight in her seat. Bernard—the Woodpecker—regarded it with the gaze of an expert.

⚬•⚬ 20 ⚬•⚬

Suspecting that the authorities might run checks on hair dye purchases, Bernard made his own coloring from roots and bark. It had a peculiar smell, but women did not find it unattractive. To Bernard, the odor evoked memories of vulture shadows and wolf howls; of cocaine, high explosives, and sure-footed steeds; of the hideout behind the waterfall. As for its effect on others, he'd been asked more than once if he didn't shampoo with root beer. He limited the dying to the hair on his head and for that reason was careful to make love only in the dark. Once, he spilled the dye all over his shoes. From then on, he dyed with his boots on.

The Twelve Most Famous Redheads:
1. Lucille Ball, comedienne
2. Gen. George Custer, military maverick
3. Lizzie Borden, hatchetwoman
4. Thomas Jefferson, revolutionary
5. Red Skelton, comic
6. George Bernard Shaw, playwright
7. Judas Iscariot, informer

8. Mark Twain, humorist
9. Woody Allen, humorist
10. Margaret Sanger, feminist
11. Scarlet O'Hara, bitch
12. Bernard Mickey Wrangle, bomber

From this list, the analytically minded might conclude that persons with red hair tend to be either dangerous or funny. But of the dozen, only one ever had to hide his or her hue. Even Judas flew his natural colors. Judas Iscarrot-top.

How did Bernard feel about dressing his woodpecker strands in suits of crow? From the admiring looks that he aimed at Leigh-Cheri's crown, and Haleakala's, a shallow observer might be inclined to compare him to a connoisseur of rubies trapped under a coal chute. Upon more careful examination, however, one would have to report that he took a very nearly delicious pleasure in smuggling his curls about, their blaze concealed from the cold eye of the law by the thinnest millimeter of pigment.

And, of course, Bernard, as all men, carried around in his trousers the most renowned redhead of all—characteristically funny and dangerous.

21

Aboard Aloha Airlines Flight 23, Bernard wasn't the only admirer of Leigh-Cheri. From the seat in front of her, a young man with a long, wavy beard, aloha shirt, and hibiscus blossoms intertwined in his ponytail had turned around to engage her in conversation. He was on his way to the Care Fest, he said, to teach meditation techniques at a workshop. The young man tried to interest Leigh-Cheri in his program. He offered to give her personal instruction in meditation, free of charge. She seemed to be seriously considering it.

Bernard leaned forward until his freckled chin rested atop Leigh-Cheri's seat. "Yum," he said.

The Princess flinched, but did not glance back. The young man in front began showing her his puka shell necklace. While fingering the pukas, he spoke quietly to her of deep relaxation, inner peace, and the wisdom of letting things flow.

"Yum," repeated Bernard. He said it very close to the royal ear.

This time she spun around. Her expression was indignant. "I beg your pardon."

Bernard smiled as sweetly as a retarded jack-o'-lantern. "It's my mantra."

Leigh-Cheri glowered at him, as only someone of the redheaded persuasion can glower. He was dressed all in black and had bad teeth. He was wearing Donald Duck sunglasses. Kiddie glasses. She turned back to the meditation instructor, who at once ceased scowling at Bernard and gave her a sympathetic look.

"There are only two mantras," said Bernard. "Yum and yuk. Mine is yum."

It sounded halfway logical, but the Princess refused to respond. She squeezed Gulietta's hand. She asked the junior guru in front how meditation could help alleviate suffering in the world.

"Yum," said Bernard. "Yuu-mmmm." Leigh-Cheri ignored him. The other passengers regarded him strangely.

"Do you need anything, sir?" asked the stewardess.

Bernard shrugged. He looked out of the window. He looked at the rosy rim of the big volcano. Haleakala—"House of the Sun." If Haleakala was where the sun called home, what was the moon's address? Did the moon live in France on Main Street?

22

It was Haleakala, erupting in tandem with a lesser volcano, that created the island of Maui. It must have been a show. The crater was seven and one half miles across, the cone more than ten thousand feet high, yet Haleakala had a presence at which even the most impressive measurements didn't hint.

Such an eerie, unfamiliar place was Haleakala that there was a tendency to associate it with other worlds, outer spaces. Indeed, an unusually large percentage of visitors who camped there overnight in order to view the famous Haleakala sunrise, the sun awakening in its own bedroom, swore to having seen oddly lighted forms in the sky. To the dormant volcano, with its crumbly cromlechs, its lunar contours, its black and red sands, supernatural properties came to be attributed. Many regarded it a universal center, an intergalactic connecting point, a cosmic beanhill, the earth terminal for spaceships of all degrees of substance and visibility. So many people claimed to have seen UFOs buzzing Haleakala that it turned into a mecca for flying-saucer fans and would-be cosmic cosmopolitans. Individuals, entire cults with outer-space orientations settled in the valleys near the base of the mountain.

When word of the impending Care Fest spread from Lahaina into the Maui interior, the various flying-saucer groups banded together to insist that they be included in the conference. The fact that Timothy Leary had been invited to the Care Fest to present his theories on orbiting space colonies pleased but didn't placate them. "The future of the earth is bound up with the future of the universe," they reasoned. Some went so far as to state that the future of the earth was entirely in the hands of superior beings on distant planets. The Care Fest would be a sham if UFO scholars and intermediaries weren't included, they said.

"The agenda is already set, and it's crowded as it is," protested the organizers.

The saucer people didn't care. They raced their kryptonite engines, billowed their green exhaust. From the thirteenth floor of the Darth Vader Building, communiqués and manifestoes issued.

A compromise was reached. The Maui saucerites were granted use of conference facilities on Sunday, the day prior to the official opening of the Care Fest, the day that Leigh-Cheri arrived in Lahaina. As the Princess and her chaperon checked into the Pioneer Inn, a UFO gathering was already in progress there. "How peculiar," remarked Leigh-Cheri, noticing the flowing robes and wide eyes of the delegates. There was no one in the lobby who looked the slightest like Ralph Nader.

What the hell, it was Sunday. Sunday is Sunday, even in Hawaii. No volume of orchid nectar, no wardrobe of o-o plumage could change the color of Sunday from that of . . . buttermilk, toothpaste, Camembert cheese. Leigh-Cheri knew better than to jump to conclusions on a Sunday. After unpacking, she seated herself out on the *lanai,* where, luxuriously awash in tropical twilight, she perused the Sunday edition of the Honolulu *Advertiser.*

A *lanai* was a veranda in Hawaii, but Lanai was also the name of one of the smallest of the Hawaiian Islands. The island of Lanai was close to Maui, a sort of veranda of Maui, and was clearly visible from Lahaina. In those days, Lanai was almost entirely in the possession of the Dole Corporation, which planted it in pineapples and limited its visitors, but Lanai hadn't always been a company island. As a matter of fact, there was a time when it was outlaw territory, a refuge for fugitives. If a Hawaiian lawbreaker could make it to Lanai, he was home free. That was the agreement. Police had voluntarily suspended their authority at the shoreline of Lanai. Moreover, if an escaped prisoner or a culprit fleeing a crime could survive seven years on the island (which had little food or fresh water), charges against him were dropped, and he could return to society a free man.

Maybe that's why Bernard Mickey Wrangle stood on the Lahaina waterfront staring at Lanai—staring hard, shifting weight from one boot to the other, occasionally saying "yum" under his breath.

The Woodpecker had been a fugitive (this last time) for more than six years. In eleven months, the statute of limitations in his case would expire, and he would become, in the eyes of the law, "free."

The Woodpecker stared at the former outlaw island until its margins melted like raw sugar into the steeping tea of night. Then he crossed the street to the Pioneer Inn, the restored old whalers' hotel, where the usual crowd of international beach bums, cool *kamaainas,* sailboat crewmen, amateur adventurers, itinerant waitresses, students on the metamorphose from Midwest bookworms into South Pacific night owls ("The University of Pineapple is my alma papaya, I graduated mango cum laude."), rock musicians of varying degrees of celebrity and expertise, young divorcées (older ones went to Waikiki), divers (coral, salvage, skin, and muff), puka salesmen, T-shirt airbrushers, and Berkeley radicals with a secret romantic streak made themselves at home, coming and going, flirting and hustling, posing and preening, scheming and letting off steam, a gin or rum never far from the lips, a fortune, a nirvana, or a revolution always just out of reach. Mingling with the regulars on this Sunday evening were freshly arrived Care Fest delegates, famous and unknown; plus a man and woman from the planet Argon who had slipped away from the UFO conference to have a piña colada. Plus the Woodpecker.

The Woodpecker did tequila drink. The Pioneer bar was so crowded that much dry time elapsed between waiter's visits, so the Woodpecker ordered triples. Lanai, that arid sanctuary, evidently had stimulated his thirst buds. Slurping his tequilas with a noise that sounded not dissimilar to "yum," he scanned the room in vain for a glimpse of long red hair and felt the seven sticks of explosive pressing, almost erotically, against the freckles of his flesh.

Now, tequila may be the favored beverage of outlaws, but that doesn't mean it gives them preferential treatment. In fact, tequila probably had betrayed as many outlaws as has the central nervous system and dissatisfied wives. Tequila, scorpion honey, harsh dew of the doglands, essence of Aztec, crema de cacti; tequila, oily and thermal like the sun in solution; tequila, liquid geometry of passion; Tequila, the buzzard god who copulates in midair with the ascending souls of dying virgins; tequila, firebug in the house of good taste; O tequila, savage water of sorcery, what confusion and mischief your sly, rebellious drops do generate!

Without doubt, it was the tequila that made Bernard impatient, that befuddled him into mistaking the UFO conference for the Geo-Therapy Care Fest.

As a consequence, the saucer conference was blown ass over teacup.

23

Even when intoxicated, Bernard Mickey Wrangle was a master of blast. He planted the dynamite in such a place and in such a way (breaking four sticks in half, then laying them outside the walls at twenty-foot intervals) that the Pioneer Inn shook like a wet mutt; every window in one end of it shattered, wallboards cracked, lighting fixtures and potted plants plummeted to the meeting hall floor, smoke and dust roiled for half an hour, and saucerites, scorched and scratched, scattered as if the Jewish Mother Ship had landed in their midst, spraying scalding jets of chicken soup—yet not one person was seriously hurt.

On one hand, it was a masterpiece of delicate dynamiting, on the other a faux pas. When he awoke Monday morning, much to his hangover's delight (a hangover without a head to torment is like a philanthropist without an institution to endow), and learned that he'd dropped his load in the wrong bin, the sheepish expression of the premature ejaculator crossed his face.

At breakfast, where, hoping to avoid attention, he tried to conceal from his fellow diners that he was pouring beer over his Wheaties, he said to himself, "Yikes." Then he said "Yikes" again, not pausing to ponder that there might be *three* mantras. "Yikes, that was close. Of course, close calls are the only calls an outlaw should accept, but O my Woodpecker, that business last night bordered on the crazed. Considering the tequila level of my gorge and the number of human coconuts that hula around Lahaina at every hour of the clock, it's a miracle I wasn't seen."

Yes, even in the last quarter of the twentieth century

miracles occurred—although this was not one of them. There *was* a witness to Bernard's deed. Old Gulietta had watched the whole thing.

❀ 24 ❀

To Gulietta, indoor plumbing was the devil's device. Of all the follies of the modern world, that one struck her as most unnecessary. There was something unnatural, foolish, and a little filthy about going indoors. On the European estates where she was reared, it was common practice for servant girls to lift their skirts outside. Gulietta had seen no reason to alter her habits in Seattle. Despite the difficulty there of doing one's natural duty without being rained upon or receiving from a blackberry bramble a bite as sharp as hemorrhoids, she felt comfortable—happy, even—when she could squat in fresh air. Besides, it was an opportune way to spy frogs.

Leaving Leigh-Cheri in their room, pouring over programs and press releases, the old woman had gone out looking for a sensible spot to void her bladder. The soft, warm, Sweet Lelani night seemed perfectly suited for that. The Pioneer Inn, unfortunately, was in downtown Lahaina and had no grounds. It had a courtyard, however, which at 11:00 p.m. on Sunday had been fairly deserted, so Gulietta had slipped into the banana trees next to a wall and dropped her drawers.

Before she could direct a stream, Bernard had slipped into the foliage not twenty feet from her. She thought he'd come for a piss as well, and that was fine with her, but the length of the thing he pulled out of his jeans almost made her gasp. When he snapped it in half, she did gasp.

She was small. She knew how to sit very still. Like a toad. Undetected, holding her water, she had watched the whole thing. After the fuse was lit, the Woodpecker flew. Yanking up her bloomers, Gulietta fled, too. She returned to the room just as the explosion sounded. Suddenly, she knew what it was like to pee indoors.

⦂ 25 ⦂

In the world according to the positivist, the inspiring thing about scrambled eggs is that any way you turn them they're sunny side up. In the world according to the existentialist, the hopeless thing about scrambled eggs is that any way you turn them they're scrambled. In the world according to the outlaw, it was Wheaties-with-beer for breakfast, and who cared which crossed the road first, the chicken or the egg. But any way you turned the Geo-Therapy Care Fest, you had to notice that Bernard's blast had indirectly scrambled it.

With Pioneer Inn's meeting hall in bad state of repair, with cops, newspeople, and curiosity-seekers milling around the place like bargain-minded lemmings at a suicide sale, and with the hotel management indulging a nasty attack of nerves, conference organizers spent all of Monday attempting to relocate. They made a halfhearted effort to obtain space at one or another of the luxury hotels a few miles up the coast at Kaanapali and were partially relieved to learn that there wasn't room. Old, wooden, and South Sea funky, the Pioneer Inn had been far better suited to the sensibilities of the Care Fest. This was, in truth, the first time since its opening in 1901 that the Pioneer was to host a formal convention, a fact that appealed to the Care Fest staff but an error the inn was not likely to repeat.

At last, on Tuesday, Lahaina officials granted permission for the world rescuers to convene under the giant banyan tree whose branches covered three-quarters of an acre in the city park. Terrific. Many considered this an even more appropriate site than the Pioneer Inn, which, after all, was built to cater originally to the whaling trade, an irony not lost on those Care Festers to whom preservation of whales and dolphins was an important and rather emotional goal. By the time anything could get organized beneath the banyan, however, it was already Wednesday, the week was half-shot, and a number of the luminaries who were to address the gathering had left or had decided not to attend. Many simply couldn't adjust their busy schedules to the amended program; a few were put off by the UFO delegates (including the visiting couple from Argon) who remained on the scene, singed and bruised, babbling rumors of the most astonishing conspiracies and plots; while others were worried about the possibility of further explosions, a not unreasonable concern considering that the Woodpecker was still on Maui with three sticks of dynamite left in his clothes.

26

For her part, Princess Leigh-Cheri spent many hours dragging a freshly sunburned finger up and down the list of scheduled speakers—Dick Gregory, Marshall McLuhan, Michio Kushi, Laura Huxley, Ram Dass, David Brower, John Lilly, Murray Gell-Mann, Joseph Campbell, Elizabeth Kübler-Ross, Marcel Marceau, et al—wondering who would or would not show.

By all rights, the Princess should have been enjoying her beloved Hawaii, Care Fest or no, but it was Gulietta who romped in the surf while her young mistress sat in the shade (redheads do burn easily) of this or that koa tree, checking and rechecking lists and pouting like the koa itself, whose leaves resemble lips or the crescents of moon. There was one black cloud in all the Hawaiian Islands, and it was parked over *her* head. She was disappointed, to say the least, by the scrambling of the Care Fest, and considering her disappointments of the past year, she was beginning to suspect that she might be jinxed. She wondered if Gulietta hadn't been bringing that frog along to protect her.

"Goddamn it," she said. "A princess deserves better than this."

As if to sandpaper her burn, an oddly beautiful woman in a turban and robe had stopped her in the lobby to inform her (above the noise of workmen busily replacing window glass) that on the planet Argon redheads were considered evil and that if she had any plans for space travel, she'd better change her ways. "Red hair is caused by sugar and lust," the woman, who was blonde, confided. "Highly evolved beings do not indulge in sugar and lust." It was a rude thing to say, particularly in Hawaii where sugar and lust surpassed even pineapples and marijuana as cash crops. And since Leigh-Cheri only recently had begun to eliminate those very sweets and meats from her life—without any thought to her status on Argon—the woman's accusations made her defensive and caused an unreasonable guilt to darken the hue of her gloom. She rolled around paradise like four bald tires on an ambulance.

Late Tuesday afternoon there occurred three events to retread her mood. One, Ralph Nader checked into the Pioneer Inn, announcing that he would speak the next evening as scheduled, in Banyan Park. Two, a reporter from *People* magazine asked her for an interview, and for the first time, she felt she had something to say to those media representatives who had tried off and on for years to make some kind of "story" out of her. Three, Gulietta, looking as skinny and blue as a jailhouse tattoo as she bounded from the ever-chill ocean in her bikini, pointed out to her a man on the beach and through gesture and omomatopoeia ("boom-boom" is "boom-boom" in any land, dynamite speaks a universal lingo) identified him as the bomber.

The Princess didn't hesitate. She walked right up to the man and placed him under citizen's arrest.

⚬⚬ 27 ⚬⚬

Little did Leigh-Cheri know that she was arresting a man whom half a dozen American sheriffs had sworn on family Bibles to see dead, that she had nabbed a fugitive who had eluded the greediest nets of the FBI for a decade, all told, although it must be admitted that in recent years, with the social climate altered and Bernard inactive, interest in his capture had waned.

Leigh-Cheri had heard of the Woodpecker, of course, but in the days when he was making headlines by blowing up draft boards and induction centers, the last days of the Vietnam War, she'd been a schoolgirl, picking blackberries, cuddling teddy bears, listening to a certain bedtime story, yellowing her nose with buttercups. Curiously excited by an enema that Gulietta had administered to her on Queen Tilli's orders, Leigh-Cheri had masturbated for the first time on the very evening of Bernard's most infamous ex-

ploit, and the confusing pleasure of secret fingering—
the fresh flush that heated her cheeks, the vague
mental images of nasty games with boys, the sticky
dew that smelled of frog water and clung like prehen-
sile pearls to the thickening fuzz around her peachfish—this mysterious and shaming little ache of ecstasy eclipsed the less personal events of the day,
including the news that the notorious Woodpecker
had demolished an entire building on the campus of a
large Midwestern university.

Bernard Mickey Wrangle had sneaked into Madison,
Wisconsin, in the deep of night. His hair was red
then, red being the color of emergency and roses;
red being the prelate's top and the baboon's bottom; red
being the blood's color, jelly's color; red maddening
the bull, red bringing the bull down; red being the
color of valentines, of left-handedness, and of a small
princess's newfound guilty hobby. His hair was red,
his cowboy boots muddy, his heart a hive of musical
bees.

Aided and abetted by the Woodpecker Gang, he
blew up the chemistry building at the University of
Wisconsin. Allegedly, work performed in that building was helpful to the war the United States government was then waging in Southeast Asia. The explosion
occurred at three o'clock in the morning. The building
was supposed to have been unoccupied. Unfortunately,
a graduate student was in one of the laboratories,
completing research that was to lead to his doctorate.

The diligent student was found in the rubble. Not
all of him, but enough to matter. Confined to a
wheelchair, he became a stereo jockey in a Milwaukee
disco, trading snappy patter with good-timing office
workers and playing Barry White records as if he
believed in them. He might have been a decent scien-
tist. His project, which was obliterated by the blast,
was the perfection of an oral contraceptive for men.

Bernard made it safely back to the West. Only the radio news reports followed him to the hideout behind the waterfall. For once, the reports failed to entertain him. "I took a man's legs," he said to Montana Judy. "I took his manhood, I took his memory, and I took his career. Worse, I took his wife, who split when he ran out of manhood and career. Worse still, I might have spoiled chances for a male pill. Yikes. I've got to pay. I deserve to pay. But I'll pay in my way, not society's. As bad as I am, there isn't a judge who's good enough to sentence me."

Another penitent might have joined a grubby religious cult or stood in a dark alley waiting for someone to come along and knock him in the head. As *his* payment, Bernard embarked on a chemical research project of his own. He tracked down, investigated, and tested various esoteric methods of birth control. "Who knows," he told Montana Judy, "maybe I'll come up with something better than that poor bozo's pill."

In herbal literature, it is written that comfrey is good for sprains and fit root for spasms; cascara will end constipation, wild cherry restore loss of speech; for nosebleed, buckthorn is recommended, and for pneumonia, try skunk cabbage. If you are stricken with sexual desire, the cure prescribed is lily root, and assuming that lily root fails, is unavailable, or is forsaken in the delirium of the illness, squaw vine, spikenard, and raspberry leaves all make childbirth a little easier. Western herbal literature is oddly lacking in contraceptive advice, Bernard discovered. Oddly lacking. He suspected tampering by the Church, but Bernard suspected the Church of a great many things.

In the anthropological texts that he pilfered from public libraries on both sides of the Rockies, it was told how the influence of tree spirits and water nymphs would promote fecundity, and though Bernard did not doubt that—female members of the Woodpecker Gang demonstrated a decided tendency toward fecundity out there in the wilderness where tree spirits abounded—he wondered where the deities were who guarded *against* the knock-up. The Eskimo of the Bering Strait, the Huichol of Mexico, the Nishinam Indians of California, the Caffre tribes of South Africa, the Basuto, the Maori, and the Anno all made dolls in the likeness of the infant that was wanted, and that act of homeopathic magic brought pregnancy galloping. But what image could be fashioned to hold would-be embryos at bay? A decoction of wasp's nest was administered internally to Lkungen brides to make them as prolific as insects. How much of a rhinoceros would a bride have to eat in order to emulate that animal's habit of infrequent offspring?

In ancient times, when a people's success—its survival, perhaps—depended upon steady multiplication, all available magic was marshaled in the promotion of fertility. It was only after the Industrial Revolution that some deterrent to fertility gradually began to become widely desirable (desirable for whole societies rather than the occasional unlucky lovers), and by the last quarter of the twentieth century, when overpopulation was a major threat to the planet, there was no longer any magic to command. Or was there? Maybe in Asia . . .

Bernard saw on television, in a bar in Boulder, on a program called "You Asked for It," some remarkable documentary footage. There was a village somewhere in India on the outskirts of which a large albino cobra lived in the rocks. For years that snake had played a starring role in a unique fertility rite. The barren women of the village had to make a pilgrimage to the white cobra's den. There they had to kiss him—on top of his head. Yet it wasn't enough to kiss him. To guarantee conception, they had to kiss the cobra twice. The village lost a good many of its infertile women.

Bernard was fascinated by that powerful scene. He thought it would make a great breath-mint commercial. You know: "If she kisses you once, will she kiss you again?" Bernard mailed a suggestion to the Certs company. Certs responded that his judgment was questionable, not to mention his taste. Montana Judy said the same.

From India, however, he gathered information that a tea brewed from pennyroyal and myrrh would interfere with conception up to seven days after the act. He went at once to an herb shop in Missoula and shoplifted the ingredients. East Indian sources also supplied the intelligence that regular ingestion of carrot seed was a birth control method whose effectiveness had been proven by countless generations of Hindu women. Reference to "countless generations" did not reassure him, but he acquired carrot seeds from a farmer's supply store near Billings, and was damn near caught in the process. Obtaining the astringent ingredients used in She-link, the traditional Chinese herbal contraceptive, further taxed the Woodpecker's ingenuity, for preparation of She-link required chi je date, She-link flower, ling-shook root, and gomsomchu leaf: the Four Immortals, for God's sake. Naturally, the Food and Drug Administration frowned upon the introduction of the She-link formula to America. Bernard was forced to jimmy the locks of Chinese doctors as far west as San Francisco to get his freckled paws on some ling-shook.

Even so, he abandoned She-link as abruptly as carrot seeds and pennyroyal when he learned of lunaception. A drugless method of pinpointing ovulation by training women to resynchronize their cycles with those of the moon, lunaception landed like an astronaut on the green cheese of Bernard's imagination. Everything about it sounded right to him, especially its lunar foundation. Outlaws, like lovers, poets, and tubercular composers who cough blood onto piano keys, do their finest work in the slippery rays of the moon. Mythologically, woodpeckers are connected to Mars, the redheaded planet, but the Woodpecker, more so than any delegate to the aborted UFO convention, had a private line to the moon.

On second thought, *everything* about lunaception didn't please Bernard. Lunaception, as did She-link, pennyroyal, and carrot seeds, placed the burden of responsibility for birth control on the woman. Thus, for all of its potential effectiveness, it failed to completely compensate for the loss of the male pill. If Bernard was bothered by that, Montana Judy was bothered more. Understandably, Bernard had scant access to subjects for contraceptive testing. Who was going to trust an amateur gynecologist? Particularly one whose credentials included the Ten Most Wanted list.

Montana Judy grew sick of being a guinea pig for Bernard's experiments. And she was unrelieved when he expanded his testing to include her younger sisters, the twins: Montana Molly and Montana Polly. Bernard, you see, personally supplied and delivered the squirmy sauce that was the activating agent in the tests. Montana Judy decided that Bernard should pay his debt to society in a more conventional fashion. Montana Judy turned him in.

That book that judges are said to throw at offenders (the rule book, presumably; a Russian novel, possibly; no elegant volume of verse, certainly) was hurled like a bean ball at the red bean of Bernard Mickey Wrangle. He was sentenced to thirty years. The last quarter of the twentieth century might be destined to limp into history, but at least there'd be no Woodpecker around to drill holes in its crutches.

Aware of his reputation for exits, the federal penitentiary at McNeil Island, Washington, locked him up quite tight. It took him more than a year to blow out.

In his absence, the world had changed. It was only fair. Bernard himself had changed. For example, observation of his colleagues in prison had convinced him that thievery, inspired by the basest human impulses, was unbecoming to an outlaw. Let businessmen and riffraff rob and cheat. He vowed never to steal again, unless it was necessary. He also vowed to behave more sensitively toward women, beginning with Montana Judy, could he find her. He couldn't. She had joined a gang of equality-minded women that spent its evenings terrorizing men, equally, regardless of their degrees of guilt or innocence. These women would accept men only as subservient flunkies, and while Bernard knew only too well that that was how many men had treated many women for many centuries, he couldn't see a mere reversal of rotten roles as being very equalizing or very helpful to *anyone*. Moreover, he was nobody's flunky. Not even the moon's. Montana Polly had joined the same mob of avengers. Montana Molly was enrolled in Spokane Success, a secretarial college. The Woodpecker Gang had disbanded. Four former members were in jail. One had been clubbed to death with folding chairs by members of an American Legion post in Jackson Hole. Three had embraced conventional politics and were working within the system to alter the system. One was selling real estate and had contracted Jesus Christ as his personal savior. Willie the Wetback was studying pre-law at Stanford. He was in a fraternity. Starving his nose, although he still smoked grass occasionally. He wanted to work for Nader one day. The world had changed.

Bernard was perplexed. He missed the thrills, chills, and spills. Just because the war was over did that mean everybody had to stop having fun?

Thanks to Montana Judy, the hideout behind the waterfall was hot. Bernard went underground in

Seattle. He got a job mixing drinks in a bar frequented by off-duty policemen. Some nights there were dozens of cops in the place. Their presence sprinkled a little spice on his life. Added a tiny tickle of amusement. He poured cheap bourbon. And bided his time.

A writer published an open letter to Bernard in a leading liberal periodical. He requested an interview. Utmost secrecy was sworn. It was on the level. The writer was a man of proven courage and integrity. The writer wanted amnesty for dissidents such as Bernard. He said that Bernard had suffered enough. He wrote that living underground was no less punishing than prison. "A person underground exists in a state of controlled schizophrenia," he wrote. "Terror never slackens." The journalist considered Bernard a victim of the Vietnam War. The fact that he had acted against the government's interests instead of in them was immaterial, the writer said. The socio-political realities that drove Bernard to risk his life bombing induction centers were essentially the same as those that led other young men to risk theirs trading shots in rice paddies. As a fugitive, on the run, living in disguise and fear, Bernard was no less a casualty than those poor veterans who had left prime cuts from their physiques to decay in Da Nang and Hue.

Ha ha.

That's how Bernard's infamous response began.

"Ha ha.

"Victim? The difference between a criminal and an outlaw is that while criminals frequently are victims, outlaws never are. Indeed, the first step toward becoming a true outlaw is the *refusal* to be victimized.

"All people who live subject to other people's laws are victims. People who break laws out of greed, frustration, or vengeance are victims. People who overturn laws in order to replace them with their own laws are victims. (I am speaking here of revolutionaries.) We outlaws, however, live beyond the law. We don't merely live beyond the letter of the law—many businessmen, most politicians, and all cops do that—we live beyond the spirit of the law. In a sense, then, we live beyond society. Have we a common goal, that goal is to turn the tables on the *nature* of society. When we succeed, we raise the exhilaration content of the universe. We even raise it a little bit when we fail.

"Victim? I deplored the ugliness of the Vietnam War. But what I deplored, others have deplored before me. When war turns whole populations into sleepwalkers, outlaws don't join forces with alarm clocks. Outlaws, like poets, rearrange the nightmare. It is elating work. The years of the war were the most glorious of my life. I wasn't risking my skin to protest a war. I risked my skin for fun. For beauty!

"I love the magic of TNT. How eloquently it speaks! Its resounding rumble, its clap, its quack is scarcely less deep than the passionate moan of the Earth herself. A well-timed series of detonations is like a choir of quakes. For all of its fluent resonance, a bomb says only one word—'Surprise!'—and then applauds itself. I love the hot hands of explosion. I love a breeze perfumed with the devil smell of powder (so close in its effect to the angel smell of sex). I love the way that architecture, under the impetus of dynamite, dissolves almost in slow motion, crumbling delicately, shedding bricks like feathers, corners melting, grim facades breaking into grins, supports shrugging and calling it a day, tons of totalitarian dreck washing away in the wake of a circular *tsunami* of air. I love that precious portion of a second when window glass becomes elastic and bulges out like bubble gum before popping. I love public buildings made public at last, doors flung open to the citizens, to the creatures, to the universe.

Baby, come on in! And I love the final snuff of smoke.

"Yes, and I love the trite mythos of the outlaw. I love the self-conscious romanticism of the outlaw. I love the black wardrobe of the outlaw. I love the fey smile of the outlaw. I love the tequila of the outlaw and the beans of the outlaw. I love the way respectable men sneer and say 'outlaw.' I love the way young women palpitate and say 'outlaw.' The outlaw boat sails against the flow, and I love it. Outlaws toilet where badgers toilet, and I love it. All outlaws are photogenic, and I love that. 'When freedom is outlawed, only outlaws will be free': that's a graffito seen in Anacortes, and I love that. There are outlaw maps that lead to outlaw treasures, and I love those maps especially. Unwilling to wait for mankind to improve, the outlaw lives as if that day were here, and I love that most of all.

"Victim? Your letter reminded the Woodpecker that he is a Woodpecker blessed. Your sympathies for my loneliness, tension, and disturbing fluctuations in indentity have some basis in fact and are humbly appreciated. But do not be misled. I am the happiest man in America. In my bartender's pockets I still carry, out of habit, wooden matches. As long as there are matches, there will be fuses. As long as there are fuses, no walls are safe. As long as every wall is threatened, the world can happen. Outlaws are can openers in the supermarket of life."

28

Was there actually an era so silly that its maidens would drop a handkerchief—a purely ornamental handkerchief, we may assume; silken, lace-trimmed, nowhere upon its perfumed surface the faintest fresco of snot—in order to make the acquaintance of the gentleman bound to retrieve it? Myth or no, it was with a studied carelessness akin to scented hankie bait that the phrase "in my bartender's pockets" was dropped by Bernard upon the verbal promenade of his reply to the well-meaning journalist. Bernard was giving his pursuers a little hint. Just to make things more interesting.

The hint may have been taken, but it failed to lead the pack to his lair. Although there were several threatening moments, such as the night a drunk doused him with beer, causing his dye to run in the presence of twenty policemen, Bernard's cover held. As years went by and matchsticks yellowed and splintered in his pockets, he was sustained in his inactivity by thoughts of what fun it would be when the statute of limitations expired and he could go flamboyantly public, rub their noses in it. There came an occasion, however, when he felt compelled to speak, or rather, to let dynamite speak for him. And now, after a slight misfire, he found himself, with but eleven months left on the fugitive calendar, arrested.

Arrested by Her Royal Highness, Princess Leigh-Cheri Furstenberg-Barcalona, deposed cheerleader, environmentalist without portfolio, blue-eyed altruist, grapefruit-breasted celibate, would-be sovereign of Mu, the only woman the Woodpecker had ever met whose hair burned as brightly at his once had.

He would not go quietly.

29

"So it's you. I might have guessed it was you."

"I'm flattered that you remember me."

"The man who goes 'yum'—"

"Only at appropriate moments."

"—and blows up hotels and disrupts the most important meeting of minds since God knows when."

"This meeting is more important. This meeting between you and me. Let's retire somewhere for a drink."

"Don't be ridiculous. You're under arrest. I'm taking you straight to the police."

"I must warn you: I won't go quietly. Criminals, because they're plagued with guilt, often will surrender and go quietly. Outlaws, because they're pure, never will."

As in a symphony the brass may suddenly blare and drown out the woodwinds and strings, so fear suddenly blared in Leigh-Cheri, drowning out the anger and frustration that in the opening bars of this concerto of confrontation had served her so well. She glanced around the beach, looking for assistance. Some young men, blonde as shampoo commercials, brown-skinned as turds, noticed her looking and waved at her.

"Don't expect any help from those beach boys. They're only interested in snatch and surf. Besides, they'd be no threat to me. I have a black belt in haiku. And a black vest in the cleaners. This morning I met a visitor from the planet Argon. She told me I have an aura like burnt rubber. Thanking her, I said black was my favorite color. Aside from red."

"So you met her, too." Leigh-Cheri didn't know what else to say. For the first time, she noticed that he was wearing black swim trunks. And on his feet black thongs. Where does one buy *black* thongs? She felt disoriented. Goose bumps popped up in her sunburn, making her hide resemble a bird's-eye view of bloody cobblestones. She felt like a street in the French Revolution. She turned to the hag in the bikini. "Gulietta, get the police," she ordered, knowing full well that the police were all in town trying to solve the case of the bombed hotel. Gulietta couldn't understand her, anyway.

"There's nothing to worry about. I won't hurt you. I'm delighted that we're getting to be friends. I would have left Maui right after the boom-boom"—he grinned at Gulietta—"if it hadn't been for you."

It was true. An old pal of his from the mainland, now a marijuana planter on the Kona coast, had agreed in advance to whisk Bernard to Honolulu aboard his smuggler's sloop. Even though the bombing was premature, the sloop could have sailed Monday morning had Bernard desired.

"I don't get it. You stayed because of me?"

"Because of you, babe. And because I have some blasting powder that I haven't used yet."

"What?" She laughed in disbelief. "I can't trust my ears. You—*maniac!*"

"Mister maniac."

"You want to blow up something else?"

"What I want is to buy you a drink."

"Buy me a drink?"

"A piña tequila or a tequila tai. If you're old enough, that is. We wouldn't want to break the law."

"I'll bet I'm as old as you are."

"I'm older than Sanskrit."

"Well, I was a waitress at the Last Supper."

"I'm so old I remember when McDonald's had only sold a hundred burgers."

"You win."

"Then I can buy you a drink?"

"What's your name?"

"Bernard."

"Bernard what?"

"Bernard Maniac."

"Listen, Mr. Maniac—"

"I'm listening to nothing unless I'm sitting across a table from you at the Lahaina Broiler. Your grandmother can come, too, although frankly I'm a bit shocked by the extent to which her bathing attire reveals her charms."

"Well," she said. She paused. She thought it best to humor him. It'd be easier to raise help in town than out there on the beach. And she must admit that despite the dental neglect it disclosed, he had a *wonderful* smile. "Well, I do need to get out of the sun. Redheads burn easily."

"I know," he said. "I know."

30

On the mainland, a rain was falling. The famous Seattle rain. The thin, gray rain that toadstools love. The persistent rain that knows every hidden entrance into collar and shopping bag. The quiet rain that can rust a tin roof without the tin roof making a sound in protest. The shamanic rain that feeds the imagination. The rain that seems actually a secret language, whispering, like the ecstasy of primitives, of the essence of things.

The rain enveloped the house—the house that King Max had come to call Fort Blackberry—like a hair spray for jellyfish. Inside, the King and his Queen struggled with an electric dishwasher. They couldn't get it to function. Neither a sherry glass nor a teaspoon had been cleaned in the three days of Gulietta's absence. Chuck might have come to the rescue, but as misfortune would have it, Chuck had been called into Seattle on Monday evening and had not returned. An ill sister was the reason given, but surely it was quite another matter. There was unrest in the Furstenberg-Barcalona homeland. Revolution was in the air. Convinced that the royal family was involved, Washington wanted to tighten security. Particularly close tabs on King Max was what the CIA had in mind. The CIA primed Chuck with a small bonus. (He would lose every cent when Max drew an inside straight to his two pairs.)

As they fiddled with the dishwasher, Max and Tilli plotted and schemed.

"She'll be twenty in April," said Max. "A year after that, she can marry. I say the sooner we get a suitor in the lineup the better our odds."

"Ja," said Tilli. "Ja, da, si. Ve know thees already a hundred times. But dat doesn't mean ve got to rush her into some flake."

"Into what?"

"A flake. A flaky guy. Like zee president's son. He ees loco gringo."

"If you're insinuating that that kid has got two strikes and no balls, you're probably correct. My point is, we can't sit around here waiting for eligible Europeans to come out picking blackberries. Now, Idaj Fizel's middle boy owns part interest in an NBA club. He's in Seattle every time his team plays the Sonics. I think I can arrange a meeting."

"Oui, but he ees not royalty."

"No, he's richer and more powerful than that."

"Arab," moaned Tilli. "Ein Arab. Oh-Oh, spaghetti-o."

The dishwasher remained inactive. It might as well have gone along to Maui. The frog could have turned it into a condominium. The royal couple huffed and puffed over it. Once it sounded as if it had begun to work, but it was merely Max's valve that was clanging. When for the third or fourth time she accidentally banged her Chihuahua's head against its lid, Tilli turned her majestic back on it.

King Max gathered up the dirty dishes. He transported them into the backyard. "We'll let the rain wash them," he said. "It ought to be good for something."

Actually, the rain has many uses. It prevents the blood and the sea from becoming too salty. It administers knockout drops to unruly violets. It manufactures the ladder that neon climbs to the moon. A seeker can go into the Great Northwest rain and bring back the Name he needs. And, indeed, the rain pried flecks of egg yolk and gravy from the crest, from the honor point, from the fess point, from the nombril of the Furstenberg-Barcalona heraldic dinner plates. When, however, Max returned the next morning to fetch the dishes, half of them were missing. The Queen put the blame on tramps or gypsies. Max knew that the blackberries had gotten them.

As they dined on canned stroganoff from paper plates, Tilli said to Max, "I weesh Leigh-Cheri vas only here."

But the King said, "Maybe it's best she's away while we recruit a suitor. At any rate, we can rest assured she's in good hands in Hawaii."

31

"I've never been kissed by a man in Donald Duck sunglasses before," said Leigh-Cheri.

"I apologize," said Bernard. "I'm sorry about the Donald Duck sunglasses. They ought to be Woody Woodpecker sunglasses, but nobody makes Woody Woodpecker sunglasses."

The Princess didn't know what he was talking about. She didn't really care. She was on her third tequila mockingbird, he on his fourth. They were floating in that blissful phase that characterizes religious transcendence and the onset of alcohol poisoning. Gulietta had turned her back on them and was watching the sunset. Some chaperon.

"Also, I don't normally kiss men who smoke," announced Leigh-Cheri. "Kissing a smoker is like licking an ashtray."

"So I've heard. I've also heard that kissing a person who's self-righteous and intolerant is like licking a mongoose's ass."

"I'm not a mongoose's ass!"

"And I'm not an ashtray." Removing the unopened pack of Camels from his shirt pocket, he tossed them over his shoulder. "I only smoke when I'm locked up. In jail, a cigarette can be a friend. Otherwise, my Camels are just a front. It's an excuse for carrying matches."

"Are you saying what I think you're saying?"

"I'm saying more than I should be saying. I think you put something in my drink to make me talkative."

"I think you put something in my drink to make me kissative."

They kissed. And giggled like cartoon mice.

"What time is it?" asked Leigh-Cheri.

"Why? The police station is open all night."

"I have an appointment with *People* magazine. At first, I was scared, but now it seems funny. Everything seems funny. Even you seem funny." She pinched the end of his nose as he leaned over to kiss her again. She looked around the room for a clock, but the lounge at the Lahaina Broiler is noted for its absence of walls. The clocks of the trees had too many hands, and the ocean was on moon time. If Bernard had his way, she'd be on moon time, too.

"When are you turning me in?"

"When you stop kissing me."

"In that case I'm a free man forever."

"Don't count on it."

She meant that. But this time when he kissed her, his astonishingly resourceful tongue managed to break through the heroic barricade that her teeth had heretofore formed. There was a clean clink of enamel against enamel, an eruption of hot saliva as his tongue made a whirlwind tour of her oral hollow. A sudden jolt shot through the peachfish, fuzz and fin, and inside her No Nukes T-shirt her nipples became as hard as nuggets of plutonium.

"Jesus," thought Leigh-Cheri, "how can men be such lummoxes, such wads of Juicy Fruit on the soles of our ballet slippers and still feel so good? Especially this one. This mad bomber."

She pulled away. With sunburned knuckles, she wiped a string of spittle—his? hers? José Cuervo's—from her chin. She asked a passing waitress for the time. She was late.

"I've got to go."

"How about dinner after your interview? There's a delicious fish called mahi mahi. The fish so nice they named it twice. Isn't it charming the way Polynesians double up their language. I'd like to keep a tête-à-tête in Pago Pago, but I'm afraid I'd contract beriberi."

"Huh-uh, huh-uh," said the Princess. "No din-din, no din-din."

"Tomorrow?"

"I'll be at the Care Fest all day."

"Tomorrow night?"

"Ralph Nader is speaking tomorrow night. I wouldn't miss that for all the mahi mahi on Maui Maui. Besides, you may be in jail tomorrow night. Maybe you better get your pack of Camels back."

"You're turning me in, then?"

"I don't know. It depends. Are you really going to use the rest of your dynamite?"

"It's likely."

"Why?"

"Because that's what I do."

"But the UFO conference is over."

"I didn't come here to bomb the UFO conference. That was a mistake. I came here to bomb the Care Fest."

"You *what?*" She felt a bomb go off in *her*.

"Boom-boom Care Fest," he said. He poured tequila through the crack of his grin.

Abruptly, she stood. "You must be crazy," she said. "You must really be fucking insane." She yanked Gulietta away from the sunset and made for the street.

"You're turning me in, then?"

"You're damned right I am," she said.

⟐ 32 ⟐

The idea for the monarchy of Mu had come to Leigh-Cheri on Maui. It visited her unexpectedly while she sat in koa shade watching Gulietta play octogenarian mermaid and worrying about what she might possibly say to *People* magazine that was neither a paraphrase of Care Fest brochures nor a violation of the Furstenberg-Barcalona code. At some moment it occurred to her that there was a fair amount of unemployed royalty in the world, royals whose thrones had gone the way of war or political upheaval, just as her family's had, and that these persons, although they'd been bred to lead, to preside, or at least to symbolize, were living for the most part the lives of the idle rich.

For example, the comte de Paris, pretender to the French throne, had eleven children who dabbled in elegant pursuits, such as publishing an art magazine (the duke of Orléans) and running a painting gallery (Prince Thibaut). In Brazil, there were among the royal Orleans Braganza family no fewer than eighteen young cousins with time, energy, and money. Otto von Hapsburg, entitled to be emperor were there any longer an Austrian Empire, had seven sons and daughters riding to the hounds of dilettante culture. Italy's Prince Enrico D'Assia and Prince Amedeo Savoy managed the family holdings and shared Queen Tilli's devotion to opera. To the list could be added Yugoslavia's Prince Alexander, King Leka I of Albania (a relative of hers), and Japan's imperial family, among others.

Since deposed royalty no longer had individual kingdoms to serve, why not band together to serve the world? The earth could be their kingdom. And they could combine their talents and skills, their illustrious names and considerable wealth (the Furstenberg-Barcalona clan was by far the poorest of the lot), their influence and glamour in a royal crusade on behalf of ecology, conservation, and preservation; on behalf of the sweet kingdom of Earth. They would aim to be efficient and effective. They would, of course, be celebrated. And if it was crowns they wanted, she'd supply them with crowns. Collectively, they would be known as the monarchy of Mu, after the lost continent, the mother island; the homeland of sing-song, whose fragrant temples drowned one day in the sea. Each member of the monarchy would be equally a ruler of Mu, each sovereign in a nation without boundaries.

"Since the Hawaiian Islands are tips of the drowned peaks of Mu," explained Leigh-Cheri, "the monarchy should consider setting up headquarters, court, if you will, in Hawaii, perhaps right here in Lahaina, because Lahaina was the royal capital of old Hawaii and is no stranger to the privileges of queens and kings."

"That's a fascinating idea," gushed Reed Jarvis, the reporter from *People*. Indeed, Jarvis was pleased. The monarchy of Mu concept gave him a hard kernel of news, a nucleus of serious purpose around which to shape his confection. Now he could layer the goo. On to the human interest stuff—"What was it like for you, a blue-blooded princess, to grow up in a drafty old house in Washington State, attending public schools, becoming a cheerleader?"—and on, farther, to the subjects in which editors and readers of celebrity magazines were almost exclusively interested: money and sex.

"Are you ever bitter about the loss of your family fortune?"

"That was a long time ago. Before I was born. There are more important things than fortunes."

"Who is your current boy friend? Is there any one beau who is special?"

"I have no boy friends."

"None?"

"None."

"But, my dear, you're so attractive and intelligent. Have you no love life?"

"Who does have a love life anymore? These days people have sex lives, not love lives. Lots of them are even giving up sex. I don't have a love life because I've never met a man who knew *how* to have a love life. Maybe I don't know how, either."

With that, teardrops bucked out of Leigh-Cheri's eyes like bronco amoebae leaving the chutes in a biology lab rodeo.

Had Reed Jarvis been aware that Leigh-Cheri's blue

blood was at that instant tinted with streaks of tequila, he might have attributed her tears partially to booze, thus painting her to resemble less a snow statue in a furnace room. As it was, Jarvis's portrait of her in *People* as a misty-eyed romantic was still more accurate than the descriptions the gossipmongers would write—"tragic beauty," "tormented princess"—when she took to her attic.

There are essential and inessential insanities.

The latter are solar in character, the former are linked to the moon.

Inessential insanities are a brittle amalgamation of ambition, aggression, and pre-adolescent anxiety—garbage that should have been dumped long ago. Essential insanities are those impulses one instinctively senses are virtuous and correct, even though peers may regard them as coo coo.

Inessential insanities get one in trouble with oneself. Essential insanities get one in trouble with others. It's always preferable to be in trouble with others. In fact, it may be essential.

Poetry, the best of it, is lunar and is concerned with the essential insanities. Journalism is solar (there are numerous newspapers named *The Sun,* none called *The Moon)* and is devoted to the inessential.

About Leigh-Cheri, it would have made more sense to write a poem than an article. Reed Jarvis, with his Remington SL3, wrote an article. Others would follow. It remained for Bernard Mickey Wrangle, with his dynamite, to write the poem.

After the interview, the Princess went directly to bed. Gulietta told her a bedtime story. It had the desired effect. She fell quickly asleep and dreamt of Ralph Nader. During the night she awoke but once: when Nader entered a dream restaurant and ordered frog's legs. "Oh," she gasped and sat straight up in bed.

Leigh-Cheri had intended to go to the police the next morning between breakfast and the belated official opening of the Care Fest, but by the time she'd been served in the overcrowded Pioneer Inn dining room, she'd been barely able to eat and get across Hotel Street for the invocation in Banyan Park. Soon she was immersed in Dr. John Lilly's lecture on the role of marine mammals in the future of the human race. Predictably, the park was jammed. Leigh-Cheri hadn't arrived early enough to get within the cover of the banyan tree, though its shadow darkened deliciously the better part of an acre. She could hear well enough and with minor optic stress could make out the images that Dr. Lilly projected on a screen, but she was marooned in hot sunbeams. The sun raked her exposed flesh. It made her feel slightly faint. Reed Jarvis had reminded her that she was entitled to VIP privileges at the Care Fest. Ever reluctant to exploit her title, she was reaching the point where she'd pull rank like a little red wagon if it'd get her a place in the shade.

As if by genie service, a shadow fell over her. Initially, she feared it was the jinx cloud, moving in for the kill. It wasn't. Bernard was standing beside her, holding above her head a tattered parasol.

"What are you doing here?" Her whisper didn't sound half as hostile as she'd have liked it to.

He nodded his dark curls at the podium screen, upon which an image of a porpoise was projected. "Sharks are the criminals of the sea," he said. "Dolphins are the outlaws."

"You're bananas," she said.

"Then split with me."

"Huh-uh. Bananas is not the color of my true love's hair."

The reference to hair color caused him to flinch. She didn't notice. She'd returned her attention to Dr. Lilly.

"Okay. If you want to see me, just look up my address."

"I don't want to see you, although the authorities might. Anyhow, where would I look up your address? In the Banana Directory? And I don't mean the Yellow Pages."

"Look up. Look *up*."

She looked up. She couldn't help it. Chalked in a nasty scrawl on the underside of the parasol were the words LAHAINA SMALL BOAT HARBOR, THE SLOOP *HIGH JINKS*.

He shoved the parasol handle into her hand. He leaned his ravaged teeth close to her ear. "Yum," he whispered. Then he was gone.

⚬⚬ 34 ⚬⚬

She lunched on papaya poo poo or mango mu mu or some other fruity foo foo bursting with overripe tropical vowels. In hot climates, *A* provides a shady arch, *O* is a siphon through which to suck liquids, *U* a cool cave or tub to slide into; *A* stands like a surfer with its legs apart, *O* hangs like a citrus from a bough, *U* rolls its hula hips—and *I* and *E* mimic the cries of monkeys and jungle birds from which they were derived. Consonants, like fair-skinned men, do not thrive in torrid zones. Vowels are built for southern comfort, consonants for northern speed. But O how the natives do bOOgIE-wOOgIE while the planters WaLTZ.

She dined on avocado aloha or, perhaps, guava lava. Gulietta gummed roast veal à la missionary. Beach boys ringed their table, speaking indecencies. Repeatedly, Gulietta flailed her mop-stick arms, waving the young dogs away. Gulietta appeared to be enjoying it. Shooing surfers off the Princess was clearly more fun than shooing flies off the Queen. Leigh-Cheri paid scant attention. She was trying to decide whether to turn in Bernard during the lunch break.

Okay, so he had saved her from the sun. That princess cannot expect a happy ending who has been rescued by the dragon. Okay, so his exuberant spirits lent him a superficial charm. Lucifer was the cutest angel in heaven, they say, and every death's head wears a grin. This Bernard character was a menace. Two whole days of the Care Fest had been lost on his account, and who could guess what further outrage he might commit. Her duty was plain. The only question was: now or later?

"Now," she snapped. "If I hurry." She handed Gulietta a bank note with which to settle the check. Gulietta was attacking her missionary veal with missionary zeal. "I'll meet you in the park in twenty minutes," said Leigh-Cheri, not forgetting to make the appropriate hand signs.

As she sped out of the dining room, one of the beach boys called after her, "Hey, Red, where's the fire? Between your legs? Ha ha."

And as she crossed the *lanai*, she encountered the

fair-skinned extraterrestrials from Argon. "Mutant," hissed the turbaned woman. "You're branded on every planet in the system," said the fez-topped man. "Don't you understand that you've been mutated by solar radiation acting upon the excessive sugars and sex hormones in your body? You can't fool the sun."

"Jesus!" swore the Princess. She hurried across the street toward the docks. "Sometimes I feel like buying a quart of Lady Clairol and just changing my god-damned color."

When she arrived at the sloop christened *High Jinks,* she was stunned to find that the familiar face that answered the cabin door was now wearing hair at least as red as her own.

35

"If you've come to arrest me again," said Bernard, twirling his trigger finger in his brilliant curls, "then you should be aware of my true identity. It's a wise cop who knows her own prisoner. On the other hand, if you've come because you like me, it might make you like me more to see what we have in common."

"Yeah," said Leigh-Cheri. "We're both mutants."

"I beg your pardon?"

"Nothing. Nothing. You're one of the redheads, all right. Is this really your natural shade?"

"You mean can I trace my roots back to Henna? This is the color I busted out of the womb with. The last of the black dye just washed down the drain and out to sea. Jacques Cousteau is probably swimming through it, thinking that some squid is writing with a leaky pen again."

"Okay, I guess you are as red as I am. But that's *all* we have in common."

"What makes you so sure?"

"There are two kinds of people in this world: those who're part of the solution and those who're part of the problem."

"I see. I make messes, you clean 'em up? Well, let me tell you, there are two kinds of people in this world: those who look at life and see the frost on the pumpkin and those who look and see the drool on the pie."

(Actually, there *are* two kinds of people in this world: those who believe there are two kinds of people in this world and those who are smart enough to know better. However, Leigh-Cheri and Bernard were occupied with the nuances of an intricate dance, so let's be generous and cut them some slack.)

They were on the deck in the noonday sun, but Leigh-Cheri had raised the parasol, and Bernard crouched in the pencil-nub shadow of the mainsail gaff. The Pacific, tranquilized here by a broken-square jetty, rocked them as sweetly as winos rock wine. "You look familiar now, with your hair red. I think I've seen pictures of you."

"I do have a good agent. My publicity photos get around."

"Where? On post office walls? You're some kind of infamous hoodlum, aren't you?"

"I wouldn't put it that way. When I was younger, I did have a slight brush with the law. You know how boys are."

"No. Tell me about it."

"Nothing much to tell. A misunderstanding involving a city councilman's daughter and a borrowed car. But the aftermath . . . it did leave a mark. After thirty days in the sissies and snitches tank, which is another story, I was made a trustee. The trustee quarters were on the second floor, the same as the jail kitchen. All the trustees had access to the kitchen.

Well, I'd been a trustee less than a week when three kitchen knives and a seventeen-inch in diameter meat-slicing blade turned up missing. Naturally, every trustee was suspected of stealing the knives. They completely tore apart our sleeping quarters, and the TV room, too. But they didn't find the knives. So they lined us up in the hallway, watched over by a squad of guards armed with riot guns and Mace. One by one, we were marched into a small room, where, in front of several more guards and a captain with a flashlight, we were made to strip. They made me turn around, grab the cheeks of my ass and bend over, so they could look up my rectum to make sure I wasn't hiding three kitchen knives and a seventeen-inch in diameter meat-slicing blade. Of course, they didn't find the missing cutlery in any of us. But they did find four bars of soap, a *Playboy* centerfold, three ice cubes, five feathers, Atlantis, the Greek delegate to Boys' Nation, a cake with a file in it, a white Christmas, a blue Christmas, Pablo Picasso and his brother Elmer, one baloney sandwich with mustard, two Japanese infantrymen who didn't realize that World War II was over, Prince Buster of Cleveland, a glass-bottom boat, Howard Hughes's will, a set of false teeth, Amelia Earhart, the first four measures of 'The Impossible Dream' sung by the Black Mountain College choir, Howard Hughes's will (another version), the widow of the Unknown Soldier, six passenger pigeons, middle-class morality, the Great American Novel, and a banana."

"Jesus!" swore Leigh-Cheri. She didn't know whether to laugh or jump overboard. "Look, who are you, anyway? And what's your game?"

"Woodpecker's the name, and outlawing's the game. I'm wanted in fifty states and Mexico. It's nice to feel wanted, and I'd like to be wanted by you. In fact, I just blew my disguise in the hopes that it would open

your eyes and soften your heart. There. My cards are
on the table. An expression your old daddy would
surely understand."

"Jesus! The Woodpecker. Bernard Wrangle. I should
have guessed."

His cocky smile was finally gone. If smiles had
addresses, Bernard's would have been General Delivery, the Moon. He looked at her with that kind of
painted-on seriousness that comedians shift into when
they get their chance to play Hamlet. Still, there was
genuine tenderness and longing.

"This is too much for me to deal with right now,"
said Leigh-Cheri. Despite the heat waves that hootchy-
kootchied all around her, she trembled. Why had she
come to the boat in the first place? She could have
just sent the police. "I'm due back at the Care Fest."
Indeed, the panel discussion on birth control was scheduled to begin in seven minutes.

He attempted to help her onto the dock, but she
spurned his hand. Hustling away, the tattered parasol flapping like a werewolf's shirttail, she called back,
"They're going to get you again, you know."

Bernard's smile came partway home. "They never
got me, and they never will. The outlaw is someone
who cannot be gotten. He can only be punished by
other people's attitudes. Just as your attitudes are
punishing me now."

⚬⚬⚬ 36 ⚬⚬⚬

When the organizers of the Geo-Therapy Care Fest
announced their intentions, they were blizzarded by
applications from manufacturers and salespeople of
"ecologically sound" stuff who wished concessions to
peddle their New Age wares—teas and herbs, sleep-

ing bags and hot tubs, tipis and windmills, water distillers and air purifiers, wood stoves and frozen yogurt, arts and crafts, books and kits, bio-magnetic underwear and carob chip cookies—on the premises. The organizers refused. They had no complaint against ecology fairs or the cosmic profits to be reaped from them. It was just that their Care Fest was conceived to traffic, as they put it, "in ideas not objects."

Now, the line that separates objects from ideas can be pretty twiggy, but let's not unzip that pair of pants. Galileo was right to drop objects rather than ideas off of his tower, and the Care Fest might have been wise to stick with objects, as well. *Within the normal range of perception,* the behavior of objects can be measured and predicted. Ignoring the possibility that in the wrong hands almost any object, including this book you hold, can turn up as Exhibit A in a murder trial; ignoring, for the moment, the far more interesting possibility that every object might lead a secret life, it is still safe to say that objects, as we understand them, are relatively stable, whereas ideas are definitely unstable, they not only *can* be misused, they invite misuse—and the better the idea the more volatile it is. That's because only the better ideas turn into dogma, and it is this process whereby a fresh, stimulating, humanly helpful idea is changed into robot dogma that is deadly. In terms of hazardous vectors released, the transformation of ideas into dogma rivals the transformation of hydrogen into helium, uranium into lead, or innocence into corruption. And it is nearly as relentless.

The problem starts at the secondary level, not with the originator or developer of the idea but with the people who are attracted by it, who adopt it, who cling to it until their last nail breaks, and who invariably lack the overview, flexibility, imagination, and, most importantly, sense of humor, to maintain it in the spirit in which it was hatched. Ideas are made by masters, dogma by disciples, and the Buddha is always killed on the road.

There is a particularly unattractive and discouragingly common affliction called tunnel vision, which, for all the misery it causes, ought to top the job list at the World Health Organization. Tunnel vision is a disease in which perception is restricted by ignorance and distorted by vested interest. Tunnel vision is caused by an optic fungus that multiplies when the brain is less energetic than the ego. It is complicated by exposure to politics. When a good idea is run through the filters and compressors of ordinary tunnel vision, it not only comes out reduced in scale and value but in its new dogmatic configuration produces effects the opposite of those for which it originally was intended.

That is how the loving ideas of Jesus Christ became the sinister clichés of Christianity. That is why virtually every revolution in history has failed: the oppressed, as soon as they seize power, turn into the oppressors, resorting to totalitarian tactics to "protect the revolution." That is why minorities seeking the abolition of prejudice become intolerant, minorities seeking peace become militant, minorities seeking equality become self-righteous, and minorities seeking liberation become hostile (a tight asshole being the first symptom of self-repression).

The foregoing sermonette was brought to you by the Essential Insanities Dept. at Outlaw College. It was delivered in the hope that it might explain how the Care Fest, with so many masters on the roster, so many juicy ideas on the grill, went haywire.

At the Wednesday morning session, Dr. John Lilly had no sooner completed his lecture on sea mammal intelligence, ending with the idea that "a continuing dialogue with cetaceans could transform our view of all living species and the planet we share," than he was challenged by a segment of the audience that considered it a waste of time and money to try to communicate with animals when we couldn't communicate with each other. "What about human communication?" they demanded. "My ex-husband," said one, "couldn't understand a word I said. Do you think he could understand a porpoise?" "Is any big fish," asked another, "gonna get my people outta the ghetto and onto the payroll? If not, I ain't wasting my breath on the sucka."

Tunnel vision.

Leigh-Cheri thought the questions made some sense, although the questioners were rude. She felt embarrassed for Dr. Lilly and was cheered when he handled the antagonists with grace. Actually, the morning session went as slick as dolphin sweat compared to the turmoil of the afternoon.

Because the Care Fest was running two days behind schedule, thanks to that birdbrained son-of-a-bitch Woodpecker, some doubling up was necessary. (If one must double up, then Hawaii, home of mahi mahi and loma loma, was the place to do it.) The panel on birth control had been combined with the panel on childcare. The platform beneath the banyan boughs was end-to-end with experts, facts and figures forming at their lips like froth. The discussion was scarcely underway before a prevailing philosophy was established. It was this: if babies aren't brought by storks, they *ought* to be, and maybe the storks could be trained to rear them, as well.

To be sure, this viewpoint was proffered by only a couple of panel members, but a large and loud contingent in the audience supported it with such volume and menace that it carried. "We don't want birth control, we want prick control!" shouted a female in the third row. The applause that followed drowned out the woman who was lecturing on, yes, carrot seeds as an oral contraceptive. "Oh, dear," thought Leigh-Cheri. "I wonder if that isn't overstating the case?"

Things were getting a trifle rowdy. The sun didn't help. Several people left for a dunk or a drink. Gulietta looked as if she wished to join them. Leigh-Cheri dangled from the stalk of her parasol, an easy target for bullets of brain Jello.

On stage, a magazine editor from New York, a chic executive of whom it had been said, "She has a mind like a steel trap—and a mouth, heart, and vagina to match," was attempting a summation. She said, first of all, that childcare began with conception and claimed that it was egregiously unfair to expect women to babysit for nine months, night and day, without relief or assistance. In a voice that reminded Leigh-Cheri of a jackhammer at work on a string of pearls, the editor described to the conference the latest techniques for obstetrics, maintaining that women would not begin to realize their personal or societal potential until artificial insemination and controlled out-of-body gestation became routine practice around the globe. The editor hadn't stopped at virgin birth. Once born, our babies must inherit the advantages of collective professionalism, she said, and urged the Care Fest to adopt a resolution petitioning the federal government to make funds immediately available for the subsidization of day-care centers where experts would insure standardized improvement for the young and independence for the parents.

The Princess was feeding this through her computer to determine how many shares she would buy when a poet, an aging humorist who'd been placed on the panel to provide a "different perspective," did. He told the editor that her notions were a sift of sulfur on the roses of the race. The poet was snockered, but that has never been considered a handicap by those in his profession.

"What kind of babies will those be who are made of the formula instead of the fuck?" asked the poet. "No doubt they'll possess two eyes each, and the recommended number of toes, but can the heat of their will be hot enough, can their imagination have all of *its* fingers, can their souls be expected to fully connect to the unraveling spool of the natural universe and not to the gunk in the bottom of the test tube? Will the infant pulled at the timer's bell from a plastic womb where it has been deprived of rhythm, mother-bond, and the jostlings of everyday life not have some small space between its eyes filled with synthetic fluid, not bear, if nowhere else, in the core of its heart, the android's mark?"

The editor shared with the audience her long look of practiced exasperation. "Are you afraid," she asked the writer, "that a child not conceived in the old way won't understand your jokes?"

From the audience, someone yelled, "Can the mystical bullshit!" at the poet, who, too determined or too drunk to heed, went on to say, "And those children reared under the watch of the state, burped by automats, tickled by technicians, comforted by recorded messages from network psychologists—what kind of society do you think those children will produce upon their maturity? Do you imagine for one moment that humans indoctrinated from birth by the government will be other than tools of that government, will not reside in and preside over a totalitarian police nation exceeding in tyrannical control the harshest nightmares of . . ."

By then the booing and catcalling had become so loud that the poet couldn't be heard past the first few rows. He produced a gin bott'e and spoke into *it*. Softly. The New York editor was smirking. Numerous accusations and at least one ripe papaya were lobbed at the podium. There followed an extended general exchange familiar to all who lived in the last quarter of the twentieth century. Women said the men had eaten the cherries out of the chocolates. Men said the women were peeing in the pool.

A teacher from the Delphian School in Sheridan, Oregon, got the mike for an instant. "It seems to me that in the midst of this bickering we are forgetting the children. When we neglect the children, we neglect the future, the future this conference is designed to serve." He wore the mildly triumphant look of a man who has led a return to reason. Someone slapped him in the face with a bloody Kotex. "Existentialist!" the teacher cried.

"If you like babies so much," a woman yelled, "have them yourself."

"Right on, sister!" encouraged a young man in her vicinity. The man and woman firmly shook hands. The solution to the overpopulation problem might rest in such handshakes.

In an attempt to restore order, a well-known yogi, a Care Fest delegate, strolled onto the platform. He assumed the lotus position. He beamed. Serenely, meticulously, he took a cobweb apart, then put it back together. (There were no parts left over.) He swallowed three butterflies, then burped them up unharmed. Only that portion of the crowd that was already orderly was impressed. The yogi had the stink of eternity about him, and in many circles eternity was simply no longer fashionable.

The situation became increasingly unsavory. Also, tedious. You'll be spared the details. Enough is enough. A banyan sends its adventitious roots to the ground, sometimes causing it to spread over a wide area. Under proper conditions, it bears figs. Thomas Jefferson was fond of figs. It was Jefferson's genius that kept the American Revolution from being sucked into the tunnel faster than it was. Jefferson had red hair. Nothing is implied here. Except the possibility that everything is connected.

With the debate on the verge of violence—or worse, of being turned over to committee—Leigh-Cheri fled the park. The palm trees she passed, the romantic palms of Hawaii, were covering their ears with their fronds. Her sentiments exactly. "Jesus," she swore. She felt like the gourmet who was goosed in Strasbourg. "It's my pâte, and I'll cry if I want to."

In the Pioneer's bar, she sat under one of the whaling harpoons that decorated the walls. She asked for a mai tai, then switched her order to tequila. Outside, the ocean banged its head against the jetty. She empathized completely. Inside, a different tide—young men with buzzing glands—swirled around her. From its eddy the news leaped like a sailfish: the police had finally solved the Lahaina bombing case. "Made da bust 'bout da hour agc," she overheard a kamaaina say.

37

Across the waves, in Seattle, it continued to rain. Late at night the rain would harden into snow drops, but by the time the morning shift of engineers, coffee thermoses in hand, sloshed up to the security gate at Boeing Aircraft, there was plain rain again and plenty of it. A gelid wind, Alaska decals on every piece of its luggage, lingered in the rain without a sneeze, muscled through the blackberry brambles without a scratch, called upon the King and Queen without an invitation.

"Little wonder the CIA has so many leaks," said Max. He was bundled against the drafts. "It knows nothing about insulation."

Chuck wrote this down in his spy book. King Max watched him laboring over the spelling. "I—n—s—u—l—a—t—i—o—n," said Max helpfully. If the King was aware of the insurrection afoot in his homeland, he kept it well hidden.

"He ain't fooling me," said Chuck. Using the kitchen extension, Chuck eavesdropped on a telephone conversation that Max had had with one A'ben Fizel.

"There's some kind of deal on with the Arabs," Chuck reported to the CIA.

"Was there any mention of arms?" asked Chuck's connection.

"Talk of jet planes and missiles, I believe."

Max had arranged for A'ben Fizel to meet Princess Leigh-Cheri when she returned from Hawaii. Chaperoned, of course. Tilli and Max would accompany their daughter and Fizel to a basketball game. Seattle Supersonics versus the Houston Rockets. In the Kingdome.

"Said something about battle in the kingdom."

"I'll be damned," swore the agent. He whistled. "This is bigger than we thought."

To her Chihuahua, whose shivering little frame she had dressed in a purple wool sweater with fur at the collar, Queen Tilli complained. "Baskeetboll. Baskeetboll. You might haf known no Arab vud vant to attend zee opera."

38

"You're crying."

"I am not."

"My mistake. You aren't crying. You aren't out of breath, either. That's fortunate because this club doesn't admit women with pants. Is that a pun in my pocket, or am I just glad to see you? Something's wrong."

Leigh-Cheri merely sniffed. "Have you got a tissue?" she asked.

"Yeah, sure. I'll find you something. Come on in."

Leigh-Cheri stooped and entered the cabin. She ripped a length of toilet paper from the roll that Bernard fetched from the head. She blew her nose, a signal for all tears to return to their homes and families.

"Well, I see you're still here."

"I am definitely here. But that's no reason to cry."

"I wasn't crying. I've had a bad day. Another one. One in a series of bad days. I'm not complaining. Bad days are my bag. They're time-consuming, however, and I'm a busy girl. I only stopped by here because I understood you'd been busted."

"Oh? You turned me in?"

"No, damn you, I didn't. Cops have busted somebody for bombing the Pioneer. Just a stab in the dark, a wild guess, I know, but I thought it might be you."

"I'm hurt that you'd think such a thing but delighted that you came by to check. It is my privilege to report that if being uncaged is being free, then I am as the birdies in the blue."

"Then who did the police arrest, I wonder?"

"I fear that there's been an international, or rather, an interplanetary incident. The police have seen fit to incarcerate our guests from the faraway world of Argon."

"No kidding? Really? How did it happen, I mean, why them?"

"Because an anonymous caller tipped off the cops, who subsequently found two sticks of dynamite in their rented Toyota. Hmmm . . ."

"Bernard!"

"Shhh. I'm trying to imagine what an Argonian driver's license looks like. One of them would have had to have a driver's license in order to rent a car."

"Bernard, that was your dynamite."

"Are you sure?"

"But two sticks. You had three."

"Go ahead, tell me I'm selfish. Call me a bum Christian. I can't help it. I couldn't bring myself to give it all away. One never knows when one might need some."

She tried to respond as if he'd made a perfectly ordinary remark. She took a slow, calming breath. "What are you trying to say? With your dynamite, I mean?"

"Say? Dynamite didn't come here to teach. It came to awaken."

"Do you think dynamite can make the world a better place?"

"A better place than *what?* Argon?"

"You evasive bastard. I'm trying to understand you, and you won't give me a straight answer." Her small sunburned fist, in frustration, crumpled the soiled toilet paper with which she'd dabbed her eyes and blown her nose.

"Maybe you're not asking the right questions. If all you're interested in is making the world a better place, go back to your Care Fest and question Ralph Nader—"

"I fully intend to go hear Ralph. Ralph Nader, I mean." She blushed, feeling, perhaps, that she'd betrayed a secret onanistic intimacy.

"Good. Do that. But if you're interested in *experiencing* the world as a better place, then stay here with me."

"Oh yeah? That'd be fine—*maybe*—for you and me, but how about the rest of humanity?"

"A better world has gotta start somewhere. Why not with you and me?"

That silenced her. She seemed pensive. She unwadded the toilet paper just to have something to do with her hands. As she did so, she was reminded of the yogi who had taken the cobweb apart. "Bernard," she said, "do you think I've been paying attention to the wrong things?"

"I don't know, babe. I don't know what you've been paying attention to, because I don't know what you've been dreaming about. We may *think* we're paying attention to this, that, or the other, but our dreams tell us what we're *really* interested in. Dreams never lie."

Leigh-Cheri thought about her dreams. Several episodes came vividly to mind. They caused her to blush again and set the peachfish to oozing from its gills. "I can't recall any dreams," she lied.

"We all dream profusely every night, yet by morning we've forgotten ninety percent of what went on. That's why poets are such important members of society. Poets remember our dreams for us."

"Are you a poet?"

"I'm an outlaw."

"Are outlaws important members of society?"

"Outlaws are *not* members of society. However, they may be important *to* society. Poets remember our dreams, outlaws act them out."

"Yeah? How about a princess? Is a princess important?"

"They used to be. A princess used to stand for beauty, magic spells, and fairy castles. That was pretty damn important."

Leigh-Cheri shook her head slowly from side to side. Her fiery tresses swung like plantation curtains—the night they drove old Dixie down. "Come on. Are you serious? That's romantic bullshit, Bernard. I can't believe the dreaded Woodpecker is such a cornball."

"Ha. Ha ha. You love the earth so much, did you know it was hollow? The earth is hollow, Leigh-Cheri. Inside the ball there's a wire wheel, and there's a chipmunk running in the wheel. One little chipmunk, running its guts out for you and for me. At night, just before I fall asleep, I hear that chipmunk, I hear its crazed chattering, hear its little heart pounding, hear the squeaking of the squirrel cage—the wheel is old and rickety now and troubled by rust. The chipmunk is doing all the work. All we have to do is occasionally oil the wheel. What do you think lubricates the wheel, Leigh-Cheri?"

"Do you really think so, Bernard?"

"Cross my heart and hope to die."

"I—I think so, too. But I feel guilty about it. I feel so fucking whimsical."

"Those who shun the whimsy of things will experience rigor mortis before death."

The *High Jinks* ran to forty feet, not including bowsprit. She slept four and could have slept more, but her cabin had been remodeled in such a way as to provide maximum cargo storage without being too obvious about her mission. She was teak with brass fittings and smelled like a spice boat, which, in a sense, she was. Leigh-Cheri sat aft, in the galley, at a glass-topped table. Beneath the glass was a nautical chart of the Hawaiian Islands. Coffee cups and tumblers of tequila had left circular stains on the glass, sticky atolls in a crumb-strewn Pacific. With those fingers that weren't gripping toilet paper, Leigh-Cheri traced the rims of the unnamed reefs. "You know," she said at last, "you make me feel good about being a princess. Most of the men I've known have made me feel guilty about it. They'd snicker up their sleeves at the mention of beauty and magic tricks and—what else did you say a princess stands for?"

"Enchantments, dramatic prophesies, swans swimming in castle moats, dragon bait—"

"Dragon bait?"

"All the romantic bullshit that makes life interesting. People need that as badly as they need fair prices at the Texaco pump and no DDT in the Pablum. The men you've been with probably wouldn't kiss your nipples correctly for fear they'd suck in some pesticide."

Upon hearing their name called, her nipples sprang to attention.

"Early in my career as an outlaw, it doesn't matter when, right after my first jailbreak, I helped hijack an airliner to Havana. Castro, that great fox, granted me sanctuary, but I hadn't been in Cuba a month before I borrowed a small boat with an outboard motor and putt-putted like hell for the Florida Keys. The sameness of the socialistic system was stifling and boring to me. There was no mystery in Cuba, no variety, no novelty and worse, no options. For all the ugly vices that capitalism encourages, it's at least interesting, exciting, it offers possibilities. In America, the struggle is at least an individual struggle. And if the individual has strength enough of character, salt enough of wit, the alternatives are thicker than polyesters in a car salesman's closet. In a socialistic system, you're no better or no worse than anybody else."

"But that's equality!"

"Bullshit. Unromantic, *unattractive* bullshit. Equality is not in regarding different things similarly, equality is in regarding different things differently."

"You may be right." She fiddled with the toilet paper. She drew it across the table top and absentmindedly wiped out a whole archipelago. Is that what an "act of God" is? "I certainly don't feel like I'm the same as everybody else. Especially when I'm around you. But that only inspires me to want to help those who aren't as lucky as me."

"There's always the same amount of good luck and bad luck in the world. If one person doesn't get the bad luck, somebody else will have to get it in their place. There's always the same amount of good and evil, too. We can't eradicate evil, we can only evict it, force it to move across town. And when evil moves, some good always goes with it. But we can never alter the ratio of good to evil. All we can do is keep things stirred up so neither good nor evil solidifies. That's when things get scary. Life is like a stew, you have to stir it frequently, or all the scum rises to the top." He paused. "Anyway, to hear you tell it, you haven't been real lucky lately."

"That may be changing. You've reaffirmed my belief in romantic bullshit, and Ralph Nader speaks in forty minutes. But answer me one more question before I go. If I stand for fairy-tale balls and dragon bait— *dragon bait*—what do you stand for?"

"Me? I stand for uncertainty, insecurity, surprise, disorder, unlawfulness, bad taste, fun, and things that go boom in the night."

"You've really bought the desperado package, haven't you? I mean, you've actually done those big bad things. Hijacked planes, blown-up banks—"

"No. No banks. I leave banks to the criminal types. Without and within. Outlaws never—"

"You make outlaw sound so special."

"Oh, it's not all that special, I suppose. If you're honest, you sooner or later have to confront your values. Then you're forced to separate what is right from what is merely legal. This puts you metaphysically on the run. America is full of metaphysical outlaws. I've simply gone one step farther."

"Out of the frying pan and into the crossfire, eh, Bernard? I admire the courage of that. I do. But, frankly, it seems to me that you've turned yourself into a stereotype."

"You may be right. I don't care. As any car freak will tell you, the old models are the most beautiful, even if they aren't the most efficient. People who sacrifice beauty for efficiency get what they deserve."

"Well, you may get off on being a beautiful stereotype, regardless of the social consequences, but my conscience won't allow it. And I goddamn *refuse* to be dragon bait. I'm as capable of rescuing you as you are of rescuing me."

"I'm an outlaw, not a hero. I never intended to rescue you. We're our own dragons as well as our own heroes, and we have to rescue ourselves from ourselves. Even outlaws perform services, however, and I brought my dynamite to Maui to remind the Care Fest that good can be as banal as evil. As for you, well . . . did you really expect me to keep my senses after taking a look at your hair?"

Leigh-Cheri held a strand of her hair to her eyes. As if in comparison, she reached across the table to where Bernard sat opposite her and examined one of his unruly ringlets. The hair of most so-called redheads actually is orange, but it was red, first color in the spectrum and the last seen by the eyes of the dying, it was true-blue red that clanged like fire bells about the domes of Bernard Mickey Wrangle and Princess Leigh-Cheri.

There followed an embarrassed silence, tense and awkward, broken finally with a snap by the Woodpecker's abrupt plunging of his hand into his jeans. Patterning his gesture after the successful Jack Horner, he pulled out a single hair and held it aloft. It glowed like a copper filament. "Can you match that?" he challenged.

Okay, buster. Okay okay okay okay okay *okay*.

Beneath the table, beneath a map of Hawaii with extraneous atolls, she submarined a hand into the depths of her skirt and slid it along the flat of her thigh. It winnowed into her panties. She yanked. Ouch! Damn it! She yanked again. And presto, there it was, curly and stiff, and as red as a thread from a socialist banner.

"What do you think of that?" she asked brightly. Then she noticed that from the tip of the hair there hung, like a tadpole's balloon, a tiny telltale bead of fishy moisture. O sweet Jesus, no! She released her grip on the crumpled toilet paper. It fluttered to the deck like a stricken dove. Her face heated as crimson as the hair, and then some. She could have died.

"What do I think of that?" The Woodpecker's voice was very very gentle. "I think it could make the world a better place."

39

"Vertical integration by food conglomerates, as in the poultry industry, has moved with great speed in the last quarter of the twentieth century. Yet this incredible 'poultry peonage' of the chicken farmer has spread almost without notice by urban America."

In the moonlight that soaked through the foliage of the grand banyan tree, the Hero was addressing the multitudes. Dressed in an inexpensive gray suit and a terminally drab necktie, he might just as well have been speaking in Philadelphia as Lahaina, but so enormous was his integrity that the sound of his voice caused the mongooses to cease stalking poodledogs on the grounds of the public library, and even Montana Judy's mob, which had raised seven kinds of hell at the afternoon session of the Care Fest, sat on the grass in respectful silence. In fact, aside from several plastic Japanese fans and the Hero's dry lips, the only thing moving in Banyan Park was an ancient chaperon, cruising the crowd, row by row, searching for her responsibility.

"How, for example, can the housewife detect and do something about residues of hormones, antibiotics, pesticides, and nitrates in the meat she purchases, or the excess water added to the chickens, hams, and processed meats?"

Slurp and slobber, smack and excess water. Leigh-Cheri and Bernard kissed deliriously. They were speaking in tongues. Like an animal at a salt lick, he cleaned up the last of her tears. He even kissed a pearl of her snot away. As if his tongue weren't enough, he eased a finger as well into her mouth and read the slippery Braille being writ there. She sucked his finger, and pressed her body against his so tightly that he nearly lost balance and toppled to starboard. The ocean in the Small Boat Harbor was feisty with tide, and they hadn't gained their sea legs yet. Cautiously, centimeter by centimeter, squeezing as he went, Bernard worked a freckled hand up inside her skirt. Her panties all but dissolved in his grip. Oh my! Had King Max telephoned his bookie right then, he'd have found the odds running eight to one against celibacy.

"The chemical industry and its pushers have ensured that the government go slow on research for alternative and safer methods of pest control."

Bernard handed her a capsule and a cup of tequila with which to wash it down. "Here. Swallow this."

"What is it?"

"She-link. Chinese birth control. It's very old and very safe. One capsule lasts for months. Take it, babe."

"I don't know. . . . What's in it?"

"The Four Immortals."

"Only four. I'd feel safer with six."

"Take it."

"With six you get eggroll."

"Take it."

She took it, trying, as she swallowed, not to think of that line of marching Chinese, eight abreast, stretching completely around the globe.

"Later, I'll teach you lunaception: how to observe the way your hormonal cycle coordinates with light. You can learn to synchronize your body with moon phasing and be knock-up proof and in harmony with the universe at the same time. A whale of a bargain."

Leigh-Cheri was so pleasantly surprised by what she was hearing, so delighted by this mad bomber's concern for her womb, that she threw her arms around him and kissed him like he was going out of style, which to the thinking of many, he was. She found herself laughing, kissing and undressing, all at the same time. Former Republican presidents, eat your hearts out.

"Competition, free enterprise, and an open market were never meant to be symbolic fig leaves for corporate socialism and monopolistic capitalism."

Did the Hero realize that as he spoke of symbolic fig leaves, real fig leaves formed the canopy that shielded the sheen of his business suit from the playful rays of the moon?

Aboard the *High Jinks*, the last symbolic fig leaf had fallen. Bernard's shorts—black, naturally—hit the deck moments after Leigh-Cheri stepped out of her panties. Their underwear just lay there, gathering dust, like ghost towns abandoned when the nylon mines petered out.

They tumbled onto a lower berth. Leigh-Cheri had been this aroused before but never this relaxed about it. Her knees framed her smiling face. She presented a target difficult to miss. The moon, bright as a lemon, entered the sloop via porthole and sparkled on the dripping bull's-eye. His aim was true. He sank to the hilt. "Sweet Jesus!" she cried. "Yum-mm," he moaned. The sea rocked the boat, as if egging them on.

"Rarely revealed publicly, but still operational, are corporate rationalizations that air pollution is the 'price of progress' and the 'smell of the payroll.'"

As time passed, the air in the cabin was composed of two parts oxygen, one part nitrogen, and three parts slish vapor, French mist, and Cupid fumes. Their funk billowed over them like a sail. It carried them across the crest of spasm after spasm. The aroma of her cunt knocked the hatches back. The scent of his semen swamped the bilges.

"Ooh," she marveled. "Don't we smell *pretty?*"

"Good enough to eat," he answered. He thought about what he had said. It gave him ideas.

"In all the current environmental concern and groping for directions by students and citizen's groups, one major institution has been almost ignored or shunted aside as irrelevant."

They had been still for a while, catching their breath, letting the tempo of their blood drums slacken, gazing into each other's eyes in perfect manifestation of hypnotic universal peeper-lock love trance, when Leigh-Cheri said, "You know, Bernard, that was not very nice what you did."

"I'm sorry. I thought you liked it. Some women are inhibited about having ... that part of them loved— maybe it hurts them—but I tried to be gentle, and you certainly sounded like you were liking it."

"Not *that*, silly. I'm not talking about that. I did like it. It was my first time. Not even a finger, can you believe it? It probably never occurred to my boyfriends that princesses even *have* assholes." She kissed Bernard appreciatively.

"I wasn't talking about that, you silly bomber. I

meant your frame job. The poor ambassadors from Argon."

"Them. Well, first of all, babe, if they really got here all the way from Argon, they shouldn't have any trouble getting out of the Lahaina jail. Second, the things they were saying about redheads constituted a crime against nature. Nature demanded retribution. Third, the Woodpecker is proud of his deeds, even those that have a certain overtone of fuck-up about them. He's not gonna let any glory hogs from outer space take credit for what was a rather fine piece of journeyman dynamiting. One day he'll set the record straight. But not right away. There're eleven months to go before the statute of limitations expires, at which time he plans to enjoy some especially amusing public appearances."

"In eleven months you'll be free?"

"If that's freedom, yeah."

"For some reason that makes me happy."

"I can't imagine why."

They snuggled closer, and when they were as close as they could get without being behind one another, they commenced to kiss again. His middle finger began to disappear into her vagina, but she pulled it out and forced it instead—with some discomfort and some ecstasy—deep into the royal rectum.

"Outlaw territory," she whispered.

"What is needed is a sustained public demand for a liberation of law and technology that will disarm the corporate power that turns nature against man. Thank you, ladies and gentlemen. Good night."

Did the banyan tree believe that the cheering was for it? Surely, the moon realized that in the last quarter of the twentieth century it could expect no applause. The Hero, nodding more than bowing, stepped down from the podium and in scruffed shoes strode modestly from Banyan Park.

If success is clapped and failure booed, then Gulietta deserved but catcalls for *her* evening's work. An hour's diligent searching had not located her mistress and charge. Gulietta also left the park.

Bernard and Leigh-Cheri might legitimately have applauded themselves, but freshly fucked lovers seldom acknowledge "success" in those terms, and besides, they were too pooped to give themselves the standing ovation they deserved. They, too, were preparing to take their leave.

They sat on the berth. They shared a cup of tequila and a package of Hostess Twinkies. As if they were tourists at a geological site, they watched a flow of translucent lava inch its way down the inside of her leg.

"You sure were full of it," she said.

"A regular Hostess Twinkie," he replied.

She dipped a thumb into the flow and stuck it in her pretty mouth. It made her giggle.

"I hear it tastes like plastic," Bernard said.

"Cream of bomber soup. Someday I want a whole bowl full."

"You know how to open the can."

Dreamily, the Princess stood up. "I'm not sure if I can walk," she said.

"Then I'll carry you."

"Is that what love is?"

"I no longer know what love is. A week ago I had a lot of ideas. What love is and how to make it stay. Now that I'm in love, I haven't a clue. Now that I'm in love, I'm completely stupid on the subject."

Leigh-Cheri was feeling stupid, as well. Look as she might, she couldn't find her underpants. "They must have melted," she joked as she hugged Bernard goodbye, but secretly she suspected that the gods had vaporized them as a warning, a sign of divine displeasure for her having given her heart and her ass to the outlaw rather than her mind and her soul to a cause. In actual fact, a mongoose, attracted by the primal fragrance emanating from the sloop, had come aboard and carried them off. Having chewed all of the salt out of them, the mongoose abandoned the panties in a gutter along Hotel Street, where, the following morning, the Hero, hailing a taxi for the airport, stepped on them without noticing, although the lace cried out sweetly to his purposeful shoes.

40

She was queen of Hawaii at last. Hawaii opened up to her as she had opened up to Bernard, like a flower whose bell is deep and sticky, like a book with satin pages, like a fruit so swollen with juice it moans for the prick of the knife. Despite Gulietta's halfhearted objections, Leigh-Cheri spent Thursday with Bernard, and everywhere the two redheads went, Hawaii was there to receive them.

They picnicked in a forest beneath the volcano. Ants, perhaps bearing tiny leis, swarmed to greet them. Bernard bit into a tomato. He spit out its seeds. The seeds formed a circle on the ground. They sat inside the circle. Intent on wishing them "aloha," the ants stormed the circumference, but the circle would not yield. Leigh-Cheri passed Bernard the pickles. Bernard handed Leigh-Cheri the cheese. From somewhere in the jungle, the wind knocked bamboo together, making a musical clack-clack-clack like the teeth of a wooden idol. Doors of yellow ginger blossoms, on hinges that never need oiling, opened and closed in the wind.

Bernard popped a can of Primo, the native Hawaiian beer. Although beer is one of the few neutral foods, being neither yin nor yang, acidic nor alkaline, solar nor lunar, masculine nor feminine, wholly dynamic nor wholly inert, although beer perpetually idles in neutral and therefore may be the perfect beverage for the dispassionate and indecisive last quarter of the twentieth century, the Princess did not drink beer. She was content to drink the warm zephyrs of Maui. And after lunch, the ants looking on in a state of frenzy, she drank her lover's come. "Hmmm. It doesn't taste like plastic," she thought. "It tastes a lot like poi." Ah, Hawaii.

There is lovemaking that is bad for a person, just as there is eating that is bad. That boysenberry cream pie from the Thrift-E Mart may appear inviting, may, in fact, cause all nine hundred taste buds to carol from the tongue, but in the end, the sugars, the additives, the empty calories clog arteries, disrupt cells, generate fat, and rot teeth. Even potentially nourishing foods can be improperly prepared. There are wrong combinations and improper preparations in sex as well. Yes, one must prepare for a fuck—the way an enlightened priest prepares to celebrate mass, the way a great matador prepares for the ring: with intensification, with purification, with a conscious summoning of sacred power. And even that won't work if the ingredients are poorly matched: oysters are delectable, so are strawberries, but mashed together ... (?!) Every nutritious sexual recipe calls for at least a pinch of love, and the fucks that rate four-star rankings from both gourmets and health-food nuts use cupfuls. Not that sex should be regarded as therapeutic or to be taken for medicinal purposes—only a dullard would hang such a millstone around the nibbled neck of a lay—but to approach sex carelessly, shallowly, with detachment and without warmth is to dine night after night in erotic greasy spoons. In time, one's palate will become insensitive, one will suffer (without knowing it) emotional malnutrition, the skin of the soul will fester with scurvy, the teeth of the heart will decay. Neither duration nor proclamation of commitment is necessarily the measure—there are ephemeral explosions of passion between strangers that make more erotic sense than many lengthy marriages, there are one-night stands in Jersey City more glorious than six-months affairs in Paris—but finally there is a commitment, however brief; a purity, however threatened; a vulnerability, however concealed; a generosity of spirit, however marbled with need; an honest *caring*, however singed by lust, that must be present if couplings are to be salubrious and not slow poison. Having consumed for years only junk-food sex (some of it undeniably finger-licking good), Princess Leigh-Cheri was now the recipient, in abundance, of both lusciousness and nourishment, and needless to say, it was agreeing with her. Trying to make love standing up in the Kaanapali surf (tourists on the sands were none the wiser), enjoying her lover's reflection (crimson pubes and all) in a jungle pool near Hana, bouncing her sex-sore bottom along a riding trail at Makawao (she'd never seen anyone stand in the saddle before or bring down a mango with a thrown blade: that Bernard!) it was as if all her travel-poster fantasies had finally come true.

❄❄ 41 ❄❄

And yet the pea under the mattress complained. It broadcast—peep peep peep—through the most luxuriant stuffing its bruising litany: poverty, waste, injustice, pollution, disease, armaments, sexism, racism, overpopulation; a boring inventory of social ills atop which princess meat could never quite get comfortable.

Nagged by the pea, she thought of returning that night to the Care Fest and to the purpose of her mission to Maui. Through the kamaaina grapevine, however, she overheard a report of the day's session in Banyan Park that inflamed the least attractive aspects of her redheadedness. It seemed that the Care Fest microphones had been seized, first by Montana Judy's gang, who harmonized on thirty-eight verses of the popular ballad, "All Men Are Rapists" (oddly enough, many men in the audience sang along); then by Gay Bob and his friends, who read aloud a long poetic manifesto entitled "Everyone Is Homosexual"; then by the Rev. Booker T. Kilimanjaro, who, Bible in one hand, machete in the other, launched into his speciality: a sermon, "Pilate Was a Honky Imperialist, Jesus Was a Nigger," delivered while performing the latest disco dances. Meanwhile, the seminar on solar energy was eclipsed, and the lecture on immortality drugs was killed. When the yogi who had taken the cobweb apart attempted, at the request of management, to cosmically charm the interlopers into relinquishing the podium, he was hurled from the stage and was last seen limping toward the first-aid tent slouched over in the Broken-Collarbone Asana.

Leigh-Cheri was furious. "You know what we should do? And I'm serious. Take that last stick of you-know-what over there and just run those rude assholes right out of the park. The Care Fest has turned into a can of worms, anyhow. We might as well finish it off."

"Oh yeah? You mean you would have me blow up something just because I didn't approve of it? What do you think I am, a vandal? A fascist? A fucking *critic*?"

"Shit," said Leigh-Cheri. "No, I don't think you're any of those things. I think you're an outlaw. And I'm starting to think that outlawism, the way you practice it, has got just as many rules as anything else."

That one hurt. They were sitting in the second-story window of the Blue Max, and as if to drive off the sting of her accusation, he was tempted to pull that last stick of you-know-what from his clothing, ignite it, and toss it into Front Street. He composed himself, though, and replied, "You obviously acquired your knowledge of explosives from watching cartoons on television. All those barnyard animals and psychopathic house pets shoving TNT in each other's beds. Well, real bombs do more than burn your fur off, I'm afraid. And there's no Hollywood animator to put you back together in the next frame. Dynamite is not some kind of custard pie in the hands of pissed-off pussycats and vengeful ducks. And it's not a practical joke—"

"All right, all right. You don't have to make excuses. Apparently an outlaw has grave responsibilities. Just like a general or a judge."

That did it. He jerked the deadly cylinder from inside his shirt and thrust its fuse-end into the candle flame that was dutifully going through the motions of romantic restaurant flick-flick upon the table top between them. Instead of throwing the dynamite into the street, however, he held it over his head like Liberty's torch while Leigh-Cheri looked on, paralyzed with horror. Other patrons of the Blue Max looked on in horror, too. A waitress found the voice to scream. A surfer dove over the bar. The fuse sputtered and sparked, like a life intensely lived. "This is the way to burn," the fuse seemed to be saying to the more docile, slow-witted candlewick. "Brilliantly, ecstatically, irrepressibly. This is the way to burn."

The fuse had an appointment and could not wait around to see if the candlewick had the courage to follow its advice.

42

At the last possible second, Bernard jammed the fuse in his mouth. It sizzled in saliva. He pulled it loose with his teeth.

"Ouch," he cried. It was the only word spoken.

Finishing his tequila mockingbird in a gulp, he assisted the stunned Princess to her feet and ushered her to the stairs. Nobody tried to stop them. The normally clamorous Blue Max was as quiet as a prayer.

He walked her to the Pioneer Inn. "Go up and pack," he said. "You and Gulietta meet me at the boat as quick as you can." He leaned forward to kiss her but thought better of it. There was a nasty burn on his tongue.

43

Sunset lingered a long while that evening. It was as if a mai tai had been spilled in the sky. Streaks of grenadine, triple sec, maraschino, and rum seeped over the horizon, puddled upon the sea. Like a moth with a sweet tooth, the *High Jinks* glided toward the spill.

The marijuana smuggler and an associate attended to the sailing. Gulietta squatted in the stern, still as a toad. Leigh-Cheri and Bernard sat in the bow and talked.

"I'm sorry that I upset you," she said. "This is not an easy time to be a princess."

"No, and it's not an easy time to be an outlaw,

either. There's no longer any moral consensus. In the days when it was generally agreed what was right and what was wrong, an outlaw simply did those wrong things that needed to be done, whether for freedom, for beauty, or for fun. The distinctions are blurred now, a deliberately wrong act—which for the outlaw is right—can be interpreted by many others to be right—and therefore must mean that the outlaw is wrong. You can't tilt windmills when they won't stand still." He gazed into the sunset briefly, then broke into his dentistry-defying grin. "But it doesn't really bother me. I've always been a square peg in every round hole but one."

"Speaking of that, this is not an easy time for lovers, either. With the divorce rate up to sixty per cent, how can anyone attend a wedding with a straight face anymore? I see lovers walking hand in hand, looking at each other as if nobody else was alive on the earth, and I can't help thinking that in a year, more or less, they'll each be with someone new. Or else nursing broken hearts. True, most lovers don't work at it hard enough, or with enough imagination or generosity, but even those who try don't seem to have any ultimate success these days. Who knows how to make love stay?"

He thought for several moments before he answered.

"I guess love is the *real* outlaw," he said.

She wanted him to say more, and perhaps eventually he would have, but the next word he uttered was "Yikes!" And her own next words were "Sweet Jesus!" Gulietta's words were beyond the capabilities of the Remington SL3, and the words of the smugglers were obscured by the whoosh.

It went "whoosh" as it shot by, a sleek panatela of frozen light, pulsating with polka dots of every color, traveling, a mere thousand feet or so above the water, at incredible speed and mopping up the last of the sunset as if it were a bar rag from outer space.

Actually, and everyone aboard agreed on this in subsequent discussions, it had not pulsated with lights of *every* color. One color was notably absent. There wasn't any red.

On the ship's radio that night, they learned that numerous other parties had reported having seen a UFO rise up from Haleakala and disappear over the Pacific. But UFO sightings were old hat around Maui, and this one received little attention on the news. Much more air play was given to a dispatch about a jailbreak in Lahaina. A man and woman charged with dynamiting the Pioneer Inn had escaped from their cell. Noting that Maui was a small island, police predicted the couple's capture within a few hours.

44

Although the passing of the spaceship, if, indeed, that's what it was (the naval weather station at Pearl Harbor claimed it had been a meteor), set the *High Jinks* compass needle spinning in wild abandon, it regained its senses after an hour and resumed its obsequious fidelity to the domineering north. In the meantime, to keep them on course, Bernard took fixes on the moon and the constellations of Orion and Buddy Holly. They breezed into Kalohi Channel, making for Honolulu. The wind had its arms around them. The sea dandled them on its knee.

"Do you suppose," asked Leigh-Cheri, "that they really were from Argon?"

"Either there or L.A."

"They had a strange smell about them."

"Moth balls."

"Was that it?"

"They got their turbans and robes out of an old Shriners trunk—or else naphthalene is used as underarm deodorant where they come from."

"Bernard, suppose they were from another planet. Could they be right about redheads? Are we really moonstruck mutants whose weaknesses are betrayed by the sun?"

"I can tell you this much. In Central America, South America, and Mexico, there are prevailing myths about a race of redheaded Caucasians who appeared thousands of years ago and conquered tribe after tribe with benevolent magic. As a matter of fact, the Incas, Aztecs, and Mayas attribute the development of their highly advanced civilization to the 'Red Beards,' as they called them. The pyramids and the other massive New World masonries were built by these demigods, the oral traditions of dozens of major ethnic groups are consistent about that. The Red Beards legend extends into Oceania, as well. The great stone heads of Easter Island are said to be portraits of those same carrot tops—"

"I hate it when people call me carrot top."

"Me, too. The carrot has never lived that could match my top."

"Well, go on."

"Myth is crystallized history. All these stories couldn't possibly be coincidence. So, assuming that there was a race of demidivine redheads, and assuming that one day it just up and vanished from the face of the earth—the accounts are consistent about that, too—that leaves us with an inviting hoop through which to slam-dunk our basketballs of romantic bullshit."

"Yes?"

"Okay, one example. The Red Beards had extraordinary abilities. They were masters of, among other things, pyramid power, an incredibly effective harnessing of natural energies so mysterious and complex that modern science hasn't begun to understand it yet. Where did the Red Beards acquire these abilities, so far removed from the mainstream of knowledge as it has evolved on earth? Could it be that they *were* extraterrestrials? If our wimpy intellects will permit us to entertain that possibility, then we could nail us together a little hypothesis. The Red Beards come here from Argon, bringing with them the keys to pyramid power and who knows what other Argonian technologies. A revolution then occurs on Argon. The redheaded ruling class is overthrown. Eventually, the rebels send a task force to earth and vaporize the redheaded colonies here. Or maybe the Red Beards were exiled to earth after a revolt or war had already taken place on Argon. Later, the new Argonian regime—it would be blonde, like the couple on Lahaina—decides that the exiles are growing too strong on our little planet and, wishing to eliminate the possibility of future counterrevolution, dispatch an army to get rid of them with some kind of device that is beyond our conception. Poof! Sayonara Red Beards. We could work up variations on this scenario. But any way you slice it, it would account for both the presence and sudden disappearance of the Red Beards, as well as for the antipathy toward red hair among contemporary Argonians. The Red Beards might have been connected to Mars, the red planet. More likely, though, the conflict on Argon would have been between lunar and solar forces. The Red Beards would have been a lunar people—mystic, occult, changeable, feministic, spiritual, pacific, agrarian, artistic, and erotic. While the Yellow Hairs would have been solar: abstract, rational, prosaic, militaristic, industrial, patriarchal, unemotional, and puritan. It's a classic struggle here on earth. Since suns and moons are universal, the struggle could extend throughout the universe, or at least throughout our own solar system. It's a conflict that goes all the way back to the riff between Lucifer and Jehovah. The sun is Jehovah's, but Lucifer rules dat ol' debil moon."

"Jesus," said Leigh-Cheri. "That's good. You ought to write for Acid Comics. But where do we present-day, earthbound redheads fit in? Are we throwbacks, descendants of the Red Beards?"

"Maybe. They could have copulated with earthlings or in some other more esoteric way have affected the gene pool. However, my guess would be that nature, under the impetus of the moon, is trying to reevolve another superior race, trying to recreate the destroyed Red Beards. It keeps planting red seeds. Some germinate, some don't. Some grow in eccentric ways. Lots of false starts and imperfections. Lunar nature is trying to get the bugs out of the new model before it moves on to the next stage of redheaded evolution. Meanwhile, the sun takes its toll."

"So redheads are either descendants of demigods or are potential demigods. That's nice. I like that." She kissed his ear. She pinched his buttocks. "One thing for sure. You and I make love better than ordinary mortals."

"That's a fact."

"But do we know how to make love stay?"

"I can't even think about it. The best I can do is play it day by day."

"In times like these, I'm not sure if *any* lovers have a chance."

"Don't let yourself be victimized by the age you live in. It's not the times that will bring us down, any more than it's society. When you put the blame on society, then you end up turning to society for the solution. Just like those poor neurotics at the Care

116

Fest. There's a tendency today to absolve individuals of moral responsibility and treat them as victims of social circumstance. You buy that, you pay with your soul. It's not men who limit women, it's not straights who limit gays, it's not whites who limit blacks. What limits people is lack of character. What limits people is that they don't have the fucking nerve or imagination to star in their own movie, let alone direct it. Yuk."

"Yuk, Bernard?"

"Yum."

"Yum?"

"Yum. We're now at the end of one epoch and well before the start of a new one. During this period of transition, there will be no moratorium on individual aliveness. In fact, momentous events are hatching in the vacuum. It's a wonderful time to be alive. As long as one has enough dynamite."

"Or enough toot," said the captain, who had just walked up with a plate of cocaine. Bernard did a line. Leigh-Cheri was hesitant. "Come on," said Bernard. "This stuff's so fine Julius Caesar called for it with his dying breath. 'A toot, Brutus,' is what he said. Come on, try it."

Leigh-Cheri did a line. Then Gulietta did one. Perhaps Gulietta was remembering the snuff her royal employers used to snort in the good old days. The days when she would watch the swans sailing in the castle moat, never dreaming that one day, frogless, she would sail a moonlit ocean with a cargo of goofiness and love.

The sloop reached Honolulu on Saturday afternoon. The following morning, the Princess and Gulietta—and Bernard Mickey Wrangle (listed once again as T. Victrola Firecracker)—flew home to whatever stings or honeys awaited them in the vibrating American hive.

ᴥᴥ 45 ᴥᴥ

Who knows how to make love stay?

1. Tell love you are going to Junior's Deli on Flatbush Avenue in Brooklyn to pick up a cheesecake, and if love stays, it can have half. It will stay.

2. Tell love you want a momento of it and obtain a lock of its hair. Burn the hair in a dime-store incense burner with yin/yang symbols on three sides. Face southwest. Talk fast over the burning hair in a convincingly exotic language. Remove the ashes of the burnt hair and use them to paint a mustache on your face. Find love. Tell it you are someone new. It will stay.

3. Wake love up in the middle of the night. Tell it the world is on fire. Dash to the bedroom window and pee out of it. Casually return to bed and assure love that everything is going to be all right. Fall asleep. Love will be there in the morning.

Bernard the Woodpecker, who had mocked if not broken the behavioral codes of an entire civilization, rebelled, naturally enough, against the notion that he must obey the rules and regulations of a house of second-rate royalty. Eventually, however, he put pride aside and obeyed—for he wanted very much to make love stay.

The billionaire Arab sportsman, A'ben Fizel, was, with Max and Tilli's encouragement, paying court to Leigh-Cheri. If Bernard wanted so much as to see her, he had to formally court her, too. She loved him wildly, but rules are rules. She was not prepared to abandon royal privilege. "Changes are occurring in my family's country. It's boiling there. Perhaps someday the throne will be restored. I could eventually be queen. Think of the good I could do." When he failed to respond, she added, "Think of the fun we could have. I'd put you in charge of the arsenal."

So he paid court. He would treat her as if her crotch were a piece of Viennese wedding cake, sugar-frosted and rococo. He would behave as if toy soldiers guarded the vaginal gates.

Max and Tilli knew him only as a commoner the Princess had met in pagan Hawaii. They wouldn't have granted him suitor status had not Gulietta put in a good word for him. As a result, Gulietta was given a plastic frog full of coke (a substance for which she'd acquired a sudden fondness).

Bernard resided downtown in Pioneer Square. He leased the Charles Bukowski Suite in the Been-Down-So-Long-It-Looks-Like-Up-to-Me Hotel. A bachelor apartment in a building favored by pensioners and mice. The living room sofa turned into a bed. Sometimes, during the night, with him in it, it would try to turn back into a sofa again. In the bathroom, where he redyed his hair prior to calling on Leigh-Cheri, there were cigar burns on the toilet seat. There was rust in the tub and soot on the curtains. There were spiders, greasy drafts, and a calendar so out of date it still believed that holidays could fall in the middle of the week.

Dressed in a black suit, black shirt, black boots, socks, and tie, the outlaw drove his battered Merc convertible to the suburbs. The rain had stopped, but the sky hung low. It was the color of moles. Seattle's sky reminded Bernard of prison bedsheets. Using hindsight, we can see that that was ominous.

The King and Queen were to receive Bernard in the library. It was a musty room, but on its floor lay a very rare and very expensive white carpet. Whiter than doves, whiter than a toothache, whiter than God's own breath. Bernard hadn't seen Leigh-Cheri in nearly two weeks. He decided to attempt to smuggle a note to her via Gulietta. In the note he would recommend ingenuity. "May we be eaten by starving baby ostriches if we can't concoct a secret way to meet." Waiting for his prospective in-laws, he went to the desk and commenced to scribble the note. In his nervousness, he knocked an open bottle of ink onto that Easter-white carpet.

The puddle was large. The stain permanent.

Surely Queen Tilli was gracious about the mishap. Wrong. In fact, she made no effort to conceal her extreme vexation. She caressed her Chihuahua in ivory silence. Awkward and tense, the evening drooped like the sky.

Tea was poured from a silver pot whose spout had once bowed to Winston Churchill. It was excellent tea, but the suitor was craving tequila. The King made small talk about basketball. About blackberries. The Princess was afraid to look Bernard in the eye. Birds could not have flown through the longing between them. Blackberry briars could not have penetrated the longing. At nine o'clock sharp, the suitor was dismissed. Chuck tried to follow him home but lost him when in a snit he ran six red lights, the last two backwards.

The next day, Bernard managed to get Leigh-Cheri on the telephone. She told him that Queen Tilli was inconsolable. He would not be invited back. "You've got to think of something."

"I already have. Let's go live in a gypsy cave on an island off the coast of Panama. I'll play my harmonica for you and tie your hair in knots with coca leaves."

"Nothing doing," she said. "You must make amends."

A few days later, Bernard brought two dozen roses and set out for Fort Blackberry. He knew King Max was in the hospital having his valve checked. Just as well. He would call on the Queen. He rehearsed the most moving apologies. He was a trifle desperate. He would not settle for less than amends.

An uneasiness was in Gulietta's ancient eyes as she let him in. She gestured that he should wait in the music room. "Okay, but I forgot my harmonica," said Bernard. Gulietta reached for the flowers. Bernard said no, he'd just hold onto them. He went into the music room and took a seat on the couch.

As he sat, he felt something warm and heard a soft, dry snap/crackle/pop, like a singular oversized Rice Krispy being bitten into by a crocodile. He stood up slowly. The dyed hair on his neck stood up with him. Beneath him was the beloved Chihuahua. He had sat on it. And broken its neck.

There was nothing to do but lift the lid of the piano and lay the dead Chihuahua inside on the wires. He stuffed the roses in on top of it and closed the lid. He left without saying goodbye.

O sleep thy doggy nap of ages, wee beastie, yap after pharaohs' cats in the alleys of the afterworld. For Bernard Mickey Wrangle would neither sleep nor play that night. Fate had punched his ticket, love had bought him a seat on that train that only stops on the dark side of the moon.

This time, Chuck was successful in tailing him. In his haste for tequila, Bernard nipped into a Pioneer Square watering hole he normally wouldn't have frequented, the Ra Bar & Grill, owned and operated by a solar energy collective. Even the jukebox was powered by picking the sun's pockets. While Bernard was feeding that jukebox, hoping that Waylon Jennings would restore his sense of reality, Chuck was across the street in a phone booth ringing his contact in the CIA. The agent was elated. The teacup that Chuck had delivered to him two days before had yielded fingerprints. Once that same cup had worn the fingerprints of Winston Churchill, but now only the prints of the Woodpecker adorned it. "The FBI will take care of him," said the agent, "he's made monkeys of them for years. Then my office will determine what part he's been playing in the plot to restore King Max. Don't let him out of your sight."

Within an hour, Bernard was arrested—ten months to the day before the statute of limitations would have cut him loose. And although he yelled to the barroom crowd as the agents dragged him away, "They haven't got me! It's impossible to get me!" officials at McNeil Island Federal Penitentiary were already dusting out a cell from which they claimed Houdini could not have escaped.

And soon Princess Leigh-Cheri would be dusting out her attic, a cell devised to thwart love's escape, a bare museum dedicated to what each of us wants and cannot have and to the sadness and joy of that wanting.

And here might be the moment to squirt one perfect tear, all bittersweet and shimmering with dreamy resignation. Except that as the serpent once sunned its coils in Eden, patiently awaiting the opportunity to let the biggest cat in eternity out of the sturdiest bag, so a pack of Camel cigarettes stands in these wings, waiting to come on and do its most unexpected stuff.

INTERLUDE

The Remington SL3 has a new paint job. I've brushed the sucker red. Don't ask why. It's the only way I can continue with the damned machine. Externally, at least, the effect is interesting. Almost shocking. Almost intimate. Jiggling upon my table now, it's as ruddy and indiscreet as a plastic sack full of hickeys.

Internally, too, it may be destined for alterations. For better or worse, it's going to have to cope with letters, words, sentence structures with which no existing typewriter has had experience. Let me explain.

On a recent journey to Cuba, I found myself in the downtrodden plaza of an inland village, surrounded by adolescents politely requesting Chiclets. Had I imagined that Chiclets were a rare delicacy to Cubans, I might have smuggled in a few cartons from the Thrift-E Mart back home. As it was, however, I lacked both Chiclets and, as it turned out, the linguistics to say as much.

Always, I'd believed that the Spanish verb *hablar* meant "to have," so that when one said "Sí, hablo español," one was saying, "I have Spanish—I have command of the Spanish language." Operating out of that misconception, I said to the handsome young Cubans, "No hablo Chiclets." They smiled courteously.

Later, I learned that what I'd said was, of course, "I don't speak Chiclets."

At first I felt pretty dumb. But then I thought, "Well, it was an honest statement. I *don't* speak Chiclets."

Then I thought: "Why not?"

In the months since, I've been teaching myself to speak Chiclets. Let me tell you, it's easier to speak Chiclets than to read or write it.

Nevertheless, there is a definite possibility that in the remaining pages of this book I might lapse momentarily into Chiclet prose. The subject matter almost requires it.

I hope that the Remington SL3 is up to the task.

Does the moon have a purpose? Are redheads supernatural? Who knows how to make love stay? I'm going to submit those questions, and several significant others, to the Remington SL3. Like a war between magicians, it can last a long time, and even then the outcome may not be what it appears to be.

But if the Remington SL3, freshly painted, can type in Chiclets, then this enterprise may hold together. Something has got to hold it together. I'm saying my prayers to Elmer, the Greek god of glue.

PHASE III

46

After a decent interval, Queen Tilli acquired another Chihuahua. Max insisted on it. He couldn't stand it when she blubbered during dog food commercials, and the little urn of ashes was giving him the creeps. One day he simply blew out the black candles and drove her to a pet store.

An outlaw lover is not so easily replaced.

Leigh-Cheri refused to see A'ben Fizel. She refused to see the reporters who telephoned daily. The reporters didn't want to ask her about the Woodpecker—her relationship with him was still secret from the public—the reporters wanted to talk about the monarchy of Mu. Two days following Bernard's arrest, *People* magazine hit the stands with its article on her. It seemed the press thought Mu a good idea. Several deposed royals who'd been interviewed thought it a good idea. Even King Max, who'd never had the slightest interest in natural environment, beyond the blackberries that drummed their million menacing fingernails outside his walls, thought it a good idea. Max encouraged her to follow through. He encouraged her to see the reporters. He encouraged her to see A'ben Fizel. But Leigh-Cheri would see no one. She wished only to see Bernard, and so far the King County Jail, where he was being held while awaiting trial, had refused to allow him visitors.

He was not allowed bail, either. If he had been, Leigh-Cheri would have hocked what was left of Tilli's crown jewels to go it, and the Furstenberg-Barcalona code could take a flying fuck at a rolling tiara.

"The most important thing is love," said Leigh-

Cheri. "I know that now. There's no point in saving the world if it means losing the moon."

Leigh-Cheri sent that message to Bernard through his attorney. The message continued, "I'm not quite twenty, but, thanks to you, I've learned something that many women these days never learn: Prince Charming really *is* a toad. And the Beautiful Princess has halitosis. The bottom line is that (a) people are never perfect, but love can be, (b) that is the one and only way that the mediocre and the vile can be transformed, and (c) doing that makes it that. Loving makes love. Loving makes itself. We waste time looking for the perfect lover instead of creating the perfect love. Wouldn't that be the way to make love stay?"

The next day, Bernard's attorney delivered to her this reply:

> Love is the ultimate outlaw. It just won't adhere to any rules. The most any of us can do is to sign on as its accomplice. Instead of vowing to honor and obey, maybe we should swear to aid and abet. That would mean that security is out of the question. The words "make" and "stay" become inappropriate. My love for you has no strings attached. I love you for free.

Leigh-Cheri went out in the blackberries and wept. "I'll follow him to the ends of the earth," she sobbed.

Yes, darling. But the earth doesn't have any ends. Columbus fixed that.

47

Blackberries.

Nothing, not mushrooms, not ferns, not moss, not melancholy, nothing grew more vigorously, more intractably in the Puget Sound rains than blackberries. Farmers had to bulldoze them out of their fields. Homeowners dug and chopped, and still they came. Park attendants with flame throwers held them off at the gates. Even downtown, a lot left untended for a season would be overgrown. In the wet months, blackberries spread so wildly, so rapidly that dogs and small children were sometimes engulfed and never heard from again. In the peak of the season, even adults dared not go berry picking without a military escort. Blackberry vines pushed up through solid concrete, forced their way into polite society, entwined the legs of virgins, and tried to loop themselves over passing clouds. The aggression, speed, roughness, and nervy upward mobility of blackberries symbolized for Max and Tilli everything they disliked about America, especially its frontier.

Bernard Mickey Wrangle took a yum approach.

To the King, during tea, Bernard had advocated the planting of blackberries on every building top in Seattle. They would require no care, aside from encouraging them, arborlike, to crisscross the streets, roof to roof; to arch, forming canopies, natural arcades, as it were. In no time at all, people could walk through the city in the downpouringest of winter and feel not a splat. Every shopper, every theater-goer, every cop on the beat, every snoozing bum would be snug and dry. The pale green illumination that filtered through the dome of vines could inspire a whole new school of painting: centuries from now, art critics might speak, as of chiaroscuro, of "blackberry light." The vines would attract birds. Woodpeckers might not bother, but many birds would. The birds would sing. A bird full of berry pulp is like an Italian full of pathos. Small animals might move into the arches. "Look, Billy, up there, over the Dental Building. A badger!" And the fruit, mustn't forget the fruit. It would nourish the hungry, stabilize the poor. The more enterprising winos could distill their own spirits. Seattle could become the Blackberry Brandy Capital of the World. Tourists would spend millions annually on Seattle blackberry pies, the discerning toast of the nation would demand to be spread with Seattle blackberry jam. The chefs at the French restaurants would dish up duck in purplish sauces, fill once rained-on noses with the baking aromas of *gâteau mûre de ronce*. The whores might become known, affectionately, as blackberry tarts. The Teamsters could try to organize the berry pickers. And in late summer, when the brambles were proliferating madly, growing faster than the human eye can see, the energy of their furious growth could be hooked up to generators that, spinning with blackberry power, could supply electrical current for the entire metropolis. A vegetative utopia, that's what it would be. Seattle, Berry Town, encapsulated, self-sufficient, thriving under a living ceiling, blossoms in its hair, juice on its chin, more blackberries—and more!—in its future. Consider the protection offered. What enemy paratroopers could get through the briars?

The King's heart had rattled like spook chains in a horror show. Trembling, he had changed the subject to basketball.

"Oh-Oh, spaghetti-o," muttered Tilli under her breath.

Had the ink remained upright in its bottle, had the

carpet's innocence been preserved, it was still doubtful if Bernard would have been invited back to the palace.

Now, following Chihuahua slaughter and publicized arrest, it was futile for Leigh-Cheri to expect sympathy from her parents, let alone help. She wept against Gulietta's bricklike breasts. And when the tear barrel was finally empty and every available frog had been consulted, she made-up, dressed-up, and caught a bus into town. She was going to keep an appointment with Bernard's attorney. She was embracing the blackberry as her emblem, her symbol, her exemplar, her muse. In other words, she would persist to the wildest lengths of persistence. She was going to blackberry her way to her man.

48

The suburban bus let her off on First Avenue, a street as old as the city itself, though far younger than the tawdry commerce that for many Seattleites the very name of the street implied. A slim, steady rain was falling. Neon reflections on the wet concrete gave First Avenue the appearance of an underwater burial ground for parrots. As Leigh-Cheri walked south, the mood of the avenue grew increasingly rowdy. Mouth holes of saxophones and pistols gaped at her from pawnshop windows. "Adult" bookstores and porno cinemas promised further gapings. Smells of stale hot dogs and soaked mackinaws wafted by on zephyrs of exhaust. If she had drunk just one beer in each of the taverns she passed, she could have consumed a case in a very few blocks, but though beer, in its foamy neutrality, may have been the perfect beverage for the last quarter of the twentieth century, Leigh-Cheri did not drink beer and wouldn't have drunk it in the Born to Lose Tavern, the Broken Jaw Tavern, or the Sailors Have More Fun Tavern if she did.

Passing a tattoo parlor, she paused to window-shop the mermaids, screaming eagles, and macabre tributes to Mom. Through the raindrops that streaked the plate glass, she saw that phrase again, *Born to Lose*, this time on the tattoo artist's flash card: Born to Lose, a slogan so expressive, so deeply relevant that men have it permanently etched into their hides, and she thought of her own flaccid biceps, imagining the slogan stenciled there. She wondered if one lost one's royal privilege if one had one's royal epidermis inscribed. She did know that once tattooed one could no longer expect to lie for all eternity in an orthodox Jewish cemetery. They wouldn't even bury women with pierced ears. A strange theory of mutilation from the people who invented cutting the skin off the peepee.

The Princess walked on.

She met sailors who hunkered. She met lumberjacks who cursed. She met the original cast of the Food Stamp Opera, who tried to lure her up to their three-dollar hotel rooms, where the light bulbs were dying and the wallpaper was already dead. She met many winos. They were at various stages of wino development. Invariably, however, they seemed to have made peace with the rain, as if the wino ambassador had negotiated a treaty with the rulers of rain, a compromise henceforth known as the Tokay Accords. The Indian winos, in particular, were unhurried by the weather, and she recalled that Bernard had said, "White men watch clocks, but the clocks are watching the Indians."

The Princess was wearing a yellow vinyl slicker with matching hat. It looked great with her red hair. She walked on.

First Avenue lay on an incline. Steeper toward the north. Traveling south, she moved downhill. Like the rainwater. Like the twentieth century. At the foot of First, where it crossed Yesler Way, there was a small cobblestoned square, watched over by the several wooden eyes of a totem pole. There, at Pioneer Square, the mood changed abruptly. Once as rough and raunchy as upper First Avenue, Pioneer Square had been hit by restoration. Now, art galleries, boutiques, and discos were replacing the storefront churches, and the *déclassé* luncheonettes were giving way to restaurants that featured imported mineral waters and a gay waiter behind every fern.

In Pioneer Square, where the seedy collided with the chic, was where Nina Jablonski had her law office. Being somewhat of radical temperament, Nina Jablonski had volunteered to defend Bernard Mickey Wrangle against the United States of America, although Mrs. Jablonski did not fully share her client's view that he against the United States of America was a fair match. Actually, the Woodpecker regarded the contest a bit one-sided in his favor, and he would have liked to take on Japan, East Germany, and the Arab nations as well.

Nina Jablonski had red hair. Not as red as Bernard's or Leigh-Cheri's, but definitely red, and the Princess was certain that it was on account of Jablonski's hair, and perhaps the fact that she was seven months pregnant (he maintained a residue of regret about destroying the prospective male pill), that Bernard had agreed to allow her to defend him. Leigh-Cheri had to confess that she, too, was irrationally assured by Mrs. Jablonski's tresses—a fellow victim of sugar and lust? another ally against Argon and the sun?—but the swell of the attorney's belly merely reminded her that she herself hadn't had a period since she left for Maui, an omission that made her as nervous as the Queen's lapdog.

Ah, but there was good news! Jablonski, whose features were so strong that no amount of freckles could burden them, had been successful in her petition to have Bernard's rights to be visited restored. Leigh-Cheri could go see him on the following Sunday, three days away.

"There are conditions, however," said Jablonski, handing the Princess a tissue to mop up her happy tears. "Conditions set not by the court but by Mr. Wrangle and me."

"Like what?" asked Leigh-Cheri.

"My dear, you must realize that your conversation will be bugged. For some reason, Mr. Wrangle is suspected of being involved in an international plot to return your father to the throne. Anything you might say regarding your family, or, for that matter, your personal relationship with Mr. Wrangle, might be misconstrued in such a manner as to deepen those suspicions, which would hurt our chances for a minimal sentence. I wanted to establish some safe guidelines for your conversation. Mr. Wrangle went one step further. He doesn't feel it would be emotionally beneficial—for either one of you—to converse at all. He feels that poignant dialogue will merely make your separation all the more difficult. And he certainly doesn't believe the CIA should be privy to the private tenderness you share. He does very much want to see you. And he longs to hear your voice. But he desires that nothing in the way of personal conversation pass between you."

"But—what'll I do? I can't just sit there and talk about the rain on the fucking blackberries. What'll I say?" (Tears of joy, exit stage right. Tears of bewilderment, enter stage left; advance to footlights.)

"Mr. Wrangle suggests that you tell him a story."

"What? A story?"

"Yes, a story of some sort. He wishes to look at you.

He wishes to hear you speak. You'll have ten minutes. Just tell him a story. I'm sure you'll think of
something."

Leigh-Cheri stared at the antinuclear posters on
the office wall. Nuclear power was one of the most
sinister frauds ever perpetrated on the American people, and yet its implications meant little to her now.

Mrs. Jablonski removed her fashionably large spectacles and stood. "I asked Mr. Wrangle what you were
like. He said you were hornet juice and rosebuds in a
container of gazelle meat. He does speak colorfully,
doesn't he?"

Leigh-Cheri pulled on her dripping slicker and departed. As she sped back up First Avenue in a taxi—she
was not in the mood for any more Born to Lose—she
thought, "A story? I do know one story. I know one
story. It'll have to do."

49

So it came to pass that on the next Sunday afternoon,
a Sunday afternoon carved, like most Sunday afternoons, from a boiled turnip, Princess Leigh-Cheri sat
in the austere visiting room at the King County Jail,
separated from Bernard Mickey Wrangle by a panel
of thick, clear glass, telling him, through a closed-
circuit telephone, a story, the story, the story that
Gulietta had told her at bedtime almost every night
of her life.

They gazed at one another with fixed, intense smiles;
their pulses fluttered, and the ancient hormonal soup
hissed in their glands, yet Bernard was silent, and
Leigh-Cheri, in a surprisingly even tone, stuck to the
story. No sooner had she sat down across from him,
her lips aching to pucker their way through the glass,

than she picked up the phone and spoke into it brave-ly, "Once upon a time. . . ." He noticed that she had put on a few pounds, she noticed that some of his freckles looked as if they'd gone bad, but they didn't betray their observations. He listened intently, and she went on with the tale.

"Once upon a time. . . ." Just the way Gulietta would have begun, although in Gulietta's language, "Once upon a time" sounded as if it were a rubber apple on which some barnyard animal was choking.

"Once upon a time, a long time ago, when it was still of some use to wish for the thing one wanted, there lived a king whose daughters all were beautiful, but the youngest was so lovely that the sun itself, who had seen so much and forgotten so little, simply marveled each time it shone on her face.

"This daughter had a favorite plaything, a golden ball, that she loved dearly. When the days were hot, she would go out into the dark forest near the palace and spend many an hour tossing and catching her golden ball in the shade of a leafy tree. There was a spring in the forest, and usually the princess played near the brink of the spring so that when her play made her thirsty she might take a cool drink.

"Now it happened one day that the golden ball, instead of falling back into the maiden's little hands, dropped to the ground and bounced into the spring. The princess followed the ball with her eyes as it sank, but the spring was very deep, and it soon sank out of sight. The bottom of the spring could not be seen. Thereupon she began to cry, and she wailed louder and louder as if her little heart were broken.

"While she was lamenting in this way, she heard a throaty voice call to her. 'Hey now, king's daughter, what is the matter? I've never heard anyone cry so hard.'

"She looked around to see where the voice came

from, but all she saw was a frog, holding its fat, ugly head out of the water. 'Oh, it's you, you old croaker,' she said. 'Well, if you must know, I'm crying because my wonderful golden ball has fallen into the spring and has sunk so deeply I'll never get it out.'

" 'Relax, don't cry. I think I can be of some assistance. What will you give me if I can recover your toy for you?'

" 'Oh, anything, anything. Whatever you'd like most, dear frog. My fine clothes, my pearls, my carriage, even the bejeweled crown I wear.'

"The frog replied, 'I have no use whatsoever for your clothes or your pearls or even your crown, but I'll tell you what. If you will care for me and let me be your playmate and companion, let me sit beside you at your little table, eat from your little plate, drink from your little cup, and sleep in your little bed beside you, if you will promise me that, then I will dive straight down and bring back your golden ball.'

"The princess stopped weeping immediately. 'Of course,' she said. 'Of course. I promise you anything you want if you'll only bring back the ball.' But she thought, 'What nonsense that silly creature talks. As if he could do anything but swim and croak with the other frogs, as if he could possibly be anyone's companion!'

"The frog, however, as soon as he heard the promise, drew his green head under the water and sank down out of sight in the spring. After what seemed like a long while, he surfaced with a splash, the golden ball in his wide mouth. He threw the ball onto the grass.

"Needless to say, the king's daughter was overjoyed to have her ball back. She scooped it up, and tossing it and catching it, she ran off with it toward the palace.

" 'Stop, stop!' cried the frog. 'Pick me up, too. I can't run as fast as you.'

"His pleas were futile, however, for croak as he might, she paid no attention. She hurried on home and before long, forgot completely about the poor frog, who was left, presumably, to go on living in the spring.

"The next day, as the princess was sitting at table with the king and all the court, having a fine dinner, there came a pitter-patter up the marble stairs, and then there came a knocking at the door and a voice crying, 'King's youngest daughter, let me in!'

"Naturally, the princess went to the door to see who it might be, but when she found the frog sitting there, panting, she slammed the door in his face and returned to her meal, feeling quite uneasy.

"Noticing that she was acting a bit strange and that her heart was beating quickly, the king said, 'My child, what are you afraid of? Was there a giant at the door wanting to take you away?'

" 'No,' answered she. 'No giant, just a nasty frog.'

" 'Really? And what does the frog want?' asked the king.

"Tears began spilling out of the youngest daughter's eyes. She broke down and told her father everything that had happened the previous day at the spring. When she had finished, she added, 'And now he is here, outside the door, and he wants to come in to me.'

"Then they all heard the frog knocking again, and crying out:

> King's youngest daughter,
> Open to me!
> By the deep spring water
> What promised you me?

" 'That which you have promised you must always honor and perform,' said the king sternly. 'Go at once and let him in.'

"So she went and opened the door. The frog hopped in, following at her heels until she reached her chair.

Then he looked up at her and said, 'Lift me up to sit by you.' But she delayed lifting him up until the king ordered her to.

"No sooner was the frog in the chair than he demanded to get up on the table, where he sat, looking about hungrily. 'Push your plate a little nearer so that we can eat together,' he said.

"Reluctantly, she did it, and the frog feasted heartily, although for her part, every morsel seemed to stick in her throat.

" 'I'm stuffed,' said the frog at last. 'And I'm tired. You must carry me to your room and make ready your silken bed so that we can lie down and sleep.'

"The princess began to fret and moan and cry and complain. She didn't want that cold, creepy frog in her pretty, clean bed. The king became angry with her. 'You made a promise in a time of need,' he said. 'Now, as unpleasant as it might be, you must honor it.'

"Making a terrible face, she picked up the frog and carried him upstairs, where she placed him on some soiled linen in a corner. Then she slipped into bed. Before she could fall asleep, however, the frog came pitter-patter up to her bedside. 'Let me in with you or I will tell your father,' he said.

"She had had enough. Flying into a rage, she grabbed the frog. 'Get out of my life, you slimy frog!' she shouted. With all her strength, she threw him against the wall.

"When he fell to the floor, he was no longer a frog. He had become a prince with kind eyes and a beautiful smile. The frog prince took her hand and told her how a vengeful witch had bound him by her spells and how the princess alone, in her innocent beauty, could have released him. Then he asked her to marry him, which, with her father's consent, she did. And they went off to the prince's country, where they became king and queen and lived happily ever after."

As the story ended, the way that even that unhappy fartre Sartre knows that stories ought to end, a guard strode up to Bernard and tapped him on the shoulder, signaling him to return to his cell. Bernard appeared to be lost in thought. He continued to stare at Leigh-Cheri, smiling all the while, and ignoring the guard. The guard gripped him by the collar—which wasn't black—and yanked him to his feet. It was too much for Leigh-Cheri. Shrieking, she sprang up and flattened herself against the window, as if she spread herself thin enough she could squish through the loose-knit silicone molecules the way that mayonnaise squishes through the holes in Swiss cheese. Bernard elbowed the guard in the jaw and seized the telephone. He was going to speak to her! Quickly, she picked up the phone on her side of the glass and jammed it against her ear. A whistle had been blown, more guards were rushing up, and she realized that he would be able to get out only a word or two. "Yes, sweetheart, yes?"

"Whatever happened to the golden ball?" asked Bernard.

That's what he said. "Whatever happened to the golden ball? Argggg!" And then they wrestled him from the room.

⚬⚬ 50 ⚬⚬

Over the years, Leigh-Cheri had had some questions about the story herself. Mainly, she wondered why the handsome prince would want to marry a lying little amphibiaphobe who couldn't keep a promise. Leigh-Cheri had thought that frogs became princes through the transformative magic of osculation. Why did this prince escape the frog spell only after being splattered against a wall? Was he a masochist, maybe? In which case, it was small wonder that he was attracted to such an ill-tempered snip, and they probably *did* live together happily ever after, perhaps with leather accessories.

In truth, the story had never made a lot of sense to Leigh-Cheri, and she resented the Brothers Grimm for portraying a princess in such an unflattering light. It was bad enough being dragon bait. For all her reservations about the tale, however, it had never occurred to her to puzzle over the fate of the golden ball. True, the story initially made a big deal about the ball, only never to mention it again, but it was the characters who were important, the ball was just a prop, a toy, an *object*.

Maybe the princess put aside the golden ball until her own children were old enough to play with it, or maybe once she had a prince to play with she simply abandoned her beloved toy (she was certainly capable of that), and it got packed away in an attic, thrown out with the garbage, stolen by a chambermaid, or donated to Goodwill Industries. In any case, Leigh-Cheri had never been curious about it, and the psychiatrists and mythologists who'd analyzed the story— they claimed the spring ("so deep its bottom could not be seen") symbolized the unconscious mind; the frog, of course (talk about typecasting), symbolized the penis, ugly and loathsome to a girl-child, but to an emerging woman a thing of some beauty that could contribute to her happiness and fulfillment—those analysts were sure that the golden ball represented the moon, but they never asked what became of it, either.

It was Bernard who'd raised the question, and in the empty days that followed their jailhouse meeting, Leigh-Cheri wondered why it seemed so important to him. The CIA wondered, also. The CIA suspected that the story was a coded message packed with information about revolutionary activity in Max and Tilli's former kingdom. The CIA submitted its tape of the story—and Bernard's apparently urgent response—to its experts in the home office. Attorney Nina Jablonski lamented the fact that of all the stories Leigh-Cheri might have told, she had chosen one about a royal family in which a king and queen ended up happily ever after. Because of the CIA monitors, Jablonski refused to ask Bernard why he was interested in the fate of the golden ball, although Leigh-Cheri requested that she do so. "We're dropping the ball," Jablonski said flatly.

As a result of the fracas with the guards, Bernard's visitor privileges were revoked. Moreover, accounts of the incident were leaked to the press. Whereas the media had been politely interested in a beautiful young princess who wished to enlist deposed royalty in the service of environmentalism, they were savagely intrigued by a beautiful young princess who was involved, politically, romantically, or both with a notorious bomb-throwing outlaw. If the Furstenberg-Barcalona monogrammed telephone had, the previous week, frequently tinkled, it now exhausted itself in a monstrous marathon of jangling, although it sometimes could not be heard above the knockings at the door. Were it not for the blackberries, reporters would have camped in the yard.

Max was in a funk due to the constant interruption of his TV sportscasts, and both Tilli and her new Chihuahua developed nervous diarrhea. Chuck was going bananas trying to intercept all the phone calls and to photograph with a miniature camera the strangers, mostly newsmen, who rapped at the door. Gulietta kept the house running fairly smoothly, everything considered, but she had begun to toot cocaine so prodigiously that often her central nervous system was buzzing in pace with the phone. Oddly enough,

Leigh-Cheri was the calmest member of the household. In part, this could be attributed to the love that enveloped her like a silk-lined fever, but it was also due to the fact that on Wednesday, two weeks late; out of breath; embarrassed but making no excuses; flustered but offering no explanations, her menses showed up. It neither called first nor knocked, but stepped through her door, sticky, mortal, its head as red as her own, remained for five days, then disappeared again, leaving behind an exhibition of cheerfully painted tampons and a sustained series of sighs of relief that could have fluttered the flags of every used-car lot in Los Angeles.

In celebration of the proven effectiveness of She-Link, Leigh-Cheri sent out for Chinese food. Chuck snapped a whole roll of film of the Oriental boy who delivered it. "Someday, when conditions are right, I'll have Bernard's baby," thought Leigh-Cheri, chewing a mouthful of fried rice. "And it can have a golden ball to play with, or anything else its daddy gives it except dynamite. But for now . . ."

For now, her energy was devoted to pestering Nina Jablonski about schemes to see Bernard again before his trial. Jablonski didn't have the heart to tell her that there wasn't going to be any trial.

51

On Leigh-Cheri's birthday, Gulietta baked a chocolate cake and sank twenty candles into the frosting. Although they were too peeved with their daughter to promote a celebration, Max and Tilli appeared at the big oak table in the dining room, where the cake was lit up like an oil refinery, long enough to sing the traditional anthem. They lingered until, with a desperate expulsion, the Princess puffed out the candles. "Zee vhole vorld knows vat her weesh vas," complained Tilli to her pooch.

Twenty candles on a cake. Twenty Camels in a package. Twenty centuries under our belts and where do we go from here?

For her part, Leigh-Cheri went back downtown and called on Nina Jablonski.

"You have chocolate on your face," said the attorney.

"It's my birthday," said Leigh-Cheri.

"Then let me buy you a drink."

They went to a fern bar and ordered champagne cocktails.

"To justice," said Jablonski.

"To love," said Leigh-Cheri.

"You've got it bad, sister."

"No, I've got it good." The Princess downed her champagne cocktail and ordered a tequila mockingbird. "Tell me, Nina, you've been married for several years—"

"Twice. Twice for several years."

"Well, do you think it's possible to make love stay?"

"Sure. It's not at all unusual for love to remain for a lifetime. It's passion that doesn't last. I still love my first husband. But I don't desire him. Love lasts. It's lust that moves out on us when we're not looking, it's lust that always skips town—and love without lust just isn't enough."

"Anybody can fuck anybody, Nina. But how many people can play together in the fields of true love?"

"Jeez. You make true love sound like some kind of elitist picnic. That's a smug misconception. Love, of all emotions, is democratic."

Leigh-Cheri got the notion that Jablonski was chiding her for her monarchal background. She didn't care. "Oh," she said, "I'm not so sure about that. I have an idea that love is a lot more exclusive than popular songs have led us to believe. Now lust, lust is democratic, all right. Lust makes itself accessible to any clod or clone who can muster enough voltage to secrete a hormone. But like you say, it doesn't stick around for long. Maybe lust gets fed up with democracy after a while, maybe lust just gets bored with the way it's spent by mediocre people. Maybe both lust and love demand something more than most of us have the stomach for. These days, certainly, folks seem more concerned with furthering careers than with furthering romance."

"You say you're twenty today?"

The Princess registered the lawyer's insinuations of immaturity, but though she was unfamiliar with neoteny, she didn't care about that, either. "Yes, I'm twenty, and, can you believe it, I have no idea how old Bernard is. He has at least a dozen driver's licenses, each one under a different name and a different age." With ecological soundness, she diverted into her throat a quantity of tequila that otherwise might have been left to stagnate or poured down the drain to poison the fishes. "Have you ever wondered what kind of driver's licenses they have on the planet Argon?"

"I think you better let me call you a cab." Jablonski gave Leigh-Cheri that uncomfortable half-amused, half-resentful look that people always give you when they're remaining sober and you are getting looped.

As a matter of fact, Jablonski had begun to look increasingly at Bernard in that same fashion, although a rabbi's dog could score pork chops in the streets of Tel Aviv easier than Bernard could acquire tequila in the King County Jail. Jablonski had come to believe that Bernard simply had too much fun. It was one thing to be a bomber, quite another to enjoy it. "Fighting the system is serious business," the lawyer had reminded her client. "It's serious business that *creates* the system," answered Bernard. He seemed to regard his impending trial as a party the government was throwing for his amusement, to look forward to it the way a frustrated amateur actor awaits the annual skit at the Elks Club. Eventually, Jablonski decided that it would best serve her client, as well as radicalism in America, if a trial (due to changes in the social climate since Bernard's previous conviction, the judiciary had offered him a new trial) could be avoided. She asked Bernard if he would mind pleading guilty. He was delighted. "If society is considered innocent, then any person who isn't guilty isn't leading a meaningful life," he said. "Besides, an outlaw is guilty by definition." She took his admission of guilt into plea bargaining, where she traded it for a reduced sentence. It was all arranged at a meeting with the prosecutor in the judge's private chambers.

"Nina," said Leigh-Cheri, her birthday blood swarming with the liquid locusts of libation, "you've got to get me to him before the trial. And we've got to get him out, even if I have to blast him out."

"Hush!" Jablonski glanced around the bar. "Don't ever so much as mention blasting, not even in a joke. Sister, listen, I've got some good news. Bernard isn't going to have to stand trial. He's being transferred to McNeil Island. Tomorrow morning. To begin serving a ten-year sentence. That means he'll be eligible for parole in only twenty months."

Twenty candles on a cake. Twenty Camels in a pack. Twenty months in the federal pen. Twenty shots of tequila down a young girl's gullet. Twenty centuries since Our Lord's last pratfall, and after all that time we still don't know where passion goes when it goes.

⚫⚫ 52 ⚫⚫

A woodpecker's movement around a tree trunk defines a perfect spiral. To connect the hoppity helix of the woodpecker to the macrocosmic spiral of our stellar system or to the microcosmic spiral of the DNA molecule or, for that matter, to the hundreds of natural spirals in between—snail shells, crowns of daisies and sunflowers, fingerprints, cyclones, etc.—may be assigning to geometry more meaning than the mundane can abide. Suffice to say that a woodpecker is first on one side of a tree and then the other; disappearing, then reappearing at a point slightly higher up the trunk.

Bernard Mickey Wrangle had disappeared again, this time into the maximum security wing of McNeil Island Federal Penitentiary, but nobody, with the possible exception of Princess Leigh-Cheri, was expecting him to reappear any time close to soon. True, he could be paroled in twenty months, if he behaved, but who could expect Bernard to behave? Certainly not officials at McNeil. They isolated him in solitary confinement. The only person permitted to see him there was Nina Jablonski, and she saw him only once because he fired her when he found himself imprisoned without the fun of a trial. Jablonski explained that if tried he could have been made to serve the remainder of his previous thirty-year sentence plus time for his escape, or he could have drawn a new sentence that was nearly as bad, particularly had he turned the courtroom into some outlandish celebration of outlawism as he had been hinting he would do. "You're lucky," said Jablonski. "You could come out of McNeil looking more like a bald eagle than a woodpecker. This way, I'm going to have you back in circulation while your hair's still red." Bernard thanked her for her concern, but he felt betrayed, nonetheless, and he dismissed her. "That's the trouble with political people," he said. "There's not one of you, left, right, or center, who doesn't believe that the means are justified by the end."

With that, he spiraled out of view.

On the day of his transfer to McNeil, the Seattle *Post-Intelligencer* had published a one-column picture of him, grinning, as usual, as if mouthing a pulpy newsprint "yum," his snaggleteeth and freckles ghosted out but his eyes frictional, even in gray ink, with the special hungers of the terminally alive. Leigh-Cheri tore the picture out of the paper and pressed it beneath her hangover pillow. It did little, if anything, to relieve her headache—her temples were banging like her daddy's valve—but during the night she awoke to the unmistaken sound of the chipmunk that lives at the center of the earth, and it seemed unusually close to her ear.

53

That year, spring came to the Puget Sound country as it frequently does, like a bride's maid climbing a greased pole. After a gradual, precarious ascent, spring, in a triumph of frills and blooms and body heat, would seem to have finally arrived, only to suddenly slide down into the mud again, leaving winter's wet flag flapping stiffly and singularly at the top of the seasonal staff. Then, girlish bosom heaving, spring would shinny slowly back up the pole.

When Leigh-Cheri took to bed with her hangover, spring was riding high. She arose two days later to an unseasonal frost. It had numbed the bejeepers out of insects and buds. It had thrown the fear of February into batteries and birds. So inanimate was Prince Charming that Leigh-Cheri believed him deceased, although when the first sunbeam to drill through the window frost caused his flipper to twitch, she sat the terrarium in front of an open oven and watched as he stoically revived. It was the middle of April. Except for the faithful who are always sounding alarms about the return of the Ice Age, nobody in the Pacific Northwest was prepared for such a frost.

Down in Pioneer Square, where the Princess bussed for one last meeting with Nina Jablonski, frosty cobblestones gave the area the appearance of a marshmallow plantation. Shrubs and winos seemed startled in the morning light. Even the *D*-note of the ferry horn had a frosty edge as it blared up from the waterfront. As for the manholes, they looked as if they'd been snorting cocaine. The manholes, Leigh-Cheri noted, bore an enlarged resemblance to Gulietta's nostrils of late. Leigh-Cheri had been waiting to catch Gulietta when she wasn't buzzed so that she might ask the old woman if she knew whatever happened to the golden ball, but such an opportunity hadn't presented itself.

Leigh-Cheri was dressed warmly in a heavy green sweater and jeans, yet she was inadequately insulated for the coolness of Jablonski's response when she revealed to the attorney her new plans. Jablonski called the Princess selfish, frivolous, narcissistic, indulgent, and immature.

"The monarchy of Mu was a half-assed idea," said Jablonski. "It would never have worked because all those dethroned kings and deposed duchesses own chunks of the big corporations whose excessive profits are threatened by a clean, healthy environment. It'd never work, but at least it was a move in the right direction, at least it was a decent impulse, an attempt to get yourself involved with something more important than your own emotions. This, however . . ."

"You don't think love is as important as ecology?"

"I think ecology *is* love."

On the campus of Outlaw College, professors of essential insanities would characterize the conflicting attitudes of Nina Jablonski and Leigh-Cheri as indicative of a general conflict between social idealism and romanticism. As any of the learned professors would explain, plied with sufficient tequila, no matter how fervently a romantic might support a movement, he or she eventually must withdraw from active participation in that movement because the group ethic—the supremacy of the organization over the individual—is an affront to intimacy. Intimacy is the principal source of the sugars with which this life is sweetened. It is absolutely vital to the essential insanities. Without the essential (intimate) insanities, humor becomes inoffensive and therefore pap, poetry becomes exoteric and therefore prose, eroticism becomes mechanical and therefore pornography, behavior becomes predictable and therefore easy to control. As for magic, there's none at all because the aim of any social activist is power over others, whereas a magician seeks power over only himself: the power of higher consciousness, which, while universal, cosmic even, is manifest in the intimate. It would seem that a whole human being would have the capacity for both intimacy and social action, yet sad to say, every cause, no matter how worthy, eventually falls prey to the tyranny of the dull mind. In the movement, as in the bee house or the white ant's hill of clay, there is no place for idiosyncrasy, let alone mischief.

A romantic, however, recognizes that the movement, the organization, the institution, the revolution, if it comes to that, is merely a backdrop for his or her own personal drama and that to pretend otherwise is to surrender freedom and will to the totalitarian impulse, is to replace psychological reality with sociological illusion, but such truth never penetrates the Glo-Coat of righteous conviction that surrounds the social idealist when he or she is identifying with the poor or the exploited. Since, on a socio-economic level, there are myriad wrongs that need to be righted, a major problem for the species seems to be how to assist the unfortunate, throttle the corrupt, preserve the biosphere, and effectively organize for socio-economic alteration without the organization being taken over by dullards, the people who, ironically, are best suited to serving organized causes since they seldom have anything more imaginative to do and, restricted by tunnel vision, probably wouldn't do it if they had.

Dullards can put a pox on the most glorious moral enterprise by using that enterprise as a substitute for spiritual and sexual unfolding. Finally, it is dullness and not evil that begets totalitarianism, although some at Outlaw College go so far as to contend that dullness *is* evil. Of course, whether something is dull can be a matter of taste (one person's ennui is another person's coronary), and there are a lot of ostensibly boring chores that *somebody* has to attend to, but when you bring that up to a scholar at Outlaw C., you'll find the sucker has just resigned in order to enter business in Tijuana, is too stoned to talk, has been arrested on some complicated charge, or is up to his mustache in a love affair and doesn't wish to be disturbed. Well, we don't need any help from those guys to see that Leigh-Cheri, once resplendent with social idealism, had fallen off a dream cliff, slipped into the vision pit, or nibbled forbidden fruit, because Nina Jablonski's declaration that a lover is one who first of all loves the earth simply didn't move her. All she wanted from the lawyer was a detailed description of Bernard's cell.

"It's small but big enough to stretch his legs in, so they don't have to take him out for exercise. There's nothing in it but a steel cot with a piece of foam rubber on top. That's it. Guards shove in a piss pot two times a day. Ten minutes later, I think it's ten minutes, they remove it. Once a week they take him to a stall next door where he can shower."

"Any windows?"

"One tiny one, with bars on it, up near the ceiling. It lets in a little daylight, but you can't see out of it."

"Electric lighting?"

"A single bulb in the ceiling. Far too high to reach."

"What wattage?"

"How the hell would I know? I'd guess forty."

The Princess smiled mysteriously. She remembered that Bernard had told her that the light of a full moon was equivalent to a forty-watt bulb at fifteen feet. "Anything else?"

"Nothing. No books, no magazines, nothing. Except a pack of cigarettes."

Again, Leigh-Cheri smiled. "Yes, he smokes Camels when he's in jail. He said that when you're locked up, smoking a cigarette is like having a friend."

"Well, it's a lonesome friendship in this case, because he's not smoking. He demanded cigarettes, it's a prisoner's right, but they won't let him smoke them. The pack hasn't even been opened."

"Why won't they let him smoke?"

"Because they're afraid if he gets his hands on any fire, he'll make a bomb."

"Outta what? A cot? Foam rubber? His clothes? A pack of cigarettes?"

"Listen, sister, your lover has a reputation. They

say the son-of-a-bitch can make a bomb out of any-thing."

On her return trip up First Avenue, where the bride's maid was overtaking the frost on the pole, Leigh-Cheri ducked into the Born to Lose Tavern and purchased a pack of Camels.

⣿ 54 ⣿

BERNARD MICKEY WRANGLE'S FAVORITE HOMEMADE BOMB RECIPES

The hearts and diamonds bomb:

Take a deck of ordinary playing cards, the old-fashioned paper kind, cut out the red spots and soak them over-night like beans. Alcohol is the best soaking solution, but tap water will suffice. Plug one end of a short length of pipe. Pack the soggy hearts and diamonds into the pipe. On pre-plastic playing cards, the red spots were printed with a diazo dye, a chemical that has an unstable, high-energy bond with nitrogen. So you've got some nitro, of sorts, now you'll be needing glyc-erin. Hand lotion will work nicely. Glug a little lotion into the pipe. To activate the quasi-nitroglycerin, you'll require potassium permanganate. That you can find in the snake-bite section of any good first-aid chest. Add a dash of the potassium permanganate and plug the other end of the pipe. Heat the pipe. A di-rect flame is best, but simply laying the pipe atop a hot radiator will turn the trick. Take cover! The Woodpecker used a hearts and diamonds bomb to re-

lease himself from McNeil Island the first time that
he was confined there.

The Draino reefer bomb:

Acquire a can of Draino or any similar household
product that contains a high concentration of lye. Roll
the Draino in a length of aluminum foil, as if you
were rolling a reefer. If you're serious about wanting
an explosion, you'll have to submerge the reefer in
water. In jail, the ideal place for submersion is a toilet
tank. When wet lye reacts with aluminum, hydrogen
is released in the form of gas. A spark will ignite it. Taking cover is difficult with this kind of explosive. Don't
lose your head.

The jug band bomb:

You'll need gasoline for this one, but only a few drops.
When Bernard was on work detail washing the sheriff's
car, he siphoned enough through a soda straw in five
seconds to buy his way out of Cody, Wyoming, forever.
Squirt the gasoline drops into a clean jug, the glass
type in which cider is sold. Cap the jug and roll it
around so that the inside is coated with the gasoline.
Let the gasoline evaporate. Once again, you'll be
requiring a snake-bite kit for its supply of potassium
permanganate (in this world, snakes take many
forms, and if you aren't adept at charming them, you
must be prepared to counteract their venom). Add
a pinch of the p.p. and quickly recap the jug. Roll the
jug across the room with enough force so that it
will break when it strikes the opposite wall. Goodbye
wall. This is a high explosive.

The Fruit Loops and batshit bomb:

A Woodpecker original. Sugar is an unstable chemical
that loves to oxidize as passionately as sulfur does
and in much the same way. In preparing this dish,
think of sugar as sulfur. The components of gunpowder are sulfur, carbon, and saltpeter. Fruit Loops,
or any similar breakfast cereal, contains a good deal
of sugar and carbon. (Bernard endorses Fruit Loops
for bombs. For his morning repast, he prefers Wheaties.
With beer.) As for saltpeter (potassium nitrate),
batshit is a perfect source. If batshit is unavailable, bird
doo will do. The older the guano the better. Aesthetic
as well as pragmatic considerations make the fresh wet
splat inadvisable. Grind up the Fruit Loops. Mix in
the batshit thoroughly. When mixing Fruit Loops and
batshit, don't be surprised if you find the color
attractive. In fact, you may end up with a clearer
understanding of art and its origins. For that reason,
this is the bomb recommended to reviewers and critics. Place the mixture in a container and ignite it.
Gunpowder, contrary to what you might expect, is
not much of a boomer. The Fruit Loops and batshit
bomb won't flatten any buildings, but it makes a
marvelous amount of smoke. Certainly it makes more
smoke than a pack of Camels. That is, it makes more
smoke than a pack of Camels *unless* . . . unless the
missing race of redheaded Argonians gets its message
across.

❀ 55 ❀

With a bucket of black paint, Leigh-Cheri went up to
the attic. She blacked out the windows, except for one
small pane in the east. Into the overhead fixture, she
screwed a forty-watt bulb. She cleared out the royal

dressmaking dummy, Christmas tree decorations, and trunks of monogrammed junk. She moved in a chamber pot and a cot. The cot had a foam rubber mattress, the pot would be emptied by Gulietta twice a day. Gulietta, also twice daily, would bring in a plate of food. "Starchy food," ordered Leigh-Cheri. "I want to eat like he eats."

In vain, the King and Queen tried to reason with her. "It's no wonder people lack romance in their lives," said the Princess. "Love belongs to those who are willing to go to extremes for it. Goodbye."

Tilli and Max listened to the attic door slam. To Max, the door sounded like the crack of a bat when the opposition has hit a homerun to beat the Mariners in the bottom of the ninth. His heart, which would never win another pennant, cracked a tinny bat of its own. "Oh-Oh spaghetti-o," said Tilli. She did not elaborate.

Briefly, they discussed seeking professional help for the Princess, but King Max was one of those who believed that psychology was at that point in its development that surgery was at when it was practiced by barbers, so the idea was abandoned. Max put his arm halfway around his wife— halfway was as far as he could reach—and they walked out on the porch and stared at the blackberries. The blackberries, if little else in the last quarter of the twentieth century except killer bees and Arabs, were on the move.

Here, it might be worth mentioning that Bernard Mickey Wrangle, while in agreement with the King's opinion of the profession of psychology, had developed a psychological test of his own. It was short, simple, and, to the mind of its creator, infallible. To administer the test, merely ask the subject to name his or her favorite Beatle. If you are at all familiar with the distinct separate public images of the four Beatles, then you'll recognize that the one chosen—John, Paul,

George, or Ringo—reveals as much about the subject's personality as most of us will ever hope to know.

Leigh-Cheri paced the floor. She sat on the cot. She gave to foam rubber its first imprint in history of a royal behind. She walked to the windows and looked into the black. She tried out the chamber pot, although she really had nothing to contribute. She lay on the cot. Ceiling ceiling ceiling. She turned over. Floor floor floor. She got up and, like a vacuum cleaner with insomnia, roamed the room some more. For three days, she did such things. Perhaps she was coming to terms with the space, although surely she realized that space is merely a device to prevent everything from being in the same spot.

On the fourth day, she decided to think, in an organized manner, about the problem of romance. "When we're incomplete, we're always searching for somebody to complete us. When, after a few years or a few months of a relationship, we find that we're still unfulfilled, we blame our partners and take up with somebody more promising. This can go on and on— series polygamy—until we admit that while a partner can add sweet dimensions to our lives, we, each of us, are responsible for our own fulfillment. Nobody else can provide it for us, and to believe otherwise is to delude ourselves dangerously and to program for eventual failure every relationship we enter. Hey, that's pretty good. If I had pencil and paper, I'd write that down." Alas, she had no pencil, while the roll of paper that sat by the chamber pot was destined for a different end.

Next, she thought, "When two people meet and fall

in love, there's a sudden rush of magic. Magic is just naturally present then. We tend to feed on that gratuitous magic without striving to make any more. One day we wake up and find that the magic is gone. We hustle to get it back, but by then it's usually too late, we've used it up. What we have to do is work like hell at making additional magic right from the start. It's hard work, especially when it seems superfluous or redundant, but if we can remember to do it, we greatly improve our chances of making love stay." She was unsure if that idea was profound or trite. She was only sure that it mattered.

Then, she thought, "The mystics say that as soon as you give it up, you can have it. That may be true, but who wants it when you don't want it."

Leigh-Cheri tried to think more thoughts about romance. Her mind wandered. Toward dawn of the fifth day, she masturbated.

It was unintentional. She meant only to test herself for signs of numbness, atrophy, shrinkage, aridity. As the damp genital spark flashed from her fingertips, her little hand withdrew in surprise. Cautiously, it returned. It met no resistance. It slithered through the folds of saltmeat and peach. It pressed the seaweed trigger.

Afterward, she was depressed. She felt that she had violated the purity of her hermitage. Try as she might, she could not imagine Bernard masturbating in *his* cell. Bernard didn't require an ad agency to tell him the difference between the sponsor's product and Brand X. Bernard wouldn't accept an ignominious substitute. Those cherubs that circle, in an aurora of blue light, the rocking bed of true lovers, those angels do not fly for masturbators. In the future, she would try to channel her sexual energy into something more elevating than the do-it-yourself orgasm.

But what?

She tried to name the fifty states and their capitals, but she could never get past South Dakota. She tried to name the nine planets in our solar system and was bewildered to find that she could name *ten*, counting Argon. She tried to remember why George Harrison was her favorite Beatle— surely it was his sincerity, his deep spirituality, his compassion for suffering humanity—only to discover that for some reason she now preferred the rebellious explorer John Lennon. She played a game in which she was given the power to pass one law to which every person in the world must adhere. What law would she lay down? What one law could change the world? You couldn't force people to love their neighbors as themselves. There already were laws against killing, yet murders continued. Certainly, to make the internal combustion engine illegal would improve things enormously, but how long before industry would put a nuclear-powered car in every radioactive garage? Suppose she made everything illegal. Then everybody would be outlaws. Would Bernard be delighted or horrified? In another game, she could give Academy Awards to the movies of her choice, the films that really deserved them. She quickly ran out of candidates and began fantasizing a movie. She only knew one plot, however, and she could never quite handle the scene in which the frog was dashed against the wall. Besides, whatever happened to the golden ball?

Her fantasies gave way to dreams. Or was it the other way around? In either case, she lay on the cot for days and didn't open her eyes. Gulietta shook her. "Are you dyink?" the old woman asked. "Zee Queen vants to know," Gulietta said, parroting Tilli, "eef you are dyink." "Oh no," answered Leigh-Cheri dreamily. "Tell mama I am living. Living for love." She fell immediately back into communion with her private totem, a beast that was both frog and woodpecker, and, sometimes, too, the chipmunk that runs its little buns off at the center of the earth.

Time passed. It must have been a week. Maybe longer. Then, one evening she awoke, clearheaded and refreshed. She stood up and stretched. She jogged around the attic a few times. She bent down and touched her toes. With a sharp appetite, she devoured the soy burger and mashed potatoes on her dinner tray. She put the chamber pot to its proper use. She sat down on the cot. "Yes, I'm alive," she said. "Alive for love." She felt fine, although she had to confess she could still feel on her neck the tepid breath of boredom.

At that moment, something caught her eye. Something snagged the hem of her vision and yanked it like a child. A moon ray had penetrated the one clear pane and was illuminating an object. She walked over and picked the object up. For the first time, she took account of the pack of Camels.

☙ 57 ❧

The temples, the minarets, the oasis, the pyramids, the camel itself filtered through her vision without being seen. Her orbs, as if conditioned by years of literacy, settled on the message that federal law required the manufacturer to publish on the left side panel of the package.

Warning: The Surgeon General Has Determined That Cigarette Smoking Is Dangerous to Your Health.

. . . typeface, blue ink, background as white as the eye skin around her blue irises, as white as the library rug used to be.

In her mind, clumps of tumors bloomed; soft pink

lungs took on the appearance of charred firewood; grotesque tubers, oozing blood and spore jelly, spread like mushrooms across an unsuspecting lawn; arteries withered like the tendrils of parched orchids; clots resembling rotten tomatoes or the brains of diseased monkeys choked the organism, each clot emitting faint wisps of smoke from a combustion that would not die until the organism died.

Leigh-Cheri grunted in disgust. "Yuk," she said aloud, exercising the alternate mantra. "Bernard claims that a cigarette is a friend when you're locked away. With friends like these, who needs enemies?"

To the Princess, it was an enigma why anyone would smoke, yet the answer seems simple enough when we station ourselves at that profound interface of nature and culture formed when people take something from the natural world and incorporate it into their bodies.

Three of the four elements are shared by all creatures, but fire was a gift to humans alone. Smoking cigarettes is as intimate as we can become with fire without immediate excruciation. Every smoker is an embodiment of Prometheus, stealing fire from the gods and bringing it on back home. We smoke to capture the power of the sun, to pacify Hell, to identify with the primordial spark, to feed on the marrow of the volcano. It's not the tobacco we're after but the fire. When we smoke, we are performing a version of the fire dance, a ritual as ancient as lightning.

Does that mean that chain smokers are religious fanatics? You must admit there's a similarity.

The lung of the smoker is a naked virgin thrown as a sacrifice into the godfire.

Having nothing else to read, Leigh-Cheri eventually read the rest of the package. *Camel: Turkish & Domestic Blend Cigarettes: Choice: Quality: Manufactured by R.J. Reynolds Tobacco Co., Winston-Salem, N.C. 27102, U.S.A.; 20 Class A Cigarettes*; and the famous inscription that has graced the rear panel of the package since its creation in 1913 (the year, allegedly, of the last Argonian transmission to redheaded earthlings); *Don't look for premiums or coupons, as the cost of the tobaccos blended in Camel Cigarettes prohibits the use of them.*

She tried to count the *e*'s in that sentence, running into the same difficulty that has plagued many another package reader: almost nobody counts them accurately the first time. Staring at the camel, she detected a woman and a lion hidden in its body. On tiptoes, she held the pack before the one clear windowpane and saw in its reflection that the word *CHOICE* reads the same in its mirror image as it does on the pack, it is not turned around by the mirror. That might have tipped her off that the Camel package crosses dimensional boundaries, the line between matter and anti-
· matter, but she failed to grasp its significance right away. It was just another parlor game. As when she searched for additional camels on the package. (There are two behind the pyramid.)

Leigh-Cheri wondered if Bernard read his Camel pack also. She decided that he must, and she felt all the closer to him, just as daily Bible readings maintained a bond between knights and ladies separated during the Crusades.

Upon rising in the morning and before retiring

at night, the Princess read the Camel pack. Sometimes she read it during the day. The words were soothing to her. They were simple and straightforward. They did not set her mind to whizzing, as could the literature on certain other packages. Cheerios, for example.

On the right side-panel of the verbose and somewhat tautological box of Cheerios, it is written,

> If you are not satisfied with the quality and/or performance of the Cheerios in this box, send name, address, and reason for dissatisfaction— along with *entire* boxtop and price paid—to: General Mills, Inc., Box 200-A, Minneapolis, Minn., 55460. Your purchase price will be returned.

It isn't enough that there is a defensive tone to those words, a slant of doubt, an unappetizing broach of the subject of money, but they leave the reader puzzling over exactly what might be meant by the "performance" of the Cheerios.

Could the Cheerios be in bad voice? Might not they handle well on curves? Do they ejaculate too quickly? Has age affected their timing or are they merely in a mid-season slump? Afflicted with nervous exhaustion or broken hearts, are the Cheerios smiling bravely, insisting that the show must go on?

One thing you can say for the inscription, it makes you want to rush to the pantry, seize a box of Cheerios, rip back its tab (being careful not to tear it off lest there come a time to send in the boxtop, which must be *entire*), part the waxed paper inner bag with both hands, dispatch a significant minority of the Cheerio population head over heels into a bowl, douse them immediately with a quantity of milk (presumedly, they do not perform when dry), sprinkle some white sugar on top, and then, crouch, face close to the bowl, watching, evaluating, as the tiny, tan, lightweight oat doughnuts, irregular in size, tone, and texture, begin to soak up the milk and the sugar granules dissolved therein, growing soft and soggy, expanding somewhat as liquid is absorbed; and you may be thinking all the while about the toroid shape, the shape of the cyclone, the vortex, the whirlpool, the shape of a thing made of itself yet mysteriously distinct from itself; thinking about rings, halos, men overboard, the unbroken cycle of life, the void as nucleus, or, best of all, bodily orifices; thinking about whatever the trove of toroidal trinkets might inspire as, center holes flooded with sugary milk, they relax and go blobby in the bowl; but appraising, even as your mind wanders, appraising, testing, criticizing, asking repeatedly: do Cheerios measure up to Wheaties with beer, would they mix well with batshit in times of strife, would Ed Sullivan have signed them, would Knute Rockne have recruited them, how well do these little motherfuckers *perform*?

At times such as these, you understand what the man meant when he said he'd walk a mile for a Camel.

59

Leigh-Cheri began to reckon time in terms of Gulietta. When Gulietta brought lunch, it was noon. When Gulietta brought dinner, it was six in the evening. When Gulietta emptied the chamber pot, it was either 8:00 A.M. or 8:00 P.M.—for whatever the difference was worth. When Gulietta fetched her to the third-floor bath (seldom used by Max or Tilli) for a scrubbing, the Princess knew that it was Saturday and another week had passed. After ninety baths, ninety soapings

of the peachfish, her lover would be eligible for parole. Gulietta was her clock and her calendar. Time
was a skinny old woman with dilated pupils.

As for space, it came to be less defined by the walls
of the attic, more defined by the Camel pack. The
Camel pack was a rectangular solid, two and three-
quarters inches high, two and one-eighth inches wide
and three-quarters of an inch deep. Imagine Leigh-
Cheri's eyes crawling over every crinkle in the cello-
phane. Imagine Leigh-Cheri gazing expectantly, her
eyes like a couple of goldfish with insufficient water
in their bowls.

As an environmentalist, she might have been more
interested in the chamber pot. Not only did the pot
have a benevolent, ecologically sound function, but its
round shape—as biomorphic as a breast, melon, or
moon—evoked the natural world. Yet it was the Camel
pack, all right angles and parallel lines (the formal
equivalent of the rational mind); it was the Camel
pack, born on the drawing board far from the bulrushes;
it was the Camel pack, of a shape designed to shield
us from the capricious, which is to say, the inexplica-
ble; it was the logically, synthetically geometric Camel
pack that enlivened the air of her cell.

In the morning, about a quarter till Gulietta-empty-
chamber-pot, Leigh-Cheri would wake to find the
Camel pack beside her cot. It had the poise of an
animal. Some mornings, it would be lying on the foam
rubber beside her unpillowed head, like a jewel forced
out of her ear by a dream. Once, or maybe twice, lying
there of a morning, she placed the pack mischievously
in the nest of her pubis. What strange bird laid this
egg?

She spent a lot of time tossing the Camel pack in
the air and catching it. She became skilled to the
point where she could catch it behind her back, over
her shoulder, in her teeth, or with her eyes closed.

Prancing with it, she incorporated it into some old cheerleader routines. Mostly, though, she just sat holding it, staring into its exotic vistas, populating its landscape, colonizing it, learning to survive there.

When crossing the desert, she learned to swaddle herself in a burnoose, the way the natives did. Redheads burn easily. She learned which stones one could squeeze water from. She learned to appreciate the special reality of the mirage.

One day she believed that she heard the rat-a-tat of a woodpecker, but search as she might, she could find no bill holes in the trunks of the palms.

Whether on foot or camelback, Leigh-Cheri went about with eyes downcast. Leigh-Cheri was looking for matchsticks. She looked for the print of black boots in the sand.

⚬⚬ 60 ⚬⚬

Baths went by. Meals passed. Deposits were made in the chamber pot and subsequently withdrawn. The springtime turned slowly to summer. By the end of June, it was so stuffy in the attic it was difficult to breathe—but there was always a cool breeze at the oasis.

Leigh-Cheri would sit in the shade by the spring, playing toss-and-catch with her package of Camels. For hours on end, she would toss and catch, toss and catch, while from the spring waters big old green amphibians spied on her with that voyeuristic bulbousness that can trap beauty and fix a thing forever. She was reminded of A'ben Fizel, the look he had when he was courting her.

Periodically, nomads came to the spring. They, men as well as women, wore hand-hammered silver jewelry that jangled like cash registers in a shopkeeper's dream of heaven. Their antique rifles were as long as fishing poles, and the clay jugs that they filled with water were made back when Jesus was just a gleam in the One Big Eye. Berbers came, and Bedouins, driving their dromedaries to drink. Sheiks came, sheiks without oil wells or sons at Oxford, but who nevertheless wore robes that would pump up the egos of every silkworm in the East, and who vanished in clouds of perfume so thick they made the Princess cough.

Invariably, she questioned those traders, raiders, belly dancers, ali babas, and caravan executives about any red-haired outlaws they might have passed on their route, while they in turn hit her up for cigarettes.

"But I can't open the pack," she'd try to explain. "If I did, all this would collapse. A successful external reality depends upon an internal vision that is left intact."

They glared at her the way any intelligent persons ought to glare when what they need is a smoke, a bite, a cup of coffee, a piece of ass, or a good fast-paced story, and all they're getting is philosophy.

61

It was in July—about the time that King Max lost forty dollars on the All-Star Game and Gulietta ran out of cocaine—that Leigh-Cheri realized that her body had made a private compact with the moon. With a minimum of effort, she had begun to rotate on the lunar wheel.

At night, when the light was off, the attic normally was as black as the franks at a firebug's weenie roast. In that part of the world, however, the full moon always rose in the east, and on those nights when the moon was biggest and brightest, a shaft of its light would spear the one clear windowpane and pierce her sleeping body. By May, she was menstruating regularly at the new moon, just as the ancients did, and in July she observed that she had begun to ovulate when the moon was full, as will any healthy woman whose nights are not polluted by synthetic lighting. She could always tell when she was about to ovulate because her vaginal mucus would become wetter and more abundant than usual, and more smooth and slippery, too. Her glands were greasing the tracks, as it were, for the Sperm Express. Of course, testing for ovulation can be hazardous, since a primed vagina, in its enthusiasm, can mistake an exploratory finger for a serviceable phallus and try to draw it in. Her resistance was admirable, however, if not quite heroic, and the mucus tests proved that she had begun, inadvertently but successfully, to practice lunaception.

As an advocate of lunaception, Bernard would have been proud of her. Bernard would have been proud despite this irony: now that her periods were predictable and her ovulation pinpointed, now that she was capable of conceiving or not conceiving at her own discretion, now that she finally had solved the problem of birth control, it was all academic. The Sperm Express didn't run through the attic on Puget Sound.

Still, it was pleasing to her to prove Bernard's theory, and she derived, moreover, a sense of power and well-being from the sensation of being in touch with her biological cycles and of them being in harmony with the rhythms of the cosmos. She wondered how the moon, two hundred and thirty-nine thousand miles above the roof, could affect her as profoundly as it did. Being four times larger than the moon, the earth appeared to dominate. Caught in the earth's gravitational web, the moon moved around the earth and

could never get away. Yet, as any half-awake material-
ist well knows, that which you hold holds you. Neither could the earth escape the moon. The moon con-
ducts our orchestra of waters, it is keeper at the hive
of blood. In a magnetic field, every object exerts force
on every other object. The moon is an object, after all.
Like a golden ball. Like a pack of cigarettes.

The fabric of even those objects that seem densest
is, in actual fact, a loose weaving of particles and
waves. The differences and interactions between objects have their roots in the interference patterns produced along combined frequencies of vibration. What
it amounted to was that Leigh-Cheri was exerting
force on the Camel pack. And it on her. Surely, such
force had to do with the physical nature of the pack—its
size, weight, shape, chemical composition, and, above
all, proximity—and not with the pictorial content that
adorned it. Ah, but pictorial symbols have their own
weight and gravity, as the history of religion vividly
demonstrates, and while Leigh-Cheri found herself in
a relationship with the Camel pack as an object, just
as she was in relation to the moon as an object (just as
you, reader, have a relationship with this book as an
object, no matter if you can tolerate another line of its
content), she deciphered from the symbology of the
Camel pack design what appeared to be the long-lost
message from the redheads of Argon.

That might have been the major discovery of the
last quarter of the twentieth century. On the other
hand, it might have been the kind of rat hair in the
tuna tin that can eventually confront the person who
pays too close attention, who simply looks too hard.
Plato did claim that the unexamined life is not worth
living. Oedipus Rex was not so sure.

62

It would be weeks, weeks defined by starchy meals
and Saturday baths, before Princess Leigh-Cheri would
detect something Argonian about that object with which
she was sharing the bloom of her youth. Meanwhile,
summer went about its business. Blackberries multi-
plied. Chihuahuas panted. Fan blades ran around in
circles. The attic heated up. So did the revolt in Max
and Tilli's homeland. Of more concern to the King
and Queen, or so it seemed to everyone but Chuck
(Chuck believed, among other things, that Leigh-
Cheri was operating a clandestine radio transmitter
from the attic), was a rebellion that was occurring
right there in the shoebox palace on Puget Sound.

Gulietta was demanding a raise. More precisely,
Gulietta was demanding that she be put on salary,
since in the seventy-some years that she had served
the Furstenberg-Barcalona household, she had been
compensated only with room and board and had never
been paid a dime. Occasionally, the old woman received small sums from abroad, but while those mon-
ies might afford her a new bikini here, a pair of
running shoes there, a porno movie one Sunday, a
ride on a roller coaster the next, they were not nearly
enough to keep her in cocaine.

The Peruvian flake that had filled the plastic
frog—the drug had been given to Bernard by a fellow
outlaw whose life he'd once saved—would have cost
close to ten thousand dollars on the retail market,
and Gulietta had tooted through it in four months.
Now, deprived, nerve-racked, in a funk, she was demanding wages of fifty dollars a week. Retroactive to
somewhere near the beginning of the century.

"Foul!" screamed King Max. His long horse face quivered from forehead to chin. "Out of bounds," he screamed. "Dealing from the bottom of the deck." The noise that his heart valve produced sounded like two mechanical mice making love in a spoon drawer.

Queen Tilli's bulk paled. "Oh-Oh, spaghetti-o," she stammered. She elected not to develop the idea more comprehensively.

"Forget this silly notion at once," Max advised.

"In a pig's eye I'll forget," replied Gulietta. Actually, her reply has lost something in translation. "You owe me."

"Owe owe spaghetti-owe," said Tilli. The rattling of Max's heart drowned out the rest of her speech.

"No pay, no work," said Gulietta.

"You're bluffing," said Max.

"I'm on strike," said Gulietta.

"Oh-Oh, spaghetti-o," Tilli was about to declare in summary fashion. Then she saw that the others had guessed her thoughts.

63

News of the strike was a while reaching the attic. Downstairs, the place was in turmoil, it was worse than the time Gulietta went to Maui: dirty dishes piled up, dustballs rolled about freely, laundry fermented in the hamper, and the quality of meals plunged to 1.8 on the gourmet scale. What's more, Gulietta was picketing the house, marching back and forth outside, completely naked except for a pair of oven mittens. Thanks to the acres of blackberries, she could not be seen from the street, and her picket sign, composed in a language that made Serbo-Croatian seem as simple as Bozo-Cretin, was in no danger of being read by an ordinary passer-by, but her protest parade upon that miniscule portion of lawn that had not been usurped by brambles caused Max and Tilli extreme agitation. "After all these years," grumbled Max, "America has finally corrupted her." Tilli's constant comment hardly bears repeating.

Up in the attic, however, there were only a few repercussions. Gulietta continued to serve her young mistress, with whom she had no quarrel. In fact, having considerable extra time on her hands, Gulietta, out of boredom as much as anything, began paying unscheduled visits to the attic, thereby totally screwing up the Princess's clock. Once, the striking servant brought the prisoner of love a stack of magazines, including an issue of *Arizona Detective,* two issues each of *Car and Driver, Fruit and Tarantula,* and *Pork and Trichinosis,* a recent copy of *Gentlemen's Anus,* and a dog-eared issue of the *People* magazine that featured a full-page photograph of the Princess in balmier climes, lounging beneath the lippy leaves of a koa tree, her extraordinarily round breasts lending topographical grandeur to the flat cotton front of a Save-the-Whales T-shirt, her big blue eyes dreamy with visions of a modern Mu. A fifteen-round bout with literary temptation was fought before Leigh-Cheri, determined to read only the Camel pack, ordered the periodicals and their bearer back downstairs.

On another occasion, Gulietta fetched Prince Charming, terrarium and all, to the attic, insisting that it was unhealthy for a person to live completely without animate companionship. This time, Leigh-Cheri consented. For one thing, she suspected that where frogs were concerned, the old lady had arcane information that had best be heeded. For another, Leigh-Cheri rationalized that there must be something animate, a fly, a flea, a mouse, a roach, an ant, *something* breathing the air in Bernard's cell, and therefore her admission of Prince Charming wouldn't violate her vow to duplicate her lover's experience. She only insisted that Gulietta attend to the toad's daily needs, just as, in her role as surrogate jailer, she attended to Leigh-Cheri's.

If Leigh-Cheri failed to notice that Gulietta's recent appearances in the attic were *au naturel,* it probably was because she herself hadn't worn a stitch since the weather got warm back in June. When the Princess finally did learn of the strike, she was amused. She was aware of her daddy's opinion that every commoner in the USA, with the possible exception of center Jack Sikma of the Seattle Supersonics, was overpaid, and she felt that it was good, not bad, for the kingly heart to receive an occasional kick in its pants. Nevertheless, she had to recall with a twinge that Bernard hadn't much use for labor unions. It wasn't that Bernard objected to strikes—he approved of just about anything that stirred the stew—but that he believed that the time was long past when unions were effective in controlling the vices of big business, that unions, in fact, had *become* big business, had perhaps surpassed big business in relative stench of corrupt practices and violent hanky-pankies. It was the Hawaiian mongoose syndrome all over again. Who shall control those who control those who control?

As the goat feet of chaos danced on the linoleum of the kitchen below, Leigh-Cheri entertained various thoughts about labor and management. They soon faded, though. The striking crone and Prince Charming notwithstanding, her central focus was upon the Camel pack. And the Camel pack was leading her into the mysterious realm of the pyramids.

64

On an attic windowsill, which by then was about as dusty as a literal Sahara, Leigh-Cheri would set the cigarettes. Then she'd kneel so that the pack was at eye level, pyramids on the horizon. Majestic, timeless, enigmatically powerful, the pyramids pulled at her until in a semi-trance she'd strike out across the open sands, chanting the pyramid names: Tiahuanaco and Giza; Seneferu and Cheops; Teti, Pepi, and La Huaca de la Luna; Zoser, Khaba, and Ammenemes; Neferirkare and Uxmal and Chicken Itza; on Chephren, on Unas, on Donner and Blitzen; now Dancer, now Prancer, now Sesostris II.

From a distance, the pyramids gave the impression of being sleek and well-preserved, but up close they were as ravaged by time and despoilers as Gulietta. The capstones and a dozen or more courses had been removed from their apexes, and the entire facing of Tura limestone, with the exception of some sections near the base, had been stripped from the triangular facades. Tunnels had been bored into their sides by treasure hunters, while enterprising builders had hauled off random stones to shore up their bridges and domiciles. Up close, the pyramids were cakes that had been found out by freeloaders. It saddened Leigh-Cheri to think that there was not one pyramid on earth that had not been gnawed.

"I can't look at a pyramid without feeling like Perry Mason," said Leigh-Cheri, meaning that like most people, the mere sight of those immense structures set her to popping questions like a prosecuting attorney on diet pills and beer.

How were they constructed? Why were they constructed? Who constructed them? What is their strange appeal to the human psyche?

The pyramids of Egypt were said by the experts to be tombs. The pyramids of Peru, Mexico, and Central America were said to have been temples. As for the pyramids of China, Cambodia, and Collinsville, Illinois, archaeologists were reluctant to guess. And as for the four pyramidal structures photographed by Mariner 9 on its fly-by of Mars, most scientists would just as soon forget them. Pyramidologists thought that in addition to their functions as temples and/or tombs, the pyramids also served as solar and lunar observatories. With the increasing evidence of "pyramid power," that force that apparently accumulates inside the pyramidal cavity, a force that under the right conditions has the proven ability to regenerate both organic and inorganic matter, there was a modern trend to regard the pyramids as collectors or amplifiers of energy.

"It seems to me," said Leigh-Cheri, "that whether a pyramid was built over a period of decades by hundreds of thousands of laborers using primitive engineering equipment like wooden levers and ramps and sledges and stuff like that, or in a few months by spacemen with laser beams, in neither instance would they have gone to such trouble to make a six-million-ton device that did nothing but sharpen razor blades and preserve fruit."

Further, it seemed to the pyramid-gazing Princess that since the skills and sciences used by the pyramid builders were virtually identical, as were their finished products, that the motive for their construction must have been the same. Moreover, since the construction required highly advanced mathematical and astronomical calculations, some of which were clearly beyond the capabilities of those ancient civilizations, and since the civilizations were separated by thousands of miles and hundreds of years, and since no records were left that referred to the methods or purpose of construction, that unknown outsiders must have been behind them.

Could those outsiders have been the legendary Red Beards? And could the Red Beards have hailed from Argon? Was there even such a planet, or was Argon a room behind an occult bookstore in Los Angeles?

Suppose there had been a number of Argonian colonies around the ancient world, and that in each colony pyramids were erected. What would have motivated Argon to endow earthlings with pyramids and with the scientific knowledge and near-impossible mastery of masonry that their construction required? Had there been a master plan? Was it still operative?

What, if anything, did red hair have to do with it?

And why is it *nobody* knows what the hell a pyramid is doing on the American dollar bill?

For that matter, what are pyramids doing on a pack of modern-day cigarettes manufactured from a blend of American and Turkish tobaccos?

Whenever she reached that point in her questioning, Leigh-Cheri gave up. "Bernard would probably have several ideas," she said once. "I guess I'm just a dunce."

Whereupon it occurred to her that a dunce cap is shaped like a . . . ! That sent her back to the pyramids again.

65

She had pyramids on the brain like a tumor. After one too many mornings of waking up with her mind on stone monuments instead of outlaw flesh, she dispatched Gulietta to the Richmond Beach branch of the King County Public Library to pick up books on the history of package design. It wasn't strictly kosher, a book in the attic, but in the last quarter of the twentieth century what was? The Woodpecker himself had taught her that laws were like buttons—meant to be undone when the moment was ripe—and if you can't break your own rules, whose can you break?

Although Gulietta donned a dress to go to the library, she continued to carry her picket sign, not that anyone could read it. Chuck, who'd been drafted to do some minimal housework during the strike, dropped his mop and followed her. She must have known he was behind her because every block or two she'd look over her shoulder and yell "Scab!" in her inelegant tongue. Why Gulietta was bringing the sequestered Princess books on package design was beyond Chuck's comprehension, but he was to dutifully report the matter to the CIA.

While Chuck was tailing Gulietta through the library stacks, a nondescript panel truck sped up the bramble-bordered lane to the palace, intrigue hanging out of both windows. Two foreign-looking men emerged. They wore hats and long, dark raincoats, though it was a sunny day in mid-September. The men let themselves in without knocking. Stepping over mop, pail, broom, and piles of newspapers, kicking aside dustballs, Chihuahua droppings, and the occasional poker chip, they made their way straight to Tilli and Max.

66

Later that day, when there came a rapping at the attic door, Leigh-Cheri opened it without hesitation. She was expecting Gulietta. Instead, there stood her father, his noisy heart rapping upon a door of a different essence.

The King was exceedingly flustered. Initially, Leigh-Cheri attributed his embarrassment to the fact that he had violated her sanctuary, after not setting eyes on her in five months. Then she realized that she was nude. Due to the heat in the airless attic, her nipples were studded with opals of perspiration, and her pubic hair was damp and swept back from her labia, which glistened as if they'd been recently entertained. Unless shaven, the peachclam scarcely could have been more exposed.

"Excuse me," she said. She pulled on T-shirt and panties.

"Oh, I'm getting used to it. First Gulietta, now you. I trust the Queen isn't next."

"Oh-Oh, spaghetti-o!" exclaimed the Princess. They both laughed.

"You know that visitors aren't allowed."

"Sorry, dear. Gulietta was about to deliver you this volume. I thought I would bring it instead." He handed his daughter a book. *"Wrapping It: The Art of the Package*. I must say, a curious subject."

"I can think of curiouser ones. For example, a royal family in exile in America. Shall I elaborate?"

Max went to shake his head, but his head was so occupied all it did was sway. His Chaplinesque mustache swayed with it. "I shan't beat around the bush, Leigh-Cheri. I have been wondering if your mental health could be described as sound."

"By whom?"

"Interested parties."

"Depends on their criteria."

"Responsibility and—"

"Responsibility to what?"

"—leadership and—"

"Since when has leadership been a criterion for sanity? Or vice versa. Hitler was a gifted leader, even Nixon. Exhibit leadership qualities as an adolescent, they pack you off to law school for an anus transplant. If it takes, you go into government. That's what Bernard says. He says the reason so many assholes go into politics is that it's a homing instinct. At any rate, I understand that several romantics have started to follow in my footsteps. That makes me some kind of leader."

"At last count, seventeen young women and one young man have locked themselves in their rooms in emulation of your lovesick self-indulgence. Monkeys and apes will attempt to copy any moron's routine. I wouldn't be too proud. But that is not my concern. I am trying to ascertain if you are playing with a full deck."

"It may or may not be full, but at least it's *my* deck."

The King looked around the attic. The room was dusy, dim, and bare. It was stuffy and smelled like a Skid Row gymnasium. A wino wrestling team might recently have practiced there. The King thought of his beautiful daughter living nude in that filthy chamber. He wondered if she didn't get splinters. "Leigh-Cheri," he said. It was almost a moan. "Leigh-Cheri. You are wasting your life."

"My life has never been more full, daddy. And it's seldom been happier. You may tell your 'parties' that a life lived for love is the only sane life. Besides, I have other interests in here."

Again, Max surveyed the room. A chamber pot, a frog box, a cot without bedding, what appeared to be a pack of cigarettes sitting on the sill of a blackened window. Other interests? He shuddered. He kissed her damp cheek. He left without telling her that he had been visited by agents of the revolution, that they wanted her to be queen when they won back their nation.

⚬⚬⚬ 67 ⚬⚬⚬

As he was leaving, King Max called back to her. "When do you plan to come down from here?"

"When Bernard's released."

"And what will you do then?"

"Be with him."

"Doing what? A husband and wife demolition team?"

There was a long pause. "I don't know what his plans are, daddy. Bye-bye."

No, Leigh-Cheri hadn't a clue what Bernard would do when he got out of prison. He had failed to advise her of his plans, if any, or if they included her. After her father had gone, she took a moment to try to imagine what the Woodpecker might do in life, but of only a few things could she be sure. There was no burger so soggy that he would not eat it. No tequila so mean that he would not drink it. No car so covered with birdshit and rust that he would not drive it around town (and if it were a convertible, he'd have the top down, even in rain, even in snow). There was no flag he would not desecrate, no true believer he would not mock, no song he wouldn't sing off-key, no dental appointment he wouldn't break, no child he wouldn't do tricks for, no old person he wouldn't help in from the cold, no moon he wouldn't lie under, and, she hesitated to admit, no match he wouldn't strike. But what would he *do*? Perhaps he'll attempt to find out what happened to the golden ball, she thought, a little wistfully. God knows he'll stir the stew.

68

Call it intuition, divine influence, or plain dumb
luck—any way you sliced it it was still eureka. Eureka! Surely, Leigh-Cheri hadn't expected to solve cosmic riddles by consulting a book on package design.
She merely had a ... *hunch* ... that such a book
might enlighten her about the reasons for there being
pyramids on the Camel pack. As it turned out, there
was scant information, but it was pertinent enough to
make her cry "Eureka!"

Camels, it seems, hit the national market in 1914
(the year, according to interpretations of the Book of
Revelations by Jehovah's Witnesses and others, that
Jesus Christ was finally coronated as king of Heaven;
the same year, incidentally, that Tarzan of the Apes,
another king and, like Jesus, a non-smoker, appeared
on the scene). These particular cigarettes, an innova-
tive blend of Virginia burley and Carolina bright,
with imported Turkish leaf included for taste and
aroma, and with a generous amount of sweetening
added, were created personally by R.J. (Richard Joshua)
Reynolds in Winston-Salem, N.C., the previous year.
The package also was designed in 1913. It was Mr.
Reynolds's idea to name the new cigarettes "Kamel"
or "Camel" to give them an exotic mystique befitting
their Turkish ingredient, and it was Reynolds's young
secretary, Roy C. Haberkern, who talked Barnum &
Bailey into letting him photograph Old Joe, the can-
tankerous circus dromedary, for the title role on the
pack. Who placed the pyramids in the background is
unclear. The Camel label had been prepared for
Reynolds by a Richmond lithography firm, and it was
believed that an itinerant lithographer newly in the

firm's employ applied the finishing detail, including the pyramids, shortly before he walked off the job. Nobody remembered his name, but they recalled that he was a talented draftsman and had flaming red hair.

It must have occurred to Reynolds or his staff that pyramids were unknown in Turkey, yet objections were raised to the misplaced masonries neither at the home office nor anywhere else. In fact, the Camel label went on to become the most beloved in the history of packaging. When, in 1958, the manufacturer tried to alter the label—"Just a few minor changes in the familiar camel and the pyramid symbol to modernize the forty-five-year-old design"—smokers raised a stink more vile than last night's ashtray. R.J. Reynolds, Jr., son of the deceased founder, was so angry that he sold a block of his company stock, and public reaction was negative to the extent that the directors quickly returned to the original design.

After Leigh-Cheri had read the story of the Camel label three or four times, she closed the book and placed it atop the chamber pot where Gulietta would be sure to see it and carry it back to the library. Leigh-Cheri was done with the book. Leigh-Cheri had no desire to clutter the pure pyramid of her thoughts with the knowledge that the Baby Ruth candy bar was named for the daughter of President Grover Cleveland and not for the baseball player, or that Double Bubble gum was originally called Blibber Blubber. Her eureka device was jangling and flashing. She was about, as she tossed the Camel pack high in the stale attic air and caught it under her chin, to formulate a theory.

It was to be a bit on the queer side, as theories go, and a person might need to spend a few months alone in an empty attic contemplating a pack of cigarettes to appreciate it at all. Nevertheless, resonance of the theory was to reach rather far. And it would reshape the life of that princess who had given up the world for the moon, who yearned desperately to make love stay.

69

The theory arrived neither full-blown, like an orphan on the doorstep, nor sharply defined, like a spike through a shoe; nor did it develop as would a photographic print, crisp images gradually emerging from a shadowy soup. Rather, it unwound like a turban, like mummy bandage; started with the sudden loosening of a clasp, a scarab fastener, and then unraveled in awkward spirals from end to frazzled end. Several weeks went by in the unwinding. When at last it was stretched out, it looked like this:

Pyramids, although everywhere in bad repair, are not in the usual sense ruins. That is, they are not simply relics of civilizations that have gone out of business, of concern only to archaeologists, historians, and those who spend the present jacking off the past. Pyramids were built to endure, made to defy both time and humanity. Their stones, jigged into position without mortar, were fit together so snugly you could not slip a bill between them, nor for that matter, a credit card. Oriented with extraordinary precision, so that each of their angles faces one of the cardinal points, we can conclude from the pyramids that for thousands of years the position of the terrestrial axis has not appreciably varied—pyramids are great global reference points, unequaled in technology or nature. But they are more than that. Whether they were utilized as tombs, temples, or astrolabes or all three may be less significant than the discovery that pyramids, apparently as a result of properties peculiar to their particular shape, can generate or amplify an energy frequency that is restorative to what scientists call bioplasm, what philosophers call the life force, what the Chinese have always called *ch'i*. Pyramid power even enhances inorganic life. Pyramids are giant objects, affecting other objects, animate and inanimate, in ways beyond those normally attributed to gravity and electromagnetism.

Whatever the intended function of pyramids, they are not obsolete. They remain somehow relevant. In the last quarter of the twentieth century, with the current civilization staggering blindfolded down a rail strewn with banana peels, the mysteries of pyramid power, once solved, might provide an answer to the ubiquitous question, "Where do we go from here?"

Obviously, *somebody* wanted us to keep pyramids in mind, because the pyramid symbol has been placed conspicuously upon items that we regularly handle or observe. On any given day there are more than two billion one-dollar bills in circulation. For most of the century, half of the cigarettes smoked in the United States were Camels, something like thirty billion a year. It isn't likely that pyramids were chosen *arbitrarily* to adorn two of the most popular common objects of modern times. *Somebody* knew that dollars and cigarettes would be in wide circulation and saw to it that pyramids would travel with them, constantly reminding a culture separated from the original structures by distance and time that pyramids have something of value to give if we'd learn how to receive it.

Exactly who was responsible for that prominent and constant pyramidal display? Well, the committee that created the dollar bill in 1862 acted out of tradition and sentiment. It decided to include a pyramid symbol because there had been one on the last paper currency issued in America, some interest-bearing bank notes used to finance urgent undertakings such as the War of 1812. Those early bank notes had been designed by that jack-of-all-genius, the only enlightened man ever to hold high political office in the United States, Thomas Jefferson. The hand that put the pyramid on the Camel pack in 1913—almost exactly one century later—hung from the inky sleeve of a transient lithographer who departed soon afterward, perhaps to join the military forces being recruited for World War I.

Looking for connections, we find that both designs were executed in the state of Virginia, less than a hundred miles from Washington, D.C., the most powerful and influential world capital of the era. Ostensibly, the only other similarity between Jefferson and the nameless lithographer was the fact that each had red hair. That might be relegated to the realm of meaningless coincidence were it not for one thing: a certain race of red-haired Caucasians was credited in the myths, legends, hieroglyphs, and oral histories of Chavin, Mochica, Tiahuanaco, Inca, Maya, Olmec, Zapotec, Toltec, Aztec, and other New World pyramid-building peoples with having ordered and supervised pyramid construction. If no redheads are mentioned in connection with Egyptian pyramids, it may be only because not a single legend or historical account concerning pyramids has survived in Egypt. Two hundred years after the last pyramid was reared in their country, Egyptians were as baffled by the big masonries as everyone else.

Okay. Let's get this porcupine on the street. A race of carrot-topped demigods, known everywhere as Red Beards, appeared at various places in the ancient world, transforming the natives, spurring them to develop highly advanced civilizations in a very short time, leaving behind vast pyramids and other solar/

lunar architecture when they suddenly and inexplicably disappeared. That much is fact. It is also historical fact that the Chavin, Mochica, Olmec, Zapotec, and Toltec peoples also vanished abruptly and without explanation. Apparently, the Red Beards had powerful enemies, capable of zapping whole civilizations into other dimensions. If the Red Beards were extraterrestrial, a lunar race dispatched to earth, for whatever reason, from the planet Argon, then their enemy would have been a solar society, the blonde Argonian ruling class. Call them Yellow Beards. When the Yellow Beards learned what the Red Beards were up to on earth, they immediately zapped the people with whom they were conspiring. Poof! Off went the Chavin, next the Mochica, then the Olmec and so forth, transplanted, each in turn, from the universe to the anti-universe, leaving no forwarding address. Friendship with Red Beards bore a certain liability. Finally, the Red Beards themselves were zapped. This occurred shortly before the arrival of the conquistadors in the New World. When the Spanish priests heard tales of Red Beards, they naturally labeled them devils. It's no coincidence that Satan is usually depicted as being as red as boiled crabs.

Stuck in the anti-universe, still the Red Beards did not give up. They had faith in the potentiality of earthlings. Maybe they felt that alone in the universe we here on earth (perhaps because of our close proximity and special relationship to our moon) possess the humor, the playfulness, the romantic sentiment, the general warm and honorable looniness to counteract the rigid solar efficiency of the Yellow Beards. Surely the Red Beards would not accept that the pyramids have been built in vain. Therefore, they attempted to reestablish contact with earth. Of necessity, communication would have to be telepathic. And it would have to rely primarily on simple visual symbolism. Since the so-called anti-universe is a mirror image of the so-called universe, words would be reversed as they crossed from one dimension to the other, and language, even when translations were faithful, would make no sense at all.

So the Red Beards beamed their telepathic vectors into earthly dimensions. Only a few humans responded, and they exclusively redheads—maybe a trace of racial memory, an ancient residue of Argonian DNA remained in their genes—and the response was far from desirable. Reception of the extra-dimensional transmissions confused them and frequently brought them grief. For example, Vincent van Gogh, the most famous redhead omitted from the Twelve-Most-Famous-Redheads list, took to painting vases, chairs, stars, etc. as if they embodied the life force, which they likely do; as if there were vibratory fields, auras, around them, which there probably are, but everybody thought poor Vincent on the weird end of the banana, and eventually he was driven to take his own life. After several centuries of similar failures, the Red Beards refined their technique. They began to concentrate on a specific redheaded individual with a specific end in mind. Thus, they were able to influence Thomas Jefferson, an ideal receptor because of his wide-ranging sensibility, to affix a pyramid to the first American paper money issued since colonial days. When, after a century, that play hadn't turned any big tricks, they beamed to the brain of a redheaded lithographer a more ambitious transmission.

The Red Beards had established a telepathic broadcast path, a channel that cut directly and deliberately through Washington, D.C., the most important of world capitals. Development of Camel cigarettes was occurring, fortuitously, within the mainstream of that channel. In 1913, most smokers rolled their own. Manufactured brands were just barely catching on, and while Fatima in Boston and Philadelphia, and Picayune in New Orleans were gaining appeal, Camel was to be the first cigarette to shoot for national (later, international) distribution. Moreover, R.J. Reynolds's recipe for Camels called for a substantial amount of sweetener. Sugar, like lust, accentuates the reddish pigment in the hair and/or freckles of lunar-oriented people, especially when they're exposed to direct sunlight. Leigh-Cheri had learned that from bona fide Argonians.

All right. Now we're cooking, now we're dressing this alligator in gold lamé. There was something else about the new cigarette that made its package the ideal medium for a Red Beard communiqué. It already was wed to a potent symbology.

The camel has a big dumb ugly hump. But in the desert, where prettier, more streamlined beasts die quickly of thirst, the camel survives quite nicely. As legend has it, the camel carries its own water, stores it in its stupid hump. If individuals, like camels, perfect their inner resources, if we have the power *within* us, then we can cross any wasteland in relative comfort and survive in arid surroundings without relying on the external. Often, moreover, it is our "hump"—that aspect of our being that society finds eccentric, ridiculous, or disagreeable—that holds our sweet waters, our secret well of happiness, the key to our equanimity in malevolent climes. The camel symbolized a lunar truth, totemized a Red Beard lesson concerning survival in the desert, the desert being solar territory, any landscape bullied by the sun.

Transmitting to the receptive antenna on the red roof of the nameless lithographer, the Red Beards saw to it that palm trees were included on the package, for the date palm, essential to those who must dwell in deserts, underscored the symbolism of the camel itself. Every desert has its oasis, there is nourishment and shade to be found in the most barren environs if one knows where to look. Aware that hard times were coming in the last quarter of the twentieth century, times of shortages, pollutions, political betrayals, sexual confusions, and spiritual famine, the Red Beards, via the cigarette package, were projecting a moon ray through our sooty curtains. A ray of encouragement and hope.

Satisfied with the placement of the camel and the palm trees, the Red Beards turned their attention to their main concern, the pyramid. They considered the pyramid vital to the continuing evolution of earthlings, and they desired to confront earthlings with pyramids as often as possible. So successful was their telepathic prodding of the lithographer that not one but two pyramids appeared on the Camel pack.

Since the fellow was still tuned in, and responding beautifully, thank you, the Red Beards also had him work into the design a naked woman, representative of the Moon Goddess, the Great Mother, the feminine principal of creation, growth, change and renewal. The Moon Goddess is the oldest recorded and most universally common deity, and it was only fitting that her abiding fertility make its presence felt in the desert on the pack. It was the Moon Mother, perhaps, who was behind the regenerative power of the pyramids. She symbolized that power, certainly. In order not to spoil the composition, she was rendered most subtly on the package, hidden in the yellow and brown coloration in the left forequarter of the dromedary. That was apropos, for this Queen of Love, this giver of fantasies and dreams, this Shepherdess of the Stars, this healer and nurturer of all life had always made herself manifest in subtle and mysterious ways. As a reminder that the Moon Queen is ever threatened by the Solar King (we witness this cosmic drama monthly as the waning moon is consumed by the light of the sun), a yellowmaned lion, the ancient and prevalent solar symbol, was also hidden in the body of the camel, above and to the right of the woman.

That should have done it, that should have made the Camel pack a vessel of symbolic truth unprecedented in the last quarter of the twentieth century, a virtual lunar Bible, compact, accessible, and concise, as befitting a transistorized age. But the Red Beards, excited now, had a masterpiece by the tail and didn't want to turn it loose. They decided to take a further, daring step. They would try sending a *word* from their dimension into ours.

How carefully was that word chosen!

The word that allows *yes,* the word that makes *no* possible.

The word that puts the free in freedom and takes the obligation out of love.

The word that throws a window open after the final door is closed.

The word upon which all adventure, all exhilaration, all meaning, all honor depends.

The word that fires evolution's motor of mud.

The word that the cocoon whispers to the caterpillar.

The word that molecules recite before bonding.

The word that separates that which is dead from that which is living.

The word no mirror can turn around.

In the beginning was the word and the word was

CHOICE

70

Downstairs—outside—all around—the world went on wobbling and warbling through space, like a jukebox in a canoe, oblivious to her theorizing. The talk *out there* was of oil and nukes, of prices and wages, of ball scores and celebrities, of careers and illness, of, in a thousand clumsy and evasive ways, how to make love stay. A millionaire had died in a secretary's bed. Horticulturists announced the development of a square watermelon. Someone in Beverly Hills opened a disco for dogs.

On the shores of Puget Sound, October had come in like a lamb chop, breaded in golden crumbs and gently sautéed in a splash of blue oil. Indian summer, some characterized it, incorrectly, for technically, Indian summer must follow a frost, and there hadn't been a sign of frost since that freak freeze back in April. Rather, it was an extension of summer, summer had uncoiled and stretched itself out, like the garter snakes that, having heard no call to hibernate, still sunned themselves in the blackberry patch; snakes, all belt and no pants, startled from their prolonged laze only by the occasional fall of a berry, grown fat as a dove's egg and black as a curse in this longest of summers.

The confectionary odor of rotting blackberries wafted to the attic windows on breezes off the Sound, a mixture of sugar smell and salt smell that could bring out the renifleur in the primmest nostril. But the attic was shut tight, and no berry scent got in, nor did the dinosaurian squawk of the mallards, taking their time this autumn flying south. One noise that normally did penetrate the attic, the muffled raves and roars of the sporting world that leaked up through two ceilings and two floors from Max's television, was also absent. If it was strange that there was no rain that October, the lack of football cheers was stranger yet, so strange that Leigh-Cheri pried her gaze from the Camel package to ask Gulietta about it on successive weekends, but the old woman fed Prince Charming flies and could not or would not reply.

Truth was, King Max continued to spend his waking hours in front of the Magnavox. He merely neglected to turn it on.

In his homeland, the royalist revolutionaries were steamrolling. A month, six weeks at the most, the junta would crumble. For thirty years, he had dreamed, in secret and with scarcely a dab of hope, of the restoration of the monarchy. Now that skinny, furtive dream was about to come true. Only they didn't want him to be their king. There were archaic grievances against him, grudges held over like this same quasi-summer, from his previous rule. In addition, the younger revolutionary leaders felt that he had compromised with the CIA. His queen's ties to the Vatican were suspected and scorned. What his country had in mind was a socialist monarchy, somewhat on the order of Sweden or Denmark, a bit to the left of England and considerably to the left of Max. Max would be welcomed home. He would be awarded the summer palace and its grounds on the lake. An allowance substantially more luxurious than that paid him by the Americans would be granted. Tilli would preside over the opera, as she had in the past, and weekends his old cronies would gather for grouse shoots and cards. But he would not be head of state.

Someone different, someone fresh was needed, they explained. They intended to shuffle the deck. None of his worthless sons was considered. Too many scandals among them, too many land swindles, stock frauds, casino brawls, and public displays of greed. Leigh-

Cheri was the Furstenberg-Barcalona they had settled on. Young and bright and beautiful, with a strong social conscience, Leigh-Cheri would be a perfect figurehead for the new regime. Yet, unsavory stories now circulated about her, too. In Europe, in the midst of the fighting, they'd heard that she'd lost her head over a common convict. That she'd locked herself in an empty attic and wouldn't even come out to poop. They read in the gossip columns that she was "tragic." They wondered if "daffy" might not be the word.

Max longed to reassure them. How could he honestly do so? He had climbed to that attic. He had observed her, naked, dirty, and alone, yet shining with contentment, talking about "interests" when there were none to be seen.

So Max sat before a silent Magnavox, his long equine head nodding at a frozen screen.

Perhaps to the old king the screen was not empty. Perhaps he saw there, in colors more vivid than a picture tube could reproduce, the rich pageantry of his former life. Maybe he saw himself on horseback, a chestful of medals reflecting the noonday sun. Saw himself, silver saber skyward, reviewing his troops. Saw the steaming funnels of his small but seaworthy fleet. Saw the pheasant in aspic, the broad hams, the trouts in sauce, the crystal goblets awaiting wine. Dukes he saw and earls; barons and prime ministers, presidents, princes, and potentates; ambassadors, the tips of their mustaches twinkling with exotic waxes, the tips of their tongues slippery with familiar lies. Saw the white teeth of ladies, their cigarette holders of ivory and onyx, their beaded handbags concealing tiny bottles of custom-made French perfumes, and what mere king could imagine the exact kinds of laces and satins they wore beneath their gowns, next to lotioned loins? Grand parades clattered down grand boulevards (he saw this on the cold TV), private railway cars rolled through luminous acres of wheat, opera houses were strung with lights for Christmas, fine hounds pursued the fox. In Gothic state houses, the stylized din of legislation jostled the chandeliers. And late at night, in windowless rooms carpeted with the richest art of Persia's looms, over mellowed brandy and Havana cigars, the real governments convened. Strong men with wide educations and polished wits met to gossip, grapple, and plot. They spoke of precious metals, of rail lines and currencies and cattle and corn; they positioned armies at this frontier or that one, raised or lowered tariffs, arranged powerful marriages, made decisions that would affect shopgirls in Budapest or camel jockeys in Kabul. Their voices were low and grave as they pondered intrigues against them, even lower yet musical with mirth as they concocted intrigues against others. To be sure, they acted to enlarge their fortunes as much as to protect the populations who depended upon them, yet, whether the subject was commerce or war, treaties, tributes, or personal perversions of their peers, they, to a man, were consumed by a great, enormous, burning love for the drama of it all, an unrelenting passion for the secret theater of the planet.

Those days were gone. Now, the world's decisions were made by smaller men; by gray, faceless bureaucrats without vision or wit; committeemen who spoke committeespeak and thought committeethought, men who knew more of dogma than destiny, men who understood production but were ignorant of pleasure, men more comfortable with a file full of papers than a fistful of gems; unsmiling men, unmannered men, undreaming men, men who believed they could guide humanity when they could not seduce a countess nor ride a horse. Why, that bandit in black his daughter had dragged home was better fit to rule than any one of them, Communist or Fascist or Christian Democrat, alike as tasteless peas in a poisoned pod.

It was just as well that they not restore his crown. This was not a time for kings. Nor queens. Let Princess Leigh-Cheri bed down with outlaws, let her moon in an attic if that brought her joy. The gong in his heart was a soft sound now. He wouldn't respond to the queries of his countrymen. They could keep their honorary titles and their villa on the lake. Gulietta was his single remaining subject, and he'd see to it that she got the money she was due. Max, the once and never more king, would spend the golden October days right where he sat. Awaiting the rains. Awaiting the blackberries that sooner or later, like the anonymous barbarians of the last quarter of the twentieth century, would come slinking through the walls.

On Sunday, the Seattle Seahawks were to battle the Dallas Cowboys. If he could remember to turn the knob.

71

On the human head there are ninety hairs to the square inch. That's an average. In Leigh-Cheri's case, there were ninety-three or ninety-four, each redder than the last, and hovering over them, like a UFO over Haleakala, like a pan of bacon over a cook fire, there was a crown. Were they aware of the dangling diadem they might have blazed even redder in their follicles, but not one hair sensed the diamond craft that was considering landing on them, so they collected dust from Saturday bath to Saturday bath and glowed with no special effort. Beneath them, inside the skull, there was activity enough. Indeed, they feared they eventually might be driven as wild as Einstein's hairs from the reverberations of seemingly preposterous theories.

Seemingly preposterous? Hairs, you are kind. What was her theory, anyhow, but an elaborate, fanciful, and incredulous reworking of Bernard Mickey Wrangle's beliefs? The philosophy of CHOICE was outlaw philosophy, insofar as outlaws have philosophy (they are more inclined to have hangovers, herpes, and lousy credit ratings). Determinists who view the universe as an agitation of billiard balls, caroming off one another according to predetermined laws, have always been threatened by "outlaws" who insist on playing the game with their own cues. Laws describe constraint. Their purpose is to control, not to create. The universe adheres to laws only when evolution is static, catching its breath, so to speak. When things start to change again, when nature returns to its easel, its piano, its typewriter (not a Remington SL3, you better believe), as it has periodically forever, then laws give way to choice. Dullards are law-abiding because they choose not to choose. Outlaws, being less frightened by the bewildering variety of experience, being, in fact, slightly mad for encounters new and extreme, will seek to choose even when no choice readily presents itself. Leigh-Cheri, by this juncture, was familiar enough with outlaws to realize that they are living signposts pointing to Elsewhere, that they are apostles of otherness and agents of CHOICE. So what was her theory except the song of the Woodpecker, bounced a few times too many off bare attic walls? It was the Woodpecker, after all, who introduced her to the Red Beards, who suggested, if jokingly, that they might have ties to Argon.

Shut up in an attic taking lunatic lessons from a pack of cigarettes and the moon, she obviously got her lover's smartass ideas all tangled up with some archaic Indian tales and her personal meeting with a couple of self-proclaimed extraterrestrials who smelled like the cedar chests where retired pompon girls stow the prom dresses they're too old and fat to ever wear again. In her isolation and confusion, she'd decided she'd cracked a coded message from another dimension. But her hairs would have known, wouldn't they, if she was actually picking up signals from beyond the mirror?

In any event, although she was too obsessed with the implications of her theory to attribute it to a spinoff from outlaw bullshit, she felt the need for Bernard more strongly than ever. It was occurring to her that if she had cracked the code of the Camel pack in her contemplative cell, Bernard must have accomplished at least as much. Maybe Bernard had seen things there that she'd overlooked. Even if he hadn't, she was wildly anxious to share her information with him, to seek his opinions and advice. She felt as if she'd bootlegged a tape of the Golden Eternity Vibrating Ethereal Choir, that group that sings on the soundtracks of bad movies based on the Bible, and she couldn't wait to play it back on Bernard's machine to see if it still had the ring of truth, the ring of truth being the finest sound there is, although there are noises some women make in bed that are definitely in contention. The tracks of her tears led farther than the end of her nose, for a change, and she'd be damned if she could hold off another fourteen months to share her discovery with that man whose redheadedness surpassed her own.

So the Princess made a choice. She would go to him.

Nina Jablonski, the redheaded attorney, had a new baby. She was on leave from her firm. Leigh-Cheri would borrow her credentials. She would go down to McNeil Island and impersonate her. She'd wear wide spectacles, paint on extra freckles, put up her hair in a bun. Easy as toast. Although technically Jablonski was off the case, the guards wouldn't know that. Bernard would be curious enough about "Jablonski's" sudden appearance, after six months, to agree to see her. And Leigh-Cheri would end up in his cell.

Why hadn't she thought of it before? She could have been visiting him weekly in the guise of his attorney. Leigh-Cheri went limp imagining making love with Bernard every Thursday in his cubicle.

As excited as she was, it still wasn't easy, after so long a time, to just up and leave the attic. She thought perhaps she'd better come out slowly, like a diver coming up from flatfish territory, on the lookout for the bends.

Several mornings later, as preparation for her reemergence into the outside world, she walked to the window, whose nails she'd pried loose the evening before, and opened it slowly. Not slowly enough, however, to avoid dumping Chuck off the forty-foot ladder from whose top rung he'd been peering in through the single clear pane, searching for her radio transmitter—and masturbating vigorously. Chuck plummeted into the blackberry brambles, where he sank from sight, his still stiff member learning rudely and repeatedly that "prick" has more than one definition.

Dumbfounded, Leigh-Cheri listened to Chuck's moans for a minute or two before, leaning out of the window, she began to cry for help. Her cries attracted the attention of a faded man in a Sears suit and an amateur haircut who was just then shuffling up the palace lane, bringing terrible news from jail.

72

Chuck was hospitalized for nearly a month, during which time the CIA assigned a full-time professional to spy on the Furstenberg-Barcalona family. The operative kept showing up in different disguises, first as a fire inspector, then as an encyclopedia salesman, next a county health nurse wanting to put an ear to Max's valve, until Queen Tilli, petting her Chihuahua all the while, finally confronted the guy and said, "Vhy don't you just take zee leetle camera and der notebook und go leesen in on zee upstairs extension like Chucky did? You gonna get a tension headache, alvays changing your looks like dis."

It was academic, of course. Short of direct armed intervention, there was nothing further the United States could do to preserve right-wing tyranny in Tilli and Max's homeland. And Max, suspecting that right-wing tyranny would only be replaced with left-wing tyranny, as was usually the case, had washed his royal hands of the whole affair. As for Princess Leigh-Cheri, who, the CIA had learned, was an unwitting candidate for reigning monarch once the revolution was complete, Leigh-Cheri, far from getting herself prepared to rule a nation, Leigh-Cheri was in the condition a Camel pack is in once it's been dropped in a barnyard and chawed up and puked out by a goat.

As news of her self-internment had circulated, via the pages of such periodicals as *National Enquirer, Parade,* and *Cosmopolitan,* the Princess had begun to attract more and more imitators. Women whose men were in prison or military service or Alaska working on the pipeline began bolting themselves in their rooms as public proclamation of lonely devotion. Several men did the same. Eventually, misguided romantics started taking to stripped-down boudoirs, garrets, basements, woodsheds, doghouses, and fallout shelters when their lovers were not away at all but could have been in their arms nightly if they hadn't elected to sequester themselves as proof of their subjugation to the authority of Love. A wife in Unionville, Indiana, a woman known to have spent thirty dollars a week on Hallmark greeting cards, repaired to an unlighted cellar creeping with black widow spiders to demonstrate the depth of her feeling for her husband and three hungry children. Some people who locked themselves away didn't even have sweethearts. By autumn, almost a hundred "princess prisoners" were staring at wallpaper in improvised "love attics" across the land, and some sort of competition was underway, radio stations offering cash prizes for endurance records. Leigh-Cheri had an inkling of this activity, but her mind had been on pyramids and cosmic mystery, and she hadn't given it much thought. Well, the news finally traveled as far as solitary at McNeil Island, where evidently it did not sit well at all.

In fact, Bernard, who'd been behaving relatively straight in hopes of securing an early release, was so perturbed by the reports that he availed himself of the illegal but commonplace prison-system underground post office and risked his record to sneak out a letter to Leigh-Cheri. The missive, in the handwriting of the bribed guard to whom it was dictated, was delivered by Perdy Birdfeeder, a middle-aged malefactor from Tacoma freshly freed after doing fifteen years for purse-snatching. Birdfeeder, who'd grabbed hundreds of purses over a period of many years before he got careless and snatched a colostomy bag—he might have gotten away even then had he not stopped to count the change—helped tug the bleeding Chuck out of the blackberries, severely snagging his new government-grant suit in the process, and then handed over the letter to Gulietta. Birdfeeder could thank his lucky stars that the royal custom of executing messengers who bore ill tidings was no longer observed.

"Yuk!" That was how the note began.

Yuk! If you think the Black Hole is bad, you should try it with baby ferrets hanging by their teeth from the skin of your testicles. That's how I felt when I learned that our personal relationship has become public soap opera, a low-budget interview with Barbra Streisand, and a sport on the order of flagpole sitting and phone-booth stuffing. Babe, it appears that you and I are no longer sucking the same orange. Romance is not a bandwagon to be jumped on by lost souls with nothing more interesting to ride. I thought you'd learned by now that "romantic movement" is a contradiction in terms and that, if prompted, society is all too eager to turn the deepest, most authentic human experiences into yet another shallow fad. You prompted. I guess you can take the girl out of the movement, but you can't take the movement out of the girl. Even in solitary, you couldn't curb your herding instincts. Leave it to a naive world-saver like you to view our love as a Sacred Cause when in actual fact all it was was some barking at the moon.

73

The tears of the Princess, if placed end to end, would have circled Seattle like a moat.

The tears of the Princess, if dammed, would have provided refuge for the hunted whale and moorage for the *Ship of Fools.*

Among the Berbers, it was held that since there is no memory in the grave, earth from a burial mound can help a person forget his or her sorrows, especially the heartbreak of unhappy love. But Bernard included no grave dirt with his letter, and if he had, the tears of the Princess would have turned it to mud.

After she had completely soaked the foam rubber mattress with her bitter weeping, she hurled the mattress out of the window into the blackberries below. (Too bad for Chuck it hadn't been there when he fell.) Then she smashed the chamber pot against the wall. Later, pacing frantically, she slashed her feet on its shards.

Seizing the Camel pack, she squeezed it in her small fist, toppling the pyramids and busting the dromedary's hump. Mummies ran from the pyramids in panic, dragging their wrappings behind them. Water spewed from the camel's cracked hump like a fountain of tears.

For hours she would cry softly, almost imperceptively, rubbing her eyes raw with her knuckles. Then she'd leap to her feet and scream. Helpless, King Max and Queen Tilli (and the CIA agent, disguised now as a Roto-Rooter man) kept vigil at her door, while inside the attic Gulietta stood quietly, cupping Prince Charming in her hands, perhaps protecting him from red-headed rage, perhaps invoking the magic of the frog.

After three days of such carrying on, Leigh-Cheri grew calm. She was, after all, in close harmony with lunar rhythms, and that which wanes must wax. Three days of darkness is as much as the moon will tolerate before it yelps, "Enough already," and begins slowly to reopen the antique refrigerator from whose icy innards will shine the transformative light of the world.

Outside, the rains had come, the rains that like a blizzard of guppies would pelt the creaky old house until spring. There is no weeping that can compete with the Northwest rains.

So Princess Leigh-Cheri blew her nose. She sat her bare buttocks on the cot wires, careful not to snag anything. She thought for a while. She uncrumpled the Camel pack. Then she smiled. She turned to Gulietta. Her voice was determined and gay.

"Bring me A'ben Fizel," she said.

INTERLUDE

If this typewriter can't do it, then . . . what? Can the Muse punt?

The Remington SL3 needs a verb job. It clearly can't write between the lines. It's insensitive to the beauty of fungoid alkaloids—the more I ingest the more inarticulate it becomes. And despite my insistence upon traditional literary values, it remains petulantly *moderne*.

Believe me, I'd have few qualms about switching machines in the middle of the stream, but nothing's open at this hour except Mom's All Nite Diner and the contraption that taps out Mom's menu spells "greese" with three *e*'s. Besides, I've been informed that the Remington warranty doesn't cover "typing of this nature," whatever that might mean. (I suppose I shouldn't be surprised: when I went to buy a policy from Mutual of Omaha, they'd only insure my typing finger for fire and theft.)

I guess there's nothing left to do but ram in the clutch on this bourgeois paper-banger and try to coast to the finish line. In the event that I don't make it, in the event that you, dear reader, must finish without me, well, you've been a good audience, probably better than an underdeveloped novelist with an overdeveloped typewriter deserves, and I'd like to leave you with one perfect sentence, one memorable image to fold in violet silk at the back of your brain box. Something on the order of a drop of tropical jelly oozing from a love bite on a concubine's lip. Alas, there's not enough juice for us to indulge ourselves—a familiar complaint in the last quarter of the twentieth century—so at the risk of being coy, I'll thank you quickly and *arrivederci* on out of here. As they say in my country, have a nice dav.

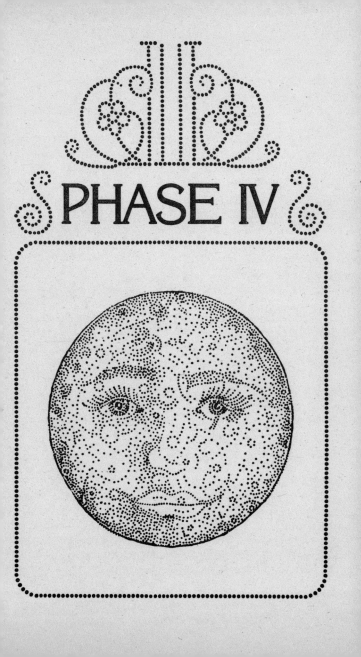

PHASE IV

74

The dawn came up like a Have-a-Nice-Day emblem. The sun shone like Mr. Happy Face himself, and the horizons were all smiles. From boundary to boundary, the people arose as if they'd been given champagne enemas, convinced that they *were* going to have a nice day. A nation traditionally, historically, anciently monarchal was about to seat its first sovereign in thirty years. It was Coronation Day, hooray.

Everyone had the day off. The hotels and boarding-houses were full. Along the procession route, crowds began thickening before dawn. All seats in the stands had been reserved as soon as booking opened, and tickets were selling on the black market for the equivalent of ninety dollars each. Balconies overlooking the route cost even more. School children had been given mugs, plates, pamphlets, and badges, and they carried them as if they had supernatural properties, pressing them to their new spring outfits. From the radio aerials of automobiles, little flags fluttered chirpily. Soldiers, heroes of the revolution, wore brand-new boots of squeaky leather, and women, young and old, smiled at them from behind bouquets. By eight o'clock, there were in the streets more flowers than people. And as common as roses were the dark blooms of cameras.

At ten, the bees inside the camera heads began to whirr furiously, announcing the approach of the State Coach, gilded, curlicued, emblazoned with baroque pastoral scenes by Cipriani, attended by scarlet-and-gold coated postilions, and drawn by six white horses. Silver trumpets blared, cathedral bells went dizzy clanging. Frightened, the capital's pigeons took to the sky, only to find the sky occupied by balloons, confetti, and the acrobatic secondhand jet planes of a fledgling air force.

In ceremonial tunic, the newly elected premier stepped from a less ornate carriage and climbed the lily-festooned stairs to the throne platform. The premier, military leader of the revolution, was cheered and cheered mightily, but it was obvious that the crowd was saving its thunder. All at once a wave of exultation akin to religious ecstasy swept through the throng. Tears catapulted like crystal jumping beans from fifty thousand sets of eyes, and in half a million breasts an enormous sigh took shape. "God save the queen!" shouted the premier, and it mattered little that the premier did not believe in God. "God save the queen!" roared the dignitaries, the soldiers, the weeping women, the workers, and the children. And there she was, ascending, her ermine train piling up behind her, a holy puppet clothed in magic robes for the comfort of the masses and the pride of the state, ascending in an aura of accumulated history, the visible and human aspect of government, the emerald cap on the toothpaste tube of nationality, the beauty mark on the contorted face of race. "God save Queen Gulietta! Long live Gulietta! Long live the queen!"

75

Max's father, King Ehrwig IV, had impregnated a kitchen maid. Captivated by the skinny child who grew from his careless seed, he went often, before Max was born, to the scullery where, among cabbage leaves and leeks, he bounced her on his elegant knee.

Ehrwig offered to adopt her, but the child's mother, as spunky and obstinate as Gulietta herself was to be, wouldn't have it. "You're content to leave me in the kitchen," she charged. "The baby stays here, too."

After Max's birth, when King Ehrwig had at last a proper heir, he sought out Gulietta, then eleven, and into her jam-sticky, bony little hand pressed a document admitting paternity. "There may come a time when you will need this," he said. A copy of the document was placed among his secret papers where many decades later it was found by a member of the revolution's monarch selection committee investigating the Furstenberg-Barcalona lineage.

All along, Gulietta had known that she was Max's half sister, but she chose to honor her mother, in life and in death, by never revealing that fact. However, when she was approached by agents of the revolution—they found her splitting cedar kindling beside a fireplace on Puget Sound—she chose to honor her father by freely confessing to the purple in her veins.

"We've lost faith in Max and Tilli," they told her, "and besides, Max has renounced the crown. Their sons are beneath consideration, they are trash. We would have liked Princess Leigh-Cheri, but you're aware of what she's gone and done. You are left. And you will be perfect. You are representative of both our proud royal heritage and our good common folk. Upon your head, the crown will not be just a piece of autocratic hardware, it will be an adjunct of democratic, socialistic rule. You will be a queen for the people because, though genetically royal, you come from among the people. Why, you even speak the mother tongue, the *old* language. On top of that, when it comes to Furstenberg-Barcalonas, you've got more sense than any of them."

At first her age had worried them, but when they observed the vim with which she swung her hatchet, they nodded at one another and smiled. "She'll outlast the twentieth century," they predicted.

So, shortly after Christmas, old Gulietta acceded to the throne, and in the spring, she publicly accepted the elaborate tokens of regal responsibility—the scepter, the ring, and last, the crown itself. It was such a glittering, emotion-charged occasion, pompous in the best sense of the word, that not a soul, not even the premier, noticed that the old woman never at any time during the coronation unclinched her left fist. And in the unlikely event that they had noticed, nobody would have suspected that inside the fist was a living frog. When the creature croaked, they attributed the sound to the excitement of ancient bowels and went right along with the ceremony.

Upon being crowned, Gulietta's first act was to reaffirm diplomatic ties with Peru and Bolivia, to whose envoys she hinted strongly that some nice fresh cocaine, for medicinal purposes only, would be regarded a proper tribute.

Her second act was to personally request of the president of the United States of America the commuting of the sentence of a certain "political prisoner" held in federal jail in Washington State. As a matter of protocol, the president had little choice but to comply.

76

"Hello, darling. Any word about the limestone?" Leigh-Cheri embraced A'ben Fizel. She kissed his mouth and welcomed the hands that slid immediately inside her negligee.

"How can one speak of stone when there is flesh at

hand?" A'ben asked. He drew her more tightly against him.

"Take it easy, darling. Don't be in such a hurry. Meat won't melt. I want to hear about the limestone."

"Okay, there is the good news, finally. The ship she passes through Suez at this hour. Should to be arrival here before two day."

"Ohh!" Leigh-Cheri squealed with happiness. "I'm so glad. Aren't you glad? Maybe we'll even finish on schedule. Do you think so?"

"You tell me take it easy. Now I tell you take it easy. Stone she not melt. Pyramid never melt. Pyramid will be here on earth long after *this* is in heaven." His fingers, dripping with jewels, closed around her groin.

"Mmmm. *This* is in heaven already. Or it soon will be." With a movement like a raccoon picking a fruit, like an outlaw striking a match, she unzipped his trousers.

❦ 77 ❧

What had disturbed Leigh-Cheri most about Bernard's note was its evidence of how poorly he knew her. Like women in general, like Aries women in particular, like redheaded Aries women in greater particular, she loathed to be misunderstood. Injustice against others outraged her, injustice against herself set her to boiling like brimstone soup. After the sacrifices she had made, after the extremity of her commitment, to then be scolded like an errant tot, to be lectured condescendingly, to have her love, their love regarded frivolously was simply intolerable. The one man who might know how to make love stay—or so she'd thought—had behaved as if the moon were his personal wheel of cheese, and once again her heart's natural inclination to contemplate romantic grandeur had been interrupted by the mundane, betrayed by the egotistical. Never again, by Jesus! Inside her, something had snapped. She couldn't say that she no longer cared about Bernard, but she could say loudly and clearly that no longer would she be victimized by caring. She was a princess, a very special entity with very special graces, and from now on, when it came to men, she would call the shots.

It occurred to her that in every relationship in which she had participated, in every union older than a year that she'd observed, imbalance existed. Of a couple, one person invariably loved stronger than the other. It seemed a law of nature, a cruel law that led to tension and destruction. She was dismayed that a law so unfair, so miserable prevailed, but since it did, since imbalance seemed inevitable, it must be easier, healthier to be the lover who loved the least. She vowed that henceforth imbalance would work in her favor.

She vowed also, caressing the warped Camel pack as she vowed, to enlarge and explore what she'd come to call her "theory." She viewed herself as some kind of Argonian link, and the vision that she'd had in that stuffy, silent attic was to be the foundation of her new life's work.

To these ends, she sent for A'ben Fizel.

When he was courting her, upon her return from Hawaii, Fizel had been a gallant but unattractive companion. Excesses of liquor and rich foods had given him bulbous jowls and a greenish complexion. He rather resembled a tall toad. But when she sent for him, suggesting that she might consent to become his wife, an amazing transformation took place. Putting aside his playboy ways, Fizel checked into a North

Dakota health ranch where he was assigned a diet of grapefruit and raw garlic cloves and made to walk twenty miles a day. At the end of thirty days, he knocked on the door at Fort Blackberry a slim and handsome figure, reeking only moderately of garlic. Leigh-Cheri was amazed. Noting the approval in her eyes, Fizel got right to business. He presented her with a diamond as big as a Ritz cracker. The Princess was not to be rushed, however.

"What do you think about the future of pyramids?" she inquired.

78

It has been estimated that it would require six years and a billion dollars to construct the Great Pyramid of Giza with modern technology. To duplicate the Great Chicken of Itza would take even more time and money—but that was Col. Sanders's problem. Leigh-Cheri's scheme was not quite so ambitious. A pyramid one-third the size of Giza would still be an enormous structure and would suit her purposes just fine.

"Your country practically borders Egypt and has much the same terrain," the Princess reminded A'ben Fizel, "but tourists never visit you because there's no attraction. In fact, when your country is mentioned, most people draw a blank. If anything comes to mind, it's oil wells, excessive profits, religious fanaticism, and vulgar taste. Suppose you were to erect the first full-sized genuine pyramid in the Levant in more than three thousand years. Not only would it attract tourists from all over the world, it would serve as a popular symbol and give your nation an identity. The pyramid could become a showplace for your culture. In addition to bringing in revenue, it would be great public relations. Folks wouldn't be so quick to think of you guys as nouveau riche barbarians with petroleum under your nails and sand between your ears."

Fizel flinched at these words, but he was fascinated nonetheless. Her proposal made some sense to him as a businessman and a patriot. The icing on the pyramid-shaped cake was that she promised to marry him when the structure was complete. His pyramid would be a celebrated monument to his love for her just as the Taj Mahal was a monument to the love of Shah Jahan for his favorite wife. Fizel was one of the few men on earth who could affort to express affection in such grandiose terms.

Following a fortnight of deliberation—and consultation with his dad—A'ben agreed. Before slipping the diamond on the Princess's finger, however, he made a stipulation of his own. It was practically common knowledge that his bride-to-be was no virgin. Fizel demanded, therefore, that while the pyramid was being built, she reside in his country, near the Fizel palace, and that one night a week she admit him to her chambers.

Since she had every intention of supervising the construction of the pyramid and since it behooved her to put distance between her and McNeil Island, Leigh-Cheri was quite willing to move to A'ben's land. As for his demand to trespass weekly in her boudoir, she put it to a vote. Her heart said no, the peachfish said it was about damn time. Ambivalent on the subject, her brain finally decided to vote with the peachfish. Thus was the betrothal announced.

79

There were moments before her mirror, brushing the hair that flowed like creeks of lava, that trailed like the woven trails of red-hot comets, when she would see a whore's face looking back at her. At those moments, she felt hard and dirty, and she'd spatter the mirror-face with tears, mourning girlish innocence, romantic dreams, the dimming of the moon. But in the square beneath her Moorish windows, real camels chewed their cuds, when she parted the brocade draperies, she could see domes, minarets, and date palms strikingly similar to those on the cigarette package, and on the far horizon, a pyramid—*her* pyramid—was swiftly rising.

It would continue to rise until reaching a height of 160.6 feet. It would spread until it covered 4.4 acres. Its four triangular faces were designed to incline at an angle of 51 degrees, 52 minutes to the ground, precisely the same as Giza's. Naturally, the pyramid would be accurately aligned to the cardinal points, while consultants from Cambridge's astronomy department were assuring that it would have solar, lunar, and stellar alignments, as well. Its outer chambers would be given over to cafes, bazaars, and nightclubs, all of highest quality, to a trade exhibit and to a small but important museum of Levantine archaeology. The inner chambers were Leigh-Cheri's alone. In them, she would oversee and conduct exhaustive experiments in pyramidology. Pyramid power, that energy frequency that preserves corpses, sharpens razor blades, amplifies thought forms, and increases sexual vitality, would be studied by the best scientific minds until it was thoroughly understood, and then every effort would be made to put it to the uses that the Argonian masters intended. Perhaps through the impetus of her pyramid, the Red Beards somehow could be retrieved from exile, or a new race of modern Red Beards would be spawned and eventually regain control over solar forces.

When she thought of things pyramidal, which was most of the time, it no longer distressed her that she was using A'ben Fizel or allowing him to use her. Then, she would look in the mirror shamelessly. She'd brush her hair as if it were the aurora of a permanent moonrise. And sometimes she'd lift the Camel pack, crinkled and bent, from her dressing table and hold it up to the looking glass, smiling at how the great word CHOICE once more defied the inversions of normal reflection. She had freely *chosen* the life she now led, and if it had unsavory aspects, well, she must be brave and bear the taint. Not that the liaisons with her fiancé were ordeals for her. *Au contraire.* Oh, very *au contraire.*

❀ 80 ❀

The first time that she spread her legs for him it had been like opening her jaws for the dentist. Clouds of dread, doubt, resentment, guilt, and sentimentality combined to shadow the faintest ray of pleasure. Eyes squeezed shut, she tried to imagine that it was Bernard inside her, but this new man felt so different, so strange that the fantasy never solidified. In the weeks that followed, she relaxed somewhat, primarily as a result of his unexpected gentleness. Eyes still tightly closed, she'd move against him as if he were a device from a sex shop, mechanically churning herself to the creamy brink of aloof orgasm. When she finally went over the brink, one twilight when incense burners were smoking up the flat and camel bells tinkled in the square below, she relaxed far more. The next time he undressed at her bedside she kept her eyes wide open—and saw what she'd been missing.

Although A'ben had resumed an active nightlife—giving the discos one last whirl before marriage, he claimed—daily workouts in the family gymnasium were keeping him trim. His Semitic beak had a strong masculine contour, the teeth that armed his shy smile were brilliant and regular (especially in comparison to Bernard's yellow wrecks), and there was a generous light in his chocolate eyes. His phallus was long, slender, and slippery, and as curved as a Phoenician eyebrow. Aroused, it stood politely on end, but bowed backward so that its head, as smooth and purple as eggplant, almost touched his belly. Even before A'ben could climb into bed, she was stroking that exotic fixture, marveling at its natural lubricity, rubbing it against her nipples, holding it against her flushed cheeks. The poor man barely got his feet off the floor before she had him in her mouth. As he throbbed in her throat, pumping jet after jet of that steamy translucent mucilage with which Cupid tries to glue the world together, she felt as if she were gulping concentrated ecstasy, and it made her blood croon. Later that evening he focused on her clitoris with unusual sensitivity, and as he was leaving to return to the palace, she hinted that one meeting a week might be shortchanging Aphrodite. "After all, you're a sheik, and I'm a redhead," she whispered. From then on, he visited her on both Wednesdays and Saturdays, and they fucked the night away.

More than once, Leigh-Cheri tried to convince herself that she'd fallen for him, but she knew that she was only in love from the waist down. No matter how ardently the peachclam might gush over him, her heart was unmoved. On those occasions when the peachfish was most ebullient, her heart would grow moody, turn up the collar on its trench coat, pull down the brim of its hat, dangle a cigarette from its sullen lips, and go walk for hours on the poorly lighted streets of the waterfront. If a heart won't listen to a vagina, what will it listen to? The question went unanswered—but Wednesday and Saturday evenings passed in physical rapture, and until there arose a difficulty procuring Tura limestone for its facing, the pyramid proceeded ahead of schedule.

81

Morality depends on culture. Culture depends on climate. Climate depends on geography. Seattle where the clams were singing, Seattle where the trolls were hiding, Seattle where the blackberries were glistening, Seattle where the bloomers of the sky were drooping, Seattle the city that washed its hands with the incessancy of a proctologist, Seattle was far behind her, at memory's rest on a dank, deep mossy bed. Now the Princess lived at the edge of a vast desert, under the seal of the sun. The change in interior geography was just the opposite. Indoors, she had traded the barren attic for a lavish flat. Her outside world and her inside world had swapped places. Had there been a corresponding psychological shift? And had its effects edited her moral code?

Perhaps. Slightly. But something had happened in the intimate immensity of the attic that, if not negating that alteration, had rendered it trivial. She had become sensitized to objecthood.

Thanks to the Camel pack, Leigh-Cheri could no longer snub an object. Thanks to the Camel pack, she had been cured of animate chauvinism. Among her acquaintances at the university, among the enlightened delegates to the Care Fest, those who railed most liberally against racism, sexism, and ageism discriminated hourly against the inanimate objects around them, denying them love, respect, and even attention. But though she'd reached no conscious conclusions on the matter, Leigh-Cheri had come to consider the smallest, deadest thing as if it had some life of its own.

During the day, out at the pyramid site, she'd find herself regarding the tools of the workmen with at least as much admiration as she regarded the workers themselves. Her grip lingered on doorknobs much longer than necessary. She patted the big granite blocks with the casual affection others might spend on a passing pooch, treating the stones as though they had individual personalities, while the wooden canteen from which she quenched her thirst became a special friend; she treasured its mouth against her mouth, was prepared to defend it against adversaries. In the evening, after she'd soaked off the desert dust and applied a fresh coat of zinc oxide to the blaze of her nose (redheads burn easily), she'd stroll through the flat (provided it wasn't Wednesday or Saturday, of course), randomly picking up ashtrays, music boxes, coffee cups, letter openers, artifacts, or candies, boring into them until each expanded into a limitless world, every bit as rich and interesting as that other more physically mobile world about which she remained curious but from which she was once again isolated.

In a society that is essentially designed to organize, direct, and gratify mass impulses, what is there to minister to the silent zones of man as an individual? Religion? Art? Nature? No, the church has turned religion into standardized public spectacle, and the museum has done the same for art. The Grand Canyon and Niagara Falls have been looked at so much that they've become effete, sucked empty by too many stupid eyes. What is there to minister to the silent zones of man as an individual? How about a cold chicken bone on a paper plate at midnight, how about a lurid lipstick lengthening or shortening at your command, how about a styrofoam nest abandoned by a "bird" you've never known, how about a pair of windshield wipers pursuing one another futilely while you drive home alone through a downpour, how about something beneath a seat touched by your shoe at the movies, how about worn pencils, cute forks, fat little radios, boxes of bow ties, and bubbles on the side of a bathtub? Yes, these are the things, these kite strings and olive oil cans and Valentine hearts stuffed with nougat, that form the bond between the autistic vision and the experiential world; it is to show these things in their true mysterious light that is the purpose of the moon.

One Wednesday evening, lying beside A'ben Fizel, at rest after a four-quarter, double-overtime copulation, Leigh-Cheri startled both herself and her intended by sitting up suddenly in bed, grasping the Vaseline jar that she'd been watching in the moonlight, and asking aloud, "Whatever happened to the golden ball?"

82

In time, Leigh-Cheri became intimate with most of the inanimate objects in her environment, including that inanimate object that controls the reproductive cycles of all living creatures, that inanimate object that choreographs the tides, that inanimate object that influences sanity, that inanimate object to which J. Isaacs was referring when he wrote, ". . . the history of poetry in all ages is the attempt to find new images for the moon." (The moon is the Empress of Objects, and as a practitioner of lunaception, Leigh-Cheri was in its league). There was one object in her domain, however, which she pointedly ignored, even though that object was particularly enlivened by moonshine. It was her engagement ring.

More than likely, she was afraid of what the ring signified. She had fully accepted A'ben Fizel as a lover, yet to contemplate their marriage made her shiver and sweat. Whenever she tried to imagine herself his lifelong bride, she grew immediately morose and set to thinking about the pyramid instead, even though the day of the pyramid's completion and her wedding day were the same.

In Fizel's country, it was taboo for an engaged couple to appear together in public, so except for slippery Wednesday evenings and slishy Saturday nights, she rarely saw him. A'ben procured materials for pyramid construction and organized the labor force. At this he was so efficient that the project, which should have taken a minimum of two years, looked as if it would be done in twenty months, the delay in delivery of limestone facing notwithstanding. But A'ben seldom appeared at the building site. An inveterate night-clubber, he frequently flew to Rome or Mikonos for a single evening's revelry, only to sleep away the mornings and devote afternoons to strenuous gymnastic sessions and meals of grapefruit and raw garlic. He had leased a satellite to relay telecasts of every game played by the American professional basketball team whose franchise he owned, and presumedly sports biz consumed a fairly large portion of his attention.

The week that Leigh-Cheri arrived in his country she was honored with a reception at the family palace, where she met the patriarch, Ihaj Fizel, one of the most financially powerful men alive. She also was introduced to A'ben's two brothers. The mother made a brief appearance, the sisters weren't seen at all. When Leigh-Cheri asked about the women, A'ben shrugged. "Is unimportant," he said. Leigh-Cheri got the impression that females counted for little in the land of the Fizels, and that, doubtlessly, was *one* reason she looked at the diamond ring with no more enthusiasm than most people looked at cigarette packages— looked but chose not to see.

"What is this golden ball of which you have the curiosity?" asked A'ben the night the subject abruptly arose.

Leigh-Cheri didn't answer. She couldn't answer. She was immersed in the silent zone, where to become motionless is to be elsewhere.

"If you want this golden ball, I buy it. Do not to worry of expense."

Still she didn't reply. Noticing that she was holding the Vaseline jar, transfixed by the bashful yet sensuous glow of its contents, and recalling that in America "ball" was a slangy euphemism for coitus, A'ben began to wonder if "golden ball" didn't refer to some special kind of sexual intercourse in which he wasn't versed. Maybe it referred to sexual perfection, the ultimate ball, and maybe he had failed to provide it, and maybe Vaseline was supposed to help. Smitten for the first time in his life with pangs of self-doubt, he asked sulkily, "This golden ball, it is something you have had with the Woodpecker man?"

A'ben had never mentioned the Woodpecker before, and it was jolting enough to cause Leigh-Cheri to come back from her reverie, although the phrase "come back" is misleading because in the realm of meditative daydream the only way to "go there" is, paradoxically, to totally "be here."

"Er, uh, not exactly," she stammered. She returned the Vaseline to the bedside table, withdrawing her gaze from the sea light of its luminous goo. "He, ah, he said something to me once. I only just now understood what he meant."

Accepting her explanation in all of its inadequacy, Fizel permitted the subject to be changed to limestone. The next morning, however, he fired messages to customs officials at every point of entry in the Arab world demanding that any traveler bearing a passport in the name of Bernard Mickey Wrangle be turned away. Forcefully, if necessary.

83

Less than a month later, believe it or not, a man bearing just such a passport stepped off a plane in Algiers. When informed that he could not enter Algeria, he put up a fight and was taken into custody.

A'ben Fizel was notified. Fizel sent the Algerian police commissioner a case of cognac, a tub of caviar, and a pearl-handled riding crop that had once belonged to King Faruk. "Wrangle is a dangerous international thug with Zionist affiliations," cabled Fizel. "He should be detained in maximum security. Indefinitely. Which most suits your taste in motor cars, commissioner, the American Lincoln Continental or the German Mercedes-Benz?"

Fizel then proceeded to add a hundred workmen to the crew at the pyramid. Work was to continue around the clock until the limestone facing was on and the inner chambers met Princess Leigh-Cheri's specifications. Fizel also ordered his palace staff to speed up preparations for the wedding.

84

You would think that an electric typewriter would know better than to bite the hand that pays the light bill. Yet the Remington SL3, in its wanton dedication to humdrum technological practicality, persists in obstructing attempts at old-fashioned literary genius. You would think that a woman obsessed with building a full-sized pyramid in the last quarter of the twentieth century would know better than to cross the one man who could make it possible. Yet Leigh-Cheri had refused A'ben's embrace and was speaking to him sharply.

"Why the hell am I being guarded?" she demanded. "Why do I trip over those two lummoxes every time I turn around?"

Leigh-Cheri's enthusiasm for sex simultaneously delighted and frightened A'ben Fizel. Months before, he had secretly assigned a eunuch to keep watch on her, assuring that her passions were not so rudderless as to allow her to drift into another's arms. She was, after all, left alone a great deal, and he was uncertain if two services a week were sufficient to cool her racy motor. Upon learning that a Bernard Mickey Wrangle had been apprehended in Algiers, A'ben had doubled the guard. It became obvious to Leigh-Cheri that the pair was camping outside her door.

"Those men of which you call dumb oxes are trusted by me. They are to—"

"Spy on me."

"No. No!" He shook his head forcefully. "They are to protect you."

"From what?"

"From the bad men. You could be kidnap. Men that

your television call 'terrorist' do such things. Ways of Middle East are not familiar to you."

That should have calmed her. She was aware that abductions and skyjackings were fairly common political tactics in that part of the globe. But red hair is slow to lay back once it's got its dandruff up, and her bitchy mood required further opportunity to express itself.

"I'm familiar enough with Middle Eastern customs to know that Moslems don't eat or make love on Saturdays. Why do you always visit me on a holy day? A day you don't dare to be seen in a disco, right? Your countrymen refuse to work on the pyramid on Saturdays, you have to hire Greeks. I'll bet they don't know how you spend *your* holy day. No meat on Saturday, A'ben. Right? No meat on Saturday."

The lids drooped like paper wrappers over his chocolate-drop eyes. A guilty tic began to palpitate in the left corner of his mouth. "Perhaps I am too long in America," he said softly. "Perhaps I am too much confuse Mecca with between your thights."

Leigh-Cheri had to laugh. "Thighs, A'ben." She opened her negligee and patted herself. "These are called thighs."

His eyes watered. His lower lip quivered like a snail that had just learned the meaning of escargot. Sorry now, she set about to kiss the quivers and tics and tears away. Soon the forgotten guards were nudging one another and grinning at the sacrilegious yet not unholy noises escaping from the flat.

85

"It won't be long now," said Leigh-Cheri to a spoon. Moorish architects were wont to make their windows look like keyholes, and the redheaded Princess stood at such a window as if she were a bloodshot eye keyhole-peeping at the pyramid while it was being dressed. It was Sunday, a day as milky and muffled in the Moslem world, oddly enough, as it was in Christendom. The day shift, made up mostly of Greek and Yugoslavian masons—the sun-wise Arabs chose to work nights—was on the job, affixing limestone facing, but Leigh-Cheri had given herself a day off.

"It won't be long now," said Leigh-Cheri. If there was a trace of anxiety in her voice, the spoon couldn't tell.

A'ben had loved her well the previous evening, and she'd slept quite late. She lingered over her breakfast tea, then devoted some time to playing with the teaspoon. It was as noon as noon could be when she stood at her window, staring across the shadowless city, low and blanched and jumbled as a boneyard, as a retirement picnic for used-up schoolroom chalk. In the noonday sun, the pyramid, too, gleamed white. Despite the intense heat, the city seemed cold. It was eternally alien to her American temperament. But the pyramid. . . . The pyramid was real to Leigh-Cheri in a way that buildings of her own society were not.

How can one thing be more real than any other? Especially when it is inscrutable and mysterious? Maybe when a thing is perceived as being absolutely direct yet absolutely unnecessary it becomes absolutely genuine. It is real unto itself and does not depend on outside attachments or associations for its reality. The more emotional values attributed to a thing, the more uses to which it can be put, the more effects it produces, then the more illusions it creates. Illusions, like many values themselves, are cloying and false. But straight lines and flat surfaces exude perpetual reality. Especially when no utilitarian function can be perceived. The geometric figure of a pyramid permits the eye to flow around its corners. We don't have to walk around it to know it completely. To see its front is to see its back. In fact, its front is its back. A pyramid is primary. It is form, not function. It is presence, not effect. We can see it in an instant, yet we continue to read it. It nourishes us over and over. A pyramid is inscrutable and mysterious not in spite of being elemental but *because* it is elemental. Free from the hypnotic hysteria of the mechanical, the numbing torpor of the electronic, and the mortal decay of the biological, it rests in vapid splendor between time and space, detached from both, representing neither, and helps to devaluate the myth of progress.

Of course, Leigh-Cheri never thought of the pyramid in terms of geometric truth. Even the mental processes that nurtured her theory hadn't carried her that far into the ozone of explanation (academic analysis is the true "outer space," frigid light years away from the solid joys of the earth), and she was too young to remember Connie Francis singing "Is it really real?" When Leigh-Cheri looked at the pyramid, her pyramid, she simply experienced the giddy sensation of having thrust her hand into the hip pocket of destiny.

She held the teaspoon in front of her eyes and moved it along the horizon lines until the distant monument appeared to be sitting in its hollow. Then she pretended to feed the pyramid to herself. "Mmmm," she said. "Needs salt."

If there was anxiety in her jest, the spoon couldn't tell.

⚬⚬⚬ 86 ⚬⚬⚬

Once upon a time (to borrow a phrase from the story with which Gulietta imprinted Leigh-Cheri) a rickety, mistreated old drudge of a truck, rusty, dusty, and packed, headlamp to tailgate, with the few possessions and many children of a family of Okie fruit-pickers, rattled to a halt across the highway from a crossroads gas station in the Walla Walla Valley. A child about two years old, still in diapers—in fact, wearing nothing but diapers—climbed down from the truck, which was beanshooting out its exhaust pipe drops of oil the size of the grapes of wrath. The child toddled across the blacktop. Although apparently male, it pushed into the station's women's toilet, where it remained for what seemed like an inordinately long time. Perhaps it was having trouble with the diaper pins. Meanwhile, the Okie at the wheel was mashing the gas feed impatiently, and the dirty kids in the rear were pounding on top of the cab. Finally, just as the bare feet of the toddler emerged from the restroom, the driver popped the clutch, and the truck lurched away. The child stared in disbelief at the disappearing vehicle, then went pattering after it. "Wait for Baby," he yelled. "Wait for Baby, you sons of bitches!"

This scene was witnessed by one Dude Wrangle, a former rodeo contender and failed Hollywood cowboy (hence the snazzy name, Dude's original moniker was something on the order of Bernie Snootch) who had become, in mid-life, a prosperous onion rancher. When the truck neither stopped nor turned around, Dude bought the tot a Pepsi and invited him to sit in his Cadillac convertible. The kid was suspicious, but the lure of the Caddy was more than he could resist. Dude both pitied the child and admired his spirit. He also liked his red curls and the freckles that were as rosy as hypodermic wounds. So he sat with him, playing the radio for him and feeding him Hostess Twinkies, until dusk. Then, convinced that the migrant family wouldn't return, Dude drove him, freckles and all, to the Cry-Me-a-River Onion Farm.

"Hi, Kathleen. Hi, Kathleen. Sorry I'm late, but it's hard work making a young'un all by yourself. Specially when the little bugger's damn near two years old. Here, come tell me how I done. Tell me how I done."

A few years before, Dude Wrangler had swept the feet out from under a young philosophy professor at Whitman College, and she'd given up Spinoza for a satin-shirted satyr, an unpainted ranch house, and all the famous Walla Walla sweet onions she could eat. (Prior to teaching at Whitman, she'd thought Walla Walla sweets played pool with Minnesota Fats.) Kathleen had a pretty face and a shiny intellect but bum plumbing. Try as they might, they couldn't get her pregnant. She was overwhelmed by this ready-made kid that Dude thrust at her. She hastened to give him a bath, then tucked him into her own bed. She stayed awake all night watching him. Baby whimpered a little before falling asleep, but morning found him cheerful and none too eager to be reunited with the sons of bitches.

This was in the Walla Walla Valley in the eastern part of Washington State, two hundred miles and two hundred yawns from Seattle, out where the apples were knocking their chins together and the sky was just too blue to be in good taste. In the dialect of the local Indians, *walla* meant water. When the Indians first discovered, cutting through the hellish hills, a fertile valley yodeling with brooks and rivers, they doubled up and called the place Walla Walla. "Water here and plenty of it," "A far greater abundance of moisture than one would have expected to find in these dusty parts," or, in the ethno-lingo that white folks enjoy, "Land of many waters." Had the valley been *really* wet, had it canals, swamps, and lagoons, they might have named it Walla Walla Walla. Maybe even Walla Walla Walla Walla. Had those same Indians ever hit Puget Sound in the rainy season, there would have been virtually no end to their *wallaing.*

Dude Wrangle had been born and raised in Walla Walla, which might account for the fact that as a child he developed a tiresome habit of saying everything twice. "Please can I? Please can I?" "I hate stinking stewed tomatoes. I hate stinking stewed tomatoes." "Pee. Pee." It was an idiosyncracy that he never outgrew, and it was his habit of repeating his lines that was as responsible as anything for his failure in the movies. No director wanted to have the posse told to "Head 'em off at the pass" two times in succession, and it somehow spoiled the mood of a tense evening in Comanche territory when the hero said, "Sure is quiet out there tonight. Sure is quiet out there tonight." Yeah, Wrangle, it was quiet until you started babbling.

Adopted by the Wrangles, Baby became accustomed to Dude's repetitions, which is probably why, years later, he had felt so at home in Hawaii with its loma loma and mahi mahi.

Growing up on the Cry-Me-a-River Onion Farm, the abandoned redhead learned philosophy from Kathleen and the wiles and ways of the drugstore cowboy from Dude. Everybody around Walla Walla called him Baby, for he had no other name until he was fifteen, at which time he was shipped off to a fancy academy in Switzerland because Kathleen didn't want him turning out to be another Walla Walla hayseed and Dude was upset by both the quantity and quality of the mischief he was getting into in public school. On the night before his departure for Geneva, Dude and Kathleen shared a quart of sourmash hootch with him and christened him Bernard Mickey.

Being a bit hungover, the three of them arrived late at the Spokane airport the next day, and Bernard Mickey had to run to catch his flight. As he dashed toward the boarding gate, he yelled, "Wait for Baby! Wait for Baby, you sons of bitches!" He looked over his shoulder at his foster parents, laughed wildly, and threw them a kiss.

They laughed and threw kisses, too.

"Keep your nose clean, darling," sang Kathleen.

And Dude bellowed, "Do us proud, you hear. Do us proud, you hear."

Now, even though he was reared amidst redundancy, it would seem that the kind of hip guy Bernard Mickey Wrangle turned out to be wouldn't have had to be ordered to halt more than once by an Algerian jailer with a machine gun. Wouldn't it seem that way?

87

Leigh-Cheri didn't learn of the shooting until a month after it happened. Then, it was Queen Tilli who informed her.

At Gulietta's request, Max's homeland paid him a substantial sum so that he might retire in dignity, independent of the American government. Max immediately divided the funds, giving half to Tilli and taking his half to Reno, where he intended to gamble until his valve blew out. He checked into a modest hotel and went every morning to the casinos, committing suicide by wheel of fortune. He telephoned Tilli twice a week, ever assuring her that he was winning money and enjoying good health. "I feel better away from the blackberries," he said. The Queen suspected that he was fibbing to ease her worry, so she arranged to stop off in Reno on her way to the Mideast for Leigh-Cheri's wedding.

To her surprise, she found her husband the toast of the town. He was the season's big winner, and everybody from casino managers to star entertainers to taxi drivers always greeted King Max. He demanded little but tipped large. He made donations to local charities. He bought drinks for doormen, sent the kind of flowers to coffee-shop waitresses that other big winners sent to showgirls. As for his heart, it was chugging along, although the doctors warned that it could derail at any moment. "I only pray that it goes at the roulette table," said Max, dropping a third lump of sugar like a depth charge into his tea. "I'll place every last cent on red thirteen and, win or lose, expire like a monarch."

It was while Tilli was sitting in the hotel lobby waiting for Max to come down for breakfast—he'd gambled until 3:00 A.M.—that she'd noticed the article. She'd picked up a copy of an underground newspaper, the Philadelphia *Drummer,* that a couple of bearded young men with backpacks had forgotten on a lobby sofa. Tilli intended to spread the paper on the floor of her room so that her Chihuahua might do its little business thereupon and not soil the rug. As she was folding the *Drummer* into her handbag, her eyes came to rest on an article concerning an incident in Algiers. According to an exclusive report, Algerian guards had

machine-gunned an American citizen, Bernard Mickey
Wrangle, thirty six, who, as the Woodpecker, had led
a notorious gang of bomb-throwing war resisters during the late sixties and early seventies. Algeria was
covering up the incident, the article said, but, it went
on to say, it was common knowledge in the Casbah
that Wrangle, arrested earlier on a passport violation,
had been killed while trying to escape.

"Oh-Oh, spaghetti-o," uttered Queen Tilli. The yelps
of her doggie as it slid off her lap made short work of
her next remark.

88

"You know, Tilli, I can't help but feel a little sad
about Wrangle." The King poured maple syrup on his
waffle. The syrup puddled the depressions in the waffle the way that desire puddles the folds in the brain.
"I detest what he stood for, but I have to admire the
fact that he stood for something, that he was prepared
to carve the roast instead of waiting for some superior
to toss him a bone. He was better company than those
serious-minded environmentalists that Leigh-Cheri was
always dragging home. Except that he wanted to plant
blackberries on the rooftops of Seattle. My God! Bar-
baric!" Max's heart valve did an imitation of a robot
having a bowel movement.

"It says in this article—pass the butter—that Wrangle was suspected of helping hijack an airliner to
Cuba back in seventy-one. Yet he was not a Marxist.
He did it out of general contempt for government.
What makes an intelligent, courageous man disrespect
the law to such an extent? In games of chance, one
plays by the rules. Rules give poker its shape, its
substance, its tension, its life. Poker without rules

would be pointless and boring. And those who cheat the rules cannot be allowed to play. In the old days they were shot. I guess that is what happened to our Mr. Wrangle. More syrup."

"In health there ees also rules," said Tilli, "und you are zee vorse ven it come to breaking dem. No! No more syrup, you break-lawer."

"When I disobey the doctor's orders, Tilli, it affects no one but me. Should I break the rules in poker, everybody at the table would feel the effects. That is what Wrangle did, and that is why he is dead. Surely I will be dead soon, too, but I am forty years older than he, and death is not my punishment, it is my reward." Like metal fatigue, a smile creased the fusilage of Max's DC-10 face. "Well, should I run into him in the next world, we shall have an amusing chat. He was—"

"All zis is not zee point," said Tilli, wiping syrup off three of her four chins. "Zee point is dat he ees killed and I spoke wif Leigh-Cheri on der phone two nights ago und she don't know nuffin of thees. Should I tell her or not?"

"Of course you should tell her. She has a right to know. There is no reason to conceal his demise. She is not in love with him any longer." A pause ensued during which Max pondered his statement. "But, uh, Tilli," he said at last, "I would wait to tell her until after she is married. Okay?"

"Eef you tink zo." Tilli wrapped bacon slices in a napkin to carry to her pooch.

"Did you read this? Allegedly, Wrangle landed in Havana in the month of December. He was surprised to find that since going Communist the Cubans no longer observed Christmas. So when he met Fidel Castro, Wrangle called him a rebel without a Claus. Ha ha. Quite the joker, eh?"

Tilli didn't get it.

89

There had to be one moment, a single isolated moment, pear-shaped, quivering, and outlined in radium, when Beethoven inked the final note of his *Fifth Symphony,* when Shakespeare chose the word ("shoot") that completed *Hamlet,* when Leonardo applied the brush stroke that shoved Mona Lisa onto the Louvre express. Such a moment occurred, at least in the mind of Princess Leigh-Cheri, when the last slab of facing was cemented in place on the capstone point of the modern pyramid. Both depressed and elated (as Beethoven, Shakespeare, and Leonardo must have been), all she could say was, "Done."

Her real task had, of course, just begun. According to Manly P. Hall, "All the wisdom possessed by the ancients seems to have been epitomized in the structure of the Great Pyramid, and he [*sic*] who solves its riddle must necessarily be as wise as he [*sic*] who contrived it."

Leigh-Cheri wasn't exactly trying to solve the riddle of the Great Pyramid, but she did aspire to understand the peculiar properties of pyramids, in general, and their application to the improvement of the human race, and she was aware that both she and her team of scientists would require capabilities beyond the ordinary. She was also aware of her lack of expertise, of the terrible ignorance she brought to this enterprise. In secret, she was counting on the Red Beards, that they would somehow intervene . . .

At any rate, it was done. And it was gorgeous. Impressive. Awesome. Hers. Well, almost hers. A'ben had promised to give it to her as a wedding present, with the stipulation that she lease, free of charge, its outer chambers to his government. So it was in two days to be her very own toy, the largest, heaviest, most expensive, most perfect toy on earth. And yet, try as she might, she couldn't think of it as exclusively hers; as much as it was the mighty egg of her dreaming, she couldn't feel close to it. The Dean of Inanimate Objects at Outlaw College would attribute the pyramid's detachment, as compared to the Camel pack's intimacy, to relative scale. Objects smaller than the human body, says the dean, possess the quality of privateness. Objects larger than the human body possess the quality of publicness. The larger the object, the less private and more public its mode. We might question the dean, provided we could get his nose out of a tequila bottle or his girlfriend's panties, about the moon. The moon is a hell of a lot bigger than the biggest pyramid and can be seen by far more people at any one time. The moon is about as public as a thing can be. Yet the moon seldom fails to invoke a sense of intimacy. We might logically assume that since two of the moon's primary characteristics—light and gravitational pull—directly, personally affect us, that that is the source of its intimate nature. Unfortunately, logic doesn't cut the mustard at Outlaw C. The dean would snort, puff his cheap cigar, and contend that the moon is as intimate as it is public because of its *markings*. As with many ornaments of tiny size, its sense of intimacy is exploited through surface detail. Surface incident sets up internal relationships, and internal relationships break down the external gestalt, the publicness. The Fizel Pyramid (as it was to be forever known), its off-white facing intact, was blank. Its profound appeal was in its constant, known physicality, for it lacked any equivalent of those enigmatic, sensuous spots that draw the moon toward intimacy.

Sure, dean, now why don't you go shoot a game of

snooker or something. Don't call us, we'll call you. The Remington SL3 is running on empty, and what with thousands of people—invited dignitaries, media representatives, and curious public—pouring in for the pyramid unveiling and the grandest wedding of the decade, we have more than we can handle right now.

Leigh-Cheri has left the pyramid site and is being driven by limousine to her flat, where she will await the two people among the wedding guests who she is excited to see: Queen Tilli and Queen Gulietta.

90

Miraculously, the pyramid had been erected in slightly less than two years. Hell, it took that long for union labor to put a fresh coat of paint on the Golden Gate Bridge. It seemed to take that long for Leigh-Cheri's limo to get back to her flat. The usual swarms of bazaar hawkers, camel drivers, snake charmers, monkey pipers, boy and girl prostitutes, beggars, dancers, shoppers, religious zealots, and soldiers had tripled. There were a half-dozen clustered around every foreign infidel, and there were more foreign infidels than the city had seen since the Crusades. A'ben Fizel had promised them foreign infidels, and there they were, cameras, spare change, and everything. The streets were festive, and traffic moved like flies through a sieve.

It was Sunday, and for once the day wasn't bleached out. Not entirely bleached, that is. The busiest, loudest Sunday will always seem subdued next to the quietest Saturday. You go to paint the town red on a Sunday, you'd better be prepared for pink. No matter. It was Sunday, and things were fairly hopping. The big day was Tuesday. In the garden of the Fizel palace,

Leigh-Cheri and A'ben would marry at dawn. The ceremony would be private and small. There would follow an equally small and private reception in the innermost chamber of the pyramid. Concealed from the condemning eyes of teetotalling Moslems, the newly married couple could wet their newly married whistles. At nine, champagne toasts dutifully drunk, the wedding party would emerge to preside over the official dedication of the pyramid. There would follow a day-long reception outside the main entrance, in attendance at which would be enough sheiks, sultans, shahs, emirs, wizirs, wazoos, and exalted omnipotent potentates to bring every Shriners' convention ever held to its knees. Plenty of European posh would also be on hand, making non-alcoholic merry until dusk, at which time Ihaj Fizel's own Boeing 747 would transport the bride and groom to Paris for a honeymoon. That was Tuesday. Monday, Leigh-Cheri could spend with Tilli and Gulietta. Provided she got back to her flat.

91

Tilli was so naive she still thought Jiminy Cricket sang songs by rubbing his hind legs together. She believed the cocaine was some kind of head-cold remedy, although it seemed a trifle odd that it came packaged in a plastic frog. Besides, neither Gulietta nor Leigh-Cheri seemed so ill that they should have to treat their noses every half hour all day. "Vhy don't I just make you a pot of camomile tea?" asked Tilli.

Her daughter and her former servant looked at each other and giggled.

> Cocaine, cocaine, the musical fruit
> The more you have the more you toot
> The more you toot the better you feel
> So sniff some wiff instead of a meal,

they harmonized. Only Leigh-Cheri's part was in English.

That's how Monday went. The three women remained in the flat all day, interrupted once by the dressmakers who came for a final fitting of Leigh-Cheri's gown. The older women wept to see her in wedding costume, but Gulietta was quickly beaming again. Her plastic frog was filled to the gills with the purest snow to sift out of the Bolivian jungle in many a winter, and she and the Princess were having themselves a party. In her fashion, Queen Tilli was enjoying herself, too. She'd splurged on a jeweled collar for her Chihuahua to wear to the ceremony, and she slipped it over the little mutt's neck several times during the day. "Zee emeralds zey go so nice mit his eyes, don't you tink?"

The queens, as well as the Princess, had been invited to numerous swell soirees, but they chose to spend this time together. Who knew when they would meet again?

Tilli had decided to move to Reno to be at Max's side when he placed his last bet. There was not a note of serious music in Reno. Tilli would have to content herself with the slot machine chorus, singing lemons, cherries, silver dollar dreams, and twenty-five-cent disappointments forever. A jackpot and a heart valve, partners in an aria, dying in each other's arms, end of Act IV, Reno Grand Opera.

Gulietta's role in the affairs of her nation had been determined by the rebels to be that of most modern-day monarchs—something more, perhaps, than a representative functionary but certainly not an initiator of political action. Yet the old woman had emerged as the most powerful figure in the government. When Gulietta decreed that there would be no nuclear plants within her borders, the ministers were forced to cancel their orders for reactors. "Our resources shall be the sun, the wind, the rivers, and the moon," she announced. "The moon?" they asked. "You can't get energy from the moon." "You are mistaken," said Gulietta. Now she had to go home and show them why they were wrong. Already, thanks to her lunar awareness program (based in part on Leigh-Cheri's attic experience), all the women in the country were menstruating simultaneously, and all babies were being born at full moon. "It will be a bit more difficult," she said, "teaching men to see in the dark."

As for Leigh-Cheri, she had to take care of some business involving a pyramid. And the bridegroom who'd paid for it.

So the three women spent this last day together. They were warm and close. Occasionally, Tilli would forget and order Gulietta to perform some menial task, whereupon Leigh-Cheri'd remind her mom just who was the reigning monarch among them, and they'd have a good laugh. Laughter came easily. Gulietta and Leigh-Cheri were as buzzed as the door button at a discount whorehouse, and Tilli was happy that the Princess was marrying a man who could afford a three-hundred-million-dollar wedding present, although his father's habit of munching sheep's eyes off the tip of a scimitar aroused misgivings in her concerning genealogy.

After an early dinner, they reluctantly broke up the party. The wedding was at dawn, and dawn had a nasty habit of showing up before breakfast. Leigh-Cheri walked Tilli and Gulietta downstairs to the limo that would drive them to their hotel. Before she maneuvered her bulk into the car, Tilli passed Leigh-

Cheri an envelope. Supposedly, it contained a personal message from King Max explaining why he hadn't come to the wedding and expressing his love for his daughter. Alas, Tilli produced the wrong missive. By mistake, she gave Leigh-Cheri an envelope containing printed accounts of the Woodpecker's death (other newspapers had picked up and amplified the original story from the *Drummer*).

Back upstairs, the Princess turned the letter opener over and over in her fingers. The letter opener was made of ivory. Its handle had been carved to resemble an animal. Exactly what kind of animal Leigh-Cheri couldn't say. It wasn't a frog. It wasn't a chipmunk, running running running at the center of the earth. Perhaps it was some kind of Arabic animal. Leigh-Cheri put the opener to its intended purpose. *Snicker snee, snicker snee.* Pushing a tiny curl of paper in front of it, the letter opener made its ragged incision. Leigh-Cheri reached in and pulled out the newsprint tumor.

92

"I don't know why I'm carrying on like this," said the Princess. "I guess Nina Jablonski was right when she called me a crybaby." She blew her nose. Sometimes a woman blowing her nose can sound as soft and poignant as a rubber horse deflating after being punctured by a seashell.

"The silly red-headed son-of-a-bitch didn't know as much about love as I thought he did. He didn't even know as much about being an outlaw as I thought he did. Done in by a stupid Arab jailer. Jeeze! But he was a genuine human being. By God, Bernard Mickey Wrangle was *real*."

How can one person be more real than any other? Well, some people do hide and others seek. Maybe those who are in hiding—escaping encounters, avoiding surprises, protecting their property, ignoring their fantasies, restricting their feelings, sitting out the Pan pipe hootchy-kootch of experience—maybe those people, people who won't talk to rednecks, or if they're rednecks won't talk to intellectuals, people who're afraid to get their shoes muddy or their noses wet, afraid to eat what they crave, afraid to drink Mexican water, afraid to bet a long shot to win, afraid to hitchhike, jaywalk, honky-tonk, cogitate, osculate, levitate, rock it, bop it, sock it, or bark at the moon, maybe such people are simply inauthentic, and maybe the jackleg humanist who says differently is due to have his tongue fried on the hot slabs of Liar's Hell. Some folks hide, and some folks seek, and seeking, when it's mindless, neurotic, desperate, or pusillanimous can be a form of hiding. But there are folks who want to know and aren't afraid to look and won't turn tail should they find it—and if they never do, they'll have a good time anyway because nothing, neither the terrible truth nor the absence of it, is going to cheat them out of one honest breath of earth's sweet gas.

"Maybe he was an insane bastard, but he was a *genuine* insane bastard," said Leigh-Cheri, "and I loved him more than I've ever loved anybody—or ever will." At that, she began to blubber again.

The clock was messing around with midnight, and midnight was messing around with her head when she found herself at the pyramid. There was no rational reason for being at the pyramid except that she couldn't sleep, didn't wish to disturb Gulietta or her mom, and from her window, she had spied the limo driver in the alley outside her flat dozing at the wheel. She wanted to say, "Drive me to Algiers to Bernard's grave." Or, "Drive me to Husky Stadium, it's time for cheerleader practice." Or, "Drive me to Hawaii, to Mu and the moon." But she'd said, "To the pyramid," and hoped against hope that there'd be solace there.

In the clear desert night, the stars were as wild as popcorn. The moon appeared to have already set, but the pyramid site was lit up like a midway. Thirty or forty workers were still on the job, applying finishing touches, readying the temporary wooden platform for the morning's ceremonies. The entrance was wide open, which was lucky because she'd forgotten her key. She walked down the long corridor to the central chamber.

Adjacent to the central chamber was a fully equipped physics laboratory and several nicely appointed offices, including an office of her own. The central chamber had been left bare, however. It was strictly unadorned stone. The central chamber was where the magic happened, and in an effort to keep it as much like the Great Pyramid's as possible, Leigh-Cheri hadn't even allowed it to be wired for electricity. There were several oil lamps affixed to the granite walls, and that was that. The lamps were antiques—they might have illuminated Cleopatra's pajama parties—and it took Leigh-Cheri five minutes of fumbling to get one burning. When it finally blazed, she shrieked—for its flare revealed a figure lurking in the chamber. She was not alone.

✦ 93 ✦

Initially, she thought it was a workman. Then the lamplight fell on his bright red beard. She shrieked again. Her spine tingled like the elements in a toaster, not that she was in any mood for rye. Holy Mother of God the Surpriser! It was one of *them!*

What do you say to an Argonian space traveler in a pyramid at midnight? Care for a Camel, sailor?

Leigh-Cheri didn't say anything. She'd lost the ability to speak. She just stood there with the toaster going, trying to decide whether to faint or not, until the Red Beard understood that if there was going to be any conversation he'd have to get the ball rolling, so he opened a mouthful of ruined teeth and said:

"Hello, dragon bait."

She fainted.

 94

She woke up with her head on a bomb. He'd made her a pillow out of his jacket and hadn't bothered to take the dynamite out of it.

"You're dead."

"Not so."

"Not so?"

"You can bank on it."

She was blinking rapidly and swallowing hard. "Well then . . . a mistake?"

"Only natural."

"Was this one of your cute tricks?"

"Nope. This was a matter of luck. Good luck for me. Bad luck for Birdfeeder."

"Who? Bernard, I haven't seen you in two and a half years. First you're dead, then you're not. Who are you talking about? What are you talking about?"

"A con named Perdy Birdfeeder did me what I *thought* was a favor. Apparently I erred—but that's another story. Perdy the Purse had a mind to retire to the French Riviera. He heard that business opportunities were handsome there. I arranged for him to meet a bartender in Pioneer Square, a pal who was minding my personal papers. Out of fourteen possible passports, Perdy chose the one with my legal alias on it—"

"Your legal alias?"

"Yeah. Alias Bernard M. Wrangle. My *real* name is Baby. Don't laugh. I'm sensitive. Anyhow, Birdfeeder didn't fare well on the Riviera. He split for North Africa, still using my passport. He didn't fare so hot there, either. Algiers must be a rotten place to die, although I suppose it's preferable to Tacoma."

"Bernard, what are you doing here?"

"Right now I'm wondering whether or not you're glad I'm undead."

Leigh-Cheri rose shakily to her feet. She was practically as tall as Bernard, and she looked him in the eye for a long time. "Once in Hawaii, before I hardly even knew you, I thought you'd been arrested, and for some reason I went running to your boat in a panic. Tonight, I thought you were dead. There wasn't any boat to run to."

She intended to continue, but the crybaby in her reared its salty head. Bernard put his arms around her. She put hers around him, and they stood that way for ... well, who knows how long. Long enough for the two eunuchs who'd followed Leigh-Cheri to the pyramid to figure it was a development worth interrupting A'ben Fizel's bachelor party for.

95

"What are you doing here, Bernard?"

"Something corny and dramatic. I have tendencies."

"Come to rescue me, have you? Peel the dragon bait off the hook?"

"I came to make boom-boom."

"Jesus! I might have guessed. Here? Right here?" She stepped out of his embrace.

"It'd take a nuke to dent this rock pile. I stopped in here for a nibble of pastry"—he gestured at the many-layered wedding cake that sat upon a table at the far end of the chamber—"while waiting for the coast to clear so I could climb to the top. I was going to blow off the point."

"Why, for God's sake?"

"A wedding present. There was nothing else I could give you that Fizel doesn't already own six of. Boom-boom. You'd have known it was me?"

"Naturally. You have a talent for bombing the wrong target."

"Ouch. That stings. But, listen, the pyramid on the dollar bill has had its top lifted off. It's tradition. Or self-fulfilling prophecy. So what do you mean wrong target?"

"Aside from being incredibly beautiful, this rock pile, as you call it, is the most important structure to be built on the planet in thousands of years. You of all people should understand that."

"How do you figure?"

"You were alone with a package of Camels. Didn't you get the message?"

"Which message? I was advised not to look for premiums or coupons and that smoking is dangerous to my health."

"I was referring to a different message."

"Which is—?"

"If you don't know—and I'm not convinced that you don't—there isn't time now for me to tell you."

"That's right. Zero hour is fast approaching. Leigh-Cheri, I can't believe you're marrying a guy with black hair."

"Hair has got nothing to do with it. But while we're

on the subject, I don't like your beard. Makes you look like Jack the Ripper."

"Jack never wore a beard. Are you hostile because I was going to knock the tip off of your pyramid?"

"That. And your note."

"Ah, the note. That note was all punch and no moves, I admit. It sounded a whole lot harsher than intended. I was annoyed at the publicity, it smacked of the old save-the-world syndrome, but I wasn't meaning to be cold—"

"Barking at the moon?"

"What about it?"

"That's all our love was to you?"

"That's all love ever is. Love is not a harpsichord concert in a genteel drawing room. And it sure as hell isn't Social Security, Laetrile, the Irish Sweepstakes, or roller disco. Love is private and primitive and a bit on the funky and frightening side. I think of the Luna card in the Tarot deck: some strange, huge crustacean, its armor glistening and its pinchers wiggling, clatters out of a pool while wild dogs howl at a bulging moon. Underneath the hearts and flowers, love is loony like that. Attempts to housebreak it, to refine it, to dress the crabs up like doves and make them sing soprano always result in thin blood. You end up with a parody. There're lots of pretty sounds that describe 'like,' but 'love' is more on the order of barking. I'm sorry about the note, though. I wrote you another, softer one, but by the time I'd lined up a postman, you'd already galloped out of Seattle on the sultan's main dromedary. Maybe I couldn't blame you—but I could ache."

Leigh-Cheri walked back into his arms. He'd been standing with them open like a bear in a taxidermist's window. Again they hugged for a long time, holding on to one another and not quite sure why. It was in that position, looking over Bernard's shoulder, that she saw A'ben Fizel at the chamber entrance. She felt the twitching of certain major nerves, but before she could direct a reaction in any one of her muscles, Fizel slammed the door. She held her breath, straining to hear if the key was going to turn in the lock.

It turned.

❀❁ 96 ❁❀

"At least it'll be awhile before we die of hunger or thirst," said Bernard. He'd popped a bottle of champagne and was making a move for the wedding cake.

"Don't," snapped the Princess. She snatched his hand away from the centerpiece.

"Excuse me. I assumed the reception had been cancelled." He replaced the champagne.

"Of course it's been cancelled. Of course it has. That was silly of me. Go ahead and eat all the goddamn cake you want. Here." She tore off a chunk and, dripping frosting, handed it to Bernard. The icing oozing between her fingers reminded him of days in the mountains when the Woodpecker Gang had had snowball fights just to keep its blood circulating.

"Well, I do have a sweet tooth. But don't worry. I'm gonna have it extracted in the morning."

"Champagne?" Before offering it to him, Leigh-Cheri took a swig from the bottle. So many bubbles shot up her nasal passages she could barely breathe. She felt as if she were Saturday night television and there were an orchestra up her nose.

"Champagne was discovered by a Catholic monk," said Bernard. "Took one swallow and burst out of his cellar yelling, 'I'm drinking stars, I'm drinking stars!' Tequila was invented by a bunch of brooding Indians.

Into human sacrifice and pyramids. Somewhere between champagne and tequila is the secret history of Mexico, just as somewhere between beef jerky and Hostess Twinkies is the secret history of America. Or aren't you in the mood for epigrams?"

"Bernard, are we in a fix?"

"You tell me. I'm unfamiliar with the gentleman's habits. How long does he carry a grudge?"

"He'll have to let us out soon. He'll have to. My mother's in town. So's Gulietta. The press is all over the place. He'll have to let us out before dawn."

"In that case, my dear, more champagne. The cake's delicious, by the way. I feel festive. Inappropriate of me, I'm sure."

Leigh-Cheri managed a small laugh. "I'm strangely elated myself. It's weird. Everything I've dreamed of and worked for and counted on is falling apart, and I'm happy. I'm also freezing."

She was wearing blue jeans and a green, sleeveless cotton blouse. Bernard wrapped his black cord jacket around her. Dynamite sticks banged her breasts. She continued to shiver, so he ripped the lace tablecloth from beneath the cake, and they both huddled under it, like a couple in a blanket at the Harvard-Princeton game. "The central chamber of the Great Pyramid is a constant sixty-four degrees Fahrenheit," she said. "I was aiming to achieve the same conditions here. Sixty-four is sure a long ways from Maui."

"Seeing as we have some time to kill, why don't you tell me about this pyramid? Why it's important and what I was supposed to learn about it from my cigarettes."

"It's a bit late, you big dummy," she said. But since the champagne was so sidereal and the cake so snowy and slick, and since it was impossible to distinguish Harvard from Princeton by the light of Cleopatra's lantern, she began to tell him. The whole story.

Meanwhile, the police were poking through her wrecked flat and A'ben Fizel was busily spreading the word that his bride-to-be had been kidnapped by Zionist terrorists.

97

Kidnapped by French champagne was more like it. The champagne had hold of them both, and not a ransom note in sight.

"I'm peeing stars!" the Princess squealed.

Bernard produced a pack of Camels from his shirt pocket. He put it through toy UFO maneuvers while making bleeping noises of the third kind.

Leigh-Cheri returned. "I got stars on my shoes," she complained.

Bernard buzzed her with the package.

"Is this your response to my theory?"

"Remember the couple from Argon? I ran into them last month in the Ranch Market on Hollywood Boulevard. Nina Jablonski wrote a film script based on my life and was peddling it to Jane Fonda and Elaine Latourelle. Teen-Aged Bomber Makes the Big Time. I went to L.A. to stop it, and there they were in the Ranch Market. Buying piña colada mix. Does that queer your theory?"

"Minor setback. What about what we saw on the *High Jinks*? That was no piña colada, mon amore."

"We saw what we saw. In the Hawaiian sky *and* at the Ranch Market. I get nervous when you talk about UFOs because I suspect you're looking for salvation from them. What I like about flying saucers is that we don't really know if they're gonna save us or sink us. Or neither. Or both. They *seem* to operate with a sense of humor. I like to think of them as outlaws of space. I like to think they could be launched from the Ranch Market as easily as from Haleakala or Argon. Damn, this stuff is tasty."

"You've opened another bottle? Bernard!"

"Yum!"

"Well, then . . . how about the Camel pack?"

"How about Adolph's Meat Tenderizer? It's a transparent door to experience, too, if you know how to look through it."

"Yeah . . . I have to go along with that. Yeah! That's it!" She clapped her hands.

"You found a key to wisdom in the Camel pack. It's certainly one of the more portentous of our sacred objects. But there're lots of others. Personally, I find the kitchen match particularly rich in symbolism, and Dippity-Do hair-set gel is an open invitation to participate in the Tantric aspects of the divine. The thing about Camels, though, is its directness. I mean, it spells it right out. CHOICE. A person's looking for a simple truth to live by, there it is. CHOICE. To refuse to passively accept what we've been handed by nature or society, but to choose for ourselves. CHOICE. That's the difference between emptiness and substance, between a life actually lived and a wimpy shadow cast on an office wall."

She kissed him impulsively. "I knew you'd understand. Where you been all my life, big boy?"

Bernard passed her the bottle. He began to sing:

Twenty froggies went to school
Come on ye Texas Rangers
Down beside a shady pool
Come on ye Texas Rangers
There they learned to work and play
Come on ye Texas Rangers
And drink Lone Star beer all day
Hee hee ye Texas Rangers.

"Bernard, I don't feel like singing."

"Sure you do.

> The river lies cold and green
> The river lies cold and green
> Leaves are dropping one by one
> And the river lies cold and green.

Funny, rivers always give us ballads. None of that E.E. Cummings stuff."

"Bernard, I want to talk some more."

"Shoot."

"You seem to be saying that the ideas I developed in the attic were intrinsic to the Camel pack, that their origins weren't necessarily Argonian."

"Maybe the Camel pack *is* Argon. In my father's house there are many mansions. Get my drift? I'm an outlaw not a philosopher, but I know this much: there's meaning in everything, all things are connected, and a good champagne is a drink."

Bernard began to sing again. Timidly, Leigh-Cheri joined in. Between verses, they opened another bottle. The popping of its cork echoed throughout the great stone chamber. Of the three billion people on earth, only Bernard and Leigh-Cheri heard the popping of the cork and its echoes. Only Bernard and Leigh-Cheri passed out under the tablecloth.

98

While they were sleeping, the lamp burned down. They awoke in a blackness so dense it would have put the fear of death into coal tar. Bernard struck a match, and Leigh-Cheri gripped his arm.

"Are you thinking what I'm thinking?" she asked.

"I doubt it. I was thinking about the origin of the word pumpkin. It's such a cute word. Kind of plump and friendly—and sexy in a farmer's daughter sort of way. Perfect. I wonder who came up with that word. Some old pumpkin-patch poet in ancient Greece, I suppose. A traveling salesman out of Babylon?"

"Bernard! Knock it off! It's been hours. I'm sure it's well past dawn."

"You'd never know in this bar. Here. Let me light a lamp." He managed to ignite another of the antique lanterns.

"If he hasn't let us out by now ... Bernard! This is no temporary pique. He means to leave us in here."

"I'm afraid you're right. There's no way he could release us now without considerable embarrassment. If he's like a lot of men, he'd rather be a murderer than a fool."

Leigh-Cheri was silent for a while. Then, abruptly, she laughed. "But it's okay, isn't it?" She flashed him a grin wide enough to deliver the Sunday New York *Times* through. "You've got your dynamite!"

"Precious little good it'll do us here."

Her smile snapped shut. Her heart called the New York *Times* and cancelled its subscription. "What ... do ... you mean?"

"Three years ago in Hawaii I tried to explain to you about dynamite. A bomb is not one of your pat solutions. Dynamite is a question not an answer. It can keep things from solidifying, it can keep the ticket open. Sometimes, just raising the question is enough to regenerate life, enough to reverse the decay that results from indifference. But dynamite is useless to us here. Sure, we could blast the door down, but there's no place for us to take cover. The explosion would kill us."

Leigh-Cheri began to weep. (For a beautiful royal princess she'd certainly shed a lot of tears in her life.)

Bernard hugged her tightly. His fingers ran like foxes through the forest fire of her hair. "You know," he said, "I'll bet pumpkin is an American word. It just sounds American to me. Sweet dumb well-fed optimistic down-home ball of fun. I think of a Midwest cheerleader getting knocked up on the back seat of a Chevy after a frosty Friday night football game. You know what I mean? American Pumpkin."

99

Outside, a dragnet was being woven. Due to the political climate of the Middle East in the last quarter of the twentieth century, everybody, including Gulietta, had swallowed A'ben Fizel's story of Zionist abduction. Police from a score of nations and troops from a dozen armies were searching for Princess Leigh-Cheri. Jew and Arab alike searched for her, and in their combined efforts achieved a kind of peaceful cooperation they had all too seldom known.

Inside, it was not unlike McNeil Island or the attic. Bernard and Leigh-Cheri were far better conditioned than most for confinement. There was even a package of Camels to keep them company. To be sure, nobody shoved in lunch plates or chamber pots, but pyramid power kept the wedding cake oven-fresh, and she had her corner for elimination and he his. As the days passed, they rationed increasingly smaller portions of cake and champagne, yet it seemed as if they had an indefinite supply. "What I miss most is the moon," said Leigh-Cheri. The outlaw said he missed it, too.

What they would do when they were freed and whether or not they'd do it together was a subject they tactically avoided. Obviously, Leigh-Cheri was washed up in that neck of the woods. She'd have to leave her pyramid as far behind as the fiancé who'd built it. And despite certain tingling memories of his long, slippery staff, of its intriguing curve and its violet crown, that could not be too far to suit her.

She might drop in on Gulietta and have a peek at her roots. (Bernard, also, had a standing invitation to visit Gulietta's palace.) After that, she'd probably return to America. Unquestionably, Bernard would. But as for a life together, well, Bernard could overlook her Arab bedmate, but he couldn't forget her inclinations toward do-good and group-think, and for her part, Leigh-Cheri had begun to suspect that in the last quarter of the twentieth century Cupid was too dazed, crazed, and generally pissed-off to stick around and finish a job. "There are three lost continents," she lamented. "We are one: the lovers."

❊⊰❁ 100 ❁⊱❊

From the invisible biogenerator of the pyramid, they derived tremendous energy, which they used up in nonstop conversations and in resisting sexual desire. There was an unspoken agreement between them that since the future of their relationship was up for reappraisal, they would not bite off any what might prove to be junk-food sex. They swapped a kiss now and then and spied on each other when they went to their respective corners to pee, but otherwise behaved as if she'd been reared in Virgin Mary, Georgia, and his after-shave cologne was No Mi Molestar. Mostly they talked.

"Leigh-Cheri, you were on the brink of marrying that man. Didn't you even know him well enough to anticipate his current display of bad manners?"

She thought it over. "Well—he did say something

spooky once. He'd been drinking, and he was sort of bragging about how powerful he and his family were. He said that they had the United States over a barrel. He said if America went to war with anybody— Russia, for example—he and his people could determine the outcome. He said they could cut off America's oil supply any time they felt like it and that it would be all over for our country. If the Arabs took a notion to withhold their oil, we couldn't resist a foreign invasion. Do you think that's possible?"

"Yeah, it probably is."

"Doesn't it upset you?"

"Hell, no. I'm not gonna worry about it. No more than I worry about *any* aspect of politics and economics."

"You're sticking your head in the sand. If Russia conquered America, it'd be terrible."

"In many ways it would be. There's nobody on earth half as boring as the Communists, no matter what their nationality, and the Slavs were on the dark and dreary side to start with. Communism is the supreme example of how political idealism can transform human beings into androids. You can bet the bright lights would dim if those robots ever got their iron paws on our switch. But I don't have to leave my house to have fun. I'd still find ways to rock and roll."

"Selfish. Frivolous. Imma—"

"Wait a minute. Hold on. What I'm saying is simply that every totalitarian society, no matter how strict, has had its underground. In fact, two undergrounds. There's the underground involved in political resistance and the underground involved in preserving beauty and fun—which is to say, preserving the human spirit. Let me tell you a story. In the nineteen-forties in Nazi-occupied Paris, an artist named Marcel Carné made a movie. He filmed it on location on the Street of Thieves, the old Parisian theater street where at one time there was everything from Shakespearean companies to flea circuses, from grand opera to girlie shows. Carné's film was a period piece and required hundreds of extras in nineteenth-century costume. It required horses and carriages and jugglers and acrobats. The movie turned out to be over three hours long. And Carné made it right under the Nazis' noses. The film is a three-hour affirmation of life and an examination of the strange and sometimes devastating magnetism of love. Romantic? Oh, babe, it's romantic enough to make a travel poster sigh and a sonnet blush. But completely uncompromising. It's a celebration of the human spirit in all of its goofy, gentle, and grotesque guises. And he made it in the very midst of Nazi occupation, filmed this beauty inside the belly of the beast. He called it *Les Enfants du Paradis—Children of Paradise*—and forty years later it's still moving audiences around the world. Now, I don't want to take anything away from the French resistance. Its brave raids and acts of sabotage undermined the Germans and helped bring about their downfall. But in many ways Marcel Carné's movie, his *Children of Paradise*, was more important than the armed resistance. The resisters might have saved the skin of Paris, Carné kept alive its soul."

Leigh-Cheri squeezed Bernard's hand until the freckles turned color. The freckles gathered up their belongings and made for the fingertips. The freckles were ready to abandon ship. "You must take me to see that movie some day. Will you promise?"

"I promise, Leigh-Cheri. And we will find a way to see it, no matter what the politicians and the generals do. Communist totalitarianism won't stop us and neither will capitalist inflation. If tickets cost a thousand dollars each, we'll pay without batting an eye. And if we can't afford to pay, we'll sneak in. Afterwards, we'll have Hostess Twinkies and a jug of wine. And if

Twinkies and wine are too expensive, we'll grow grain and grapes and make our own. And if they confiscate our little vineyard and our Twinkie patch, why we'll *steal* what we need from those who have excess. Ah, Leigh-Cheri, life is too short for us to be deprived of any one of its joys by the sad, sick androids who control laws and economics. And we won't be deprived. Not even in totalitarianism. Not even in a pyramid."

With that, he popped the last remaining bottle of champagne and swigged an amount four times the size of his daily allotment. He handed it to Leigh-Cheri, and she did the same.

"Yum," he said.

She apparently concurred.

101

For the next two days Bernard drank no champagne and Leigh-Cheri sipped only enough to wet her lips. Even so, there was so little left. . . .

Of the cake, the cake whose snowy tiers had once seemed as inexhaustible as a natural resource, only crumbs remained. Crumbs and the broken sugar wing of a confectionary cherub.

What's more, the oil had been used up in all but one of the lamps. They restricted themselves to an hour or two of lamplight daily and spent most of the time in darkness.

A month had passed—though they had no way of reckoning—and it was starting to tell on them. They seldom mentioned the possibility of death, yet it was in their eyes when the lamp flickered, it was in the way they stared at the dwindling food and drink.

They couldn't imagine why no one had come for them. The thick granite walls prevented them from hearing the workmen who swarmed over the pyramid with spray guns. A'ben Fizel was having it painted black. Nobody would ever be allowed inside the pyramid again, Fizel decreed. It was permanently closed, a memorial to his beloved.

Once, Leigh-Cheri went so far as to say, "If they should find us in here many, many years from now, we'll look the same as we do now. Thanks to pyramid power, our corpses will be perfectly preserved."

"Good," said Bernard. "Beauty like mine deserves to last. I want the children of tomorrow to be able to gaze upon my teeth."

"It's ironic, isn't it, how this starts and ends with pyramids? I mean, we wouldn't be trapped inside this thing if it weren't for the Camel pack. And, of course, your crazy story about the Red Beards from Argon. I guess it goes back further than Camels. It goes back to our red hair."

"Which will be perfectly preserved, thank God."

"Yeah, sure. But it *is* ironic. I wanted to solve the mystery of the pyramids, and here I am locked up inside one, maybe going to die in one, and I'm as far from the answer as ever."

"You mean that's all you wanted? To learn the meaning of pyramids?"

"What are you implying, *all* I wanted? That's a lot. I suppose you know the meaning of the pyramids."

"I do."

She halfway believed him. "Then will you please enlighten me? How come you found the meaning when so many others have failed?"

"Simple. It's because others—like you yourself—have looked at pyramids wrong."

"Looked at them wrong?"

"Yep. You've looked at a pyramid as if it were a finished product, the whole item, the thing itself. But a pyramid is just part of the thing, and the bottom part at that. Pyramids are pedestals, babe. A pyramid is merely a base for something else to stand on."

"Are you serious?"

"I am."

"Well, Jesus, Bernard. What stood on the pyramids?"

"Souls. Souls like you and me. And we have to stand on them now. The pyramid is the bottom, and the top is us. The top is all of us. All of us who're crazy enough and brave enough and in love enough. The pyramids were built as pedestals that the souls of the truly alive and the truly in love could stand upon and bark at the moon. And I believe that our souls, yours and mine, will stand together atop the pyramids forever."

In the darkness she found him and hugged him until once again the captain of his freckles sounded the alarm to man the lifeboats. (Freckle the lifeboats?) He hugged her back. Their lips touched, surprising them both with the volume of juice produced. Soon, faces were not spacious enough to contain their kisses, and their mouths ranged freely over one another's soiled bodies. He slipped inside of her with an audible slish, and, weakened as they were, they made love slowly and sweetly for more than an hour.

Afterward, he fell asleep on the stones beneath the tablecloth. It was when he had begun to softly snore that she slipped away and prepared the dynamite.

❀❀ 102 ❀❀

"Birds of a feather flock together," thought the Princess. "Now I'm the bomber." She had braided the fuses —not an easy feat in the darkness—and leaned the dynamite sticks against the door. "I'm the Woodpecker."

She struck one of the last of his wooden matches

and held it to the tip of the braid. When it began to sputter, she threw down the matchbox and felt her way quickly back to Bernard. She had turned the reception table, the table that had supported the cake and champagne, onto its side. It formed a flimsy barricade alongside Bernard's sleeping form. She stepped over the table and lowered herself down on top of him. He was sleeping on his back. With all of her might, she pressed her nude, goose-pimpled body against his own, shielding it, protecting it. Her face covered his face, her arms cradled his head.

Initially, he thought she had more sex on her mind, and he mumbled a happy protest. As the pressure she was exerting began to alarm him, he struggled to free his head. "Leigh-Cheri, I can't breathe," he said. His voice was muffled. She bore down harder.

"You're better equipped for this world than I am," she said. "I'm always trying to change the world. You know how to live in it."

Now he was fully awake. He smelled, then heard the sputtering fuse. He realized what she'd done. He'd been planning the same thing. Only he'd chosen to give himself one more day, one more chance to make love with her. She'd beaten him to it! She was sacrificing herself to save him. The princess as hero. "I've found one way to make love stay," she said.

He struggled to roll over, to exchange positions, but she'd braced her legs, and he couldn't turn her.

Pumping adrenaline faster than any Fizel well pumped oil, he reached for every volt and ore of strength left in him and, muscles tearing, sinews stretching, teeth grinding sparks, began willing himself to his feet. He was halfway there, Leigh-Cheri still leeched on tight, when she reached between his legs and grabbed his balls. She squeezed them so ferociously that he nearly lost consciousness. Pain rushed in the front door, and strength slipped out the back. They toppled together. Galaxies and teddy bears swooshed by as they fell, frogs leaped from star to star, the moon danced a fandango, they saw Max and Dude, Tilli and Kathleen, A'ben and Ralph Nader, blazing blackberries, solid gold onions, and the musical mountain tips of Mu.

They landed on the Camel pack with a single, painful thud. "Yum," she said, insistently, into his beard.

Then the bomb went off.

❖⊰ 103 ⊱❖

The moon can't help it. It's only an object. The moon doesn't mean to set things sloshing—in every ocean's basin, in every female's uterus, in every poet's jar of ink, in every madman's drool.

"It's only a paper moon/Sailing over a cardboard sea." The moon can't help it if the best toys are made of paper. And the best metaphors made of cheese.

They say that lost objects end up on the moon. Is a siren responsible for a sailor's taste in song?

The moon can't help it. It's only a fat dumb object, the pumpkin of the sky. The moon's a mess, to tell the truth. A burnt-out cinder the color of dishwater; a stale gray cookie covered with scars. Every loose rock in our solar system has taken a punch at it. It's been stoned, scorched, golf-clubbed, and inflicted with boils. If lovers have chosen this brutalized derelict, this tortured dustball, this pitted and pimpled parcel of wasteland as the repository of their dreams, the moon can't help it.

Solar enthusiasts are fond of pointing out that the moon merely reflects the light of the sun. Yes, the moon *is* a mirror. It can't help it. The moon is the original mirror, the first to refuse to distort CHOICE.

Objects can't think. They employ other methods. But we human beings use objects to think with. And when it comes to the moon, you are free to think as you choose.

If the moon hung over Fort Blackberry like an omen, like a cheap literary device, it couldn't help it. The moon just hung there. Bernard Mickey Wrangle and Princess Leigh-Cheri drove up in a cab.

⚬⚬⚬ 104 ⚬⚬⚬

Bernard was the first to regain consciousness. He woke up in an Arab clinic that featured goatskin bedpans and snot-green walls. It took him an hour to understand why the swarming flies didn't buzz. He was tipped off when the police began interrogating him via note pad. He was deaf.

Naturally, they believed that he was the kidnapper. They asked him if his motives were political or sexual. He wrote on the pad, "Take a flying fuck at a rolling oil barrel. Take a flying fuck at the Koran."

The police looked at one another and nodded. "Political *and* sexual," they said.

He thought only of escape. First he had to find out what they'd done with Leigh-Cheri's corpse. He intended to take her ashes to Hawaii. He'd build a sand castle in the shape of a pyramid on the beach near Lahaina. He'd sprinkle her ashes on top of the pyramid and watch as the waves came for them and carried them away to Mu.

His mind was as chained to that morbid scheme as his legs were chained to the bed. On the third day, they unlocked his leg irons. His mind remained chained.

"She say you innocent," the police wrote.

Bernard bolted up. "You mean she's alive!" he said. He couldn't hear himself say it.

They nodded. They led him down the hall to her room.

Two-thirds of her hair was singed off. Her right cheek was as torn as the moon's. But she was awake and smiling.

He pointed to his ears. She pointed to hers. She was deaf, too.

She reached for the note pad.

"Hello, dragon bait," she wrote.

⠶⢁⣀ 105 ⣀⡈⠶

The clinic wouldn't release them. A'ben Fizel ordered them held. A'ben was rushing home from an American business trip. They both knew what his return would mean.

Gulietta arrived before A'ben. Her prime minister, a bearded giant with a gun belt, accompanied her. And twenty-five rebel commandos, as well. Queen Gulietta advised Ihaj Fizel to turn over the young couple. She threatened an international incident. The old sultan followed her logic. Many times he'd warned his son that redheads were nothing but trouble. "Get them away from here at once," he told Gulietta. "I'll handle my boy. Shalom."

They recuperated at Gulietta's palace. Except for their eardrums, healing was swift.

At a desk in their room (Queen G. was no prude), Bernard wrote Leigh-Cheri a letter. Impatient, she read over his shoulder.

He was describing a dream. Or a hallucination. He wrote that when he and Leigh-Cheri fell to the floor right before the blast, he experienced the sensation that they had fallen into the Camel pack.

"All the time that I was unconscious," he wrote, "I was dreaming—I guess I was dreaming—that we had escaped through the package of Camels. That we went inside of it and caught the camel and rode it bareback to the oasis—"

She took the pad from him. "We had to ride fast," she wrote, "because we were naked and the sun was hot. Redheads burn easily."

Bernard recovered paper and pen. "Yes," he wrote. "That's right. Well, we made it to the oasis, where we rested by the water hole in the shade of the palms."

Leigh-Cheri yanked the pad back. "There was a frog in the pool. And we wondered how a frog got out there in the middle of the desert."

Bernard grabbed the pad. "How did you know that?"

It was her turn. "We ate fresh dates. You made a droll remark about dates being a laxative. Some Bedouins came through, and they gave us an old camel blanket. One blanket between us. We wrapped in it—"

"It was tan," wrote Bernard. He was so excited that the pen shook.

"With a few stripes of blue."

"How do you know this?"

"I had the same dream. It seemed more real than a dream. A hallucination? A—"

"At dusk, we made love."

"You started it by sucking my toes."

"Your toes are cute. And then the dates took effect."

The Princess laughed. "You wondered if there was a men's room over at the pyramid."

"We decided to avoid pyramids. Except as pedestals. We slept by the pool. How do you know this? How do *we* know it? Could we both have had the exact same dream?"

"Was it a dream, then?"

They were staring at one another in silent disbelief, trembling a little, when Gulietta entered. There would have been no point in her knocking first.

Gulietta brought a cable from Tilli. It was news about Max. The disappearance and resurrection of his daughter had been too much for the King. His valve had gone bingo. "I bet you zat you're soon okay," Tilli had told him when he slumped. "Two will get you five I am not," answered Max. He'd won.

For the time being, Bernard and Leigh-Cheri forgot about the Camel pack—and whether at the instant of explosion it had sheltered them from death.

They'd have the last quarter of the twentieth century, and more, perhaps, to bother their noodles with that one.

106

King Max was buried in Reno. Far from blackberries. Bernard and Leigh-Cheri attended the funeral. Later, they put Tilli on a plane for Europe. Gulietta had named her manager of the national opera. "I gun to be a vorking-o girl," said Tilli. "Oh-Oh, spaghetti-o."

Bernard and Leigh-Cheri flew to Seattle. Arriving at the Furstenberg-Barcalona house, they discovered that it had been engulfed by blackberry vines. Chuck, who still lived over the garage, had hacked a tunnel to the front door. Chuck tunneled through the brambles in order to watch game shows on Max's old Magnavox. The taxi driver offered to take Bernard and Leigh-Cheri to a hotel. They refused. They entered the tunnel by moonlight.

They set up their lives in the house. In the thorns

and berries. They seldom went out except to go shopping. They enjoyed supermarkets. Pharmacies. Vegetable stands. Tobacco shops. Val-u-Marts. Meat-o-ramas. Family Shoe Centers. Buddy Squirrel's Nuts & Candies. Appliance stores.

Wherever they looked, something momentous was happening.

They made love at all hours and in every corner of the house. Sometimes Chuck had to step over them to get to the TV.

But having acquired a taste for solitude, each of them spent days separate and alone, Leigh-Cheri in the attic, Bernard in the pantry. Funny how we think of romance as always involving two, when the romance of solitude can be ever so much more delicious and intense. Alone, the world offers itself freely to us. To be unmasked, it has no choice.

Naturally, it rained a lot. The famous Seattle rain. If love was going to stay, it better be prepared to get its feet wet.

Leigh-Cheri took up easel painting. Still lifes. She wasn't bad. Bernard carried around wooden matches. "Everybody needs a hobby," he explained.

Once, to the east, above the mountains, a strange glow science-fictioned across the sky. There were flashing lights of every color but one. When Bernard and Leigh-Cheri were certain that the thing had passed, they told each other that they were proud to be redheads. That they would be ready when the showdown came.

With her share of Max's winnings, Leigh-Cheri purchased powerful hearing aids. Hers was pink, Bernard's was black. Each hearing aid was about the size of a Camel pack. They were made from plastic and tended to squeak. They were adorable.

Even with aids, their hearing was only partially

restored. Still, they were convinced that they could hear the chipmunk at the center of the earth. They could tell that the chipmunk was running smoothly now. Its wheel spun easy and free.

EPILOGUE

Well, we made it through the night. I have to hand it to the Remington SL3, it hung in there in spite of what must have been, for a typewriter of its class, exceedingly primitive conditions.

I'll never write another novel on an electric typewriter. I'd rather use a sharp stick and a little pile of dog shit. But the Remington, although too psuedo-sophisticated for my taste, is an object, after all, and wasn't the possibility of a breakthrough in relations between animate and inanimate objects one of the subjects of this book?

Yes, this is the book that revealed the purpose of the moon. And while it may not have disclosed *exactly* what happened to the golden ball, it stated plainly why the question needed to be raised.

Objecthood was by no means our only major theme. There was, for example, the matter of the evolution of the individual, how evolving is not accomplished for a person by nature or society but is the central dimension of a personal drama to which nature and society are but spectators. Wasn't it made clear that civilization is not an end in itself but a theater or gymnasium in which the evolving individual finds facilities for practice? And when it comes to themes, how about the—but wait a minute. Hold on. I've been trapped. This is the very kind of analytical, after-the-fact goose gunk the Remington SL3 cut its teeth on. No wonder it's still yammering away, despite a lack of fuel, despite the red enamel house paint that's run down into

its guts. Enough already. I'm going to pull its plu
ug
gggg

(Ha! What's the matter, Bem, got a speech impediment?) and finish up in longhand. Not that my handwriting is any aesthetic improvement. It resembles the nasty scrawls chalked on alley walls by Mongolian monster boys. But it will encourage me to be brief. And, really, what else is there to say? If that pissant typewriter has got me in a situation where I _must_ make a closing remark, well then I guess in all fairness I should say one more thing about making love stay.

When the mystery of the connection goes, love goes. It's that simple. This suggests that it isn't love that is so important to us but the mystery itself. The love connection may be merely a device to put us in contact with the mystery, and we long for love to last so that the ecstasy

of being near the
mystery will last.
It is contrary to the
nature of mystery to
stand still. Yet it's
always there, somewhere,
a world on the other
side of the mirror
(or the Camel pack),
a promise in the
next pair of eyes
that smile at us.
We glimpse it when
we stand still.

The romance of
new love, the romance
of solitude, the romance

of objecthood, the
romance of ancient
pyramids and distant
stars are means of
making contact with
the mystery. When
it comes to perpetuating
it, however, I got
no advice. But I
can and will remind
you of two of the
most important facts
I know:

(1) Everything is
part of it.

(2) It's never
too late to have
a happy childhood.

ABOUT THE AUTHOR

TOM ROBBINS is the author of *Half Asleep in Frog Pajamas, Another Roadside Attraction, Even Cowgirls Get the Blues, Still Life with Woodpecker, Jitterbug Perfume,* and *Skinny Legs and All*—highly original novels that have left their mark on our culture. He lives near Seattle.